STARG

SG·1.

THE POWER BEHIND
THE THRONE

TEAL'C roared.

Fifty feet from the gate the blue water of the event horizon ripped out of the aperture. The way home was open. O'Neill had done it. Teal'c saw the colonel go down again. The sucking silence that followed was hideous. Then both Carter and Daniel Jackson were yelling — this time the sound was primal and filled with fear for the fallen O'Neill.

Teal'c ducked beneath a wild burst of fire from a Jaffa weapon, and ran, hard, fast, keeping low, his arms and legs pumping. A burning man staggered across his path. The flames consumed him, turning his flesh to blistered sores. Teal'c fired once, putting the Jaffa out of his misery, and was past him. He ran to O'Neill's side and gathered him into his arms. The colonel shuddered once, violently, and opened his eyes. "Go!" he rasped.

"Indeed," Teal'c said, rising. He watched Daniel Jackson's back disappear through the gate and followed him. "We do not leave men behind, O'Neill. That is the law."

But O'Neill had lapsed into unconsciousness.

STARGÅTE
SG·1

BASED ON THE HIT TELEVISION SERIES CREATED BY BRAD WRIGHT AND JONATHAN GLASSNER

Developed for television by BRAD WRIGHT & JONATHAN GLASSNER
and RICHARD DEAN ANDERSON, MICHAEL SHANKS, AMANDA TAPPING and CHRISTOPHER JUDGE

WRITTEN BY The characters of Stargate reflect certain sensibilities
with their behaviour and language which may not apply to other groups or cultures

THE POWER BEHIND
THE THRONE

STEVEN SAVILE

FANDEMONIUM BOOKS

FAN DE MON IUM

An original publication of Fandemonium Ltd, produced under license from MGM Consumer Products.

Fandemonium Books, PO Box 795A, Surbiton, Surrey KT5 8YB, United Kingdom

Visit our website: www.stargatenovels.com

S T A R G Å T E
SG·1

MGM TELEVISION ENTERTAINMENT INC. Presents
RICHARD DEAN ANDERSON
in
STARGATE SG-1™
MICHAEL SHANKS AMANDA TAPPING CHRISTOPHER JUDGE
DON S. DAVIS
Executive Producers JONATHAN GLASSNER and BRAD WRIGHT
MICHAEL GREENBURG RICHARD DEAN ANDERSON
Developed for Television by BRAD WRIGHT & JONATHAN GLASSNER

WWW.MGM.COM

ISBN: 978-1-905586-45-5 Printed in the USA

This one is for my sister
Amy
I may not see you every day but that doesn't mean
I love you any less

CHAPTER ONE

Come Up Screaming

NERYN VAR ran for her life.

The first shot fired wide, tearing into the cave wall. Stone wept as it crumbled. She threw herself forward, risking a backward glance. There were six of them. Hunters. They bore the glyphs of Jaffa on their foreheads. The lead warrior's had been inlaid with gold, marking him as First Prime. He leveled his staff weapon, taking his time with his shot. Neryn threw herself from her feet, barely avoiding the sizzling arc of blue energy as the bolt tore into the wall.

It was a long way back to the surface and the Stargate. Too far.

"Run," she pleaded, but the creature stopped to help her up. How did the Jaffa find her? Only the Tok'ra High Council knew of her mission, surely the Goa'uld did not know the true nature of Vasaveda's sole inhabitant? It didn't matter. She had been compromised. Who? When? The questions spun through her head. Someone she trusted had betrayed her to the Goa'uld. The thought paralyzed Neryn Var.

It reached down a hand for her to take. Even down here, out of the sun, the heat was searing. She pushed it away. "Just go. Run. Please. They can't take you. You have to escape."

"I can help you," it promised, even as the blast from a zat'ni'katel took it high in the chest. The creature span almost gracefully, twisting as it fell. It hit the floor hard and lay there, stunned. For a moment confusion flickered across its face. Then those features that should have been so twisted with fear appeared to melt.

Neryn looked away.

She pushed herself to her feet.

She had no weapon to return fire.

All she could do was run.

She had to reach the Stargate.

She had to escape.

She had to find out who was the traitor in their number.

And that meant she couldn't allow herself to be taken alive.

But when did she give up? When did she bite down on the false tooth in the back of her skull and release the poison that would destroy her brain? When did it become too late?

"Are you still trying to escape, Neryn Var?" the First Prime goaded. He disengaged his staff weapon as he taunted her. It was the single most insulting thing he could have done. He was telling her just how impotent she was. Shouldering the weapon meant he saw no threat. "I have such pains in store for you, Tok'ra. You will weep and you will scream as I open doorways into your flesh and mind," he promised. The malfeasance dripped from his tongue as he stepped toward her. "You should beg me to kill you now. You should fall on your knees and whimper and plead to be put out of your misery like the wretched thing you are. Do it. Beg," he paused a beat, waiting for some kind of response from her. She didn't give him the satisfaction. "No? You disappoint me, Tok'ra. I would have had some fun before I killed you. Now, I see no reason to keep you alive."

"Kill me then, Jaffa," she spat. It was little more than token resistance but she needed to show wasn't spent quite yet. Neryn Var drew herself to her full height. The heat had the sweat running in rivulets down her skin. She faced her would-be murderer across the short distance.

He chuckled mirthlessly. "Not yet, Tok'ra. I want to get inside your head first. I want to know all of your secrets."

"I will not tell you anything," she sneered. She knew he was baiting her, but knowing that didn't stop her from rising to take it. Beside her, the Mujina stirred. She didn't dare risk so much as a sideways glance toward it. Instead she darted a look toward the crystalline pillar no more than ten feet from where she stood. She wanted the Jaffa to see the look and misinterpret it. Her only hope of escape lay in his insufferable arrogance misinforming the next few moments. If he played her right she was dead but if he bought the misdirection she had a chance. It was that simple.

"Everyone talks eventually. Believe me. It might take a few hours, a day even, but in the end you will talk just to end the pain. There will be nothing left hidden between us by the time I allow you to die."

She moved slowly, as though in surrender. She had a single Tok'ra burrowing crystal in her possession from the dozen they had provided for her to excavate the tunnels during her search. All she needed was the slightest of distractions to allow her to release it unseen. It was all about creating a moment of confusion to save her life.

"Now!" Neryn Var yelled, feinting a wild lunge. Even though the creature still lay there immobile, the First Prime bought her lie and lashed around, anticipating with perfection the strike that wasn't coming. For a heartbeat he was off balance. In the space between it and the next, Neryn Var hurled the crystal at the wall. It exploded on impact, showering a kaleidoscope of color, shards of rock and light as it bit into the cavern wall.

She didn't wait to see where the tunnel would finish. She ran.

She saw the crimson light of the burning sky ahead of her. She tasted the fire of the air on her tongue and deep in the back of her throat as she forced herself to run faster.

Neryn Var dared chance a backwards glance, just once: she couldn't see the Mujina. She could only pray it had fled and not been captured.

She ran for the Stargate.

CHAPTER TWO

The Stranger

THERE WAS a sharp sound, like a fly against neon, and the artificial lights failed. The ticking of the hot bulbs filled the silence. In that moment between the lights going out and the back-up generator kicking in darkness ruled the bunker beneath Cheyenne Mountain. *Tick. Tick.* The strip lights flickered throwing a sudden flare of light across the landscape of shadow and failed again, once, twice, three times as the generator struggled to feed enough power through the base to feed all of the vital systems. *Tick. Tick.*

Then there was light.

The reserve lighting was considerably less stark than the normal fluorescents, giving the shadows somewhere to play.

O'Neill dragged back his chair and pushed aside the plate, "That *can't* be good."

"When is it ever?" Carter agreed. The softer light took the edge from the wind-swept spikes of her fringe. It did nothing for the dark smears around her eyes. She caught herself yawning and knuckled the sleep out of her eyes. "Come on then, let's go check it out."

The familiar sirens of the gate room blared before they were half way through the door. With a quick glance behind him, O'Neill was running hard before the klaxon's first wail had finished. He moved fast, without having to think because the layout of the complex was ingrained on his mind. O'Neill hit the stairwell's security door, pushing it open, and took the stairs three and four at a time. The sound of his footsteps pounded back up toward the surface. He didn't need to check if the others were with him. Not only could he hear them, he could feel them. *That* was the kind of bond they had.

The emergency lighting painted a chiaroscuro of grays the length of the corridor with darkness waiting down at the bottom by the door into the gate room. The metal stanchions bracing the tunnel stood out stark and black like the ribs of some great beast. A natural extension of that analogy would make the gate room the beating heart and the wailing siren the first seizures of a heart attack. It didn't bear thinking about. O'Neill sidestepped a worried-looking sentry, and went through the door. Alice in all of her adventures in Wonderland and behind the Looking Glass never stepped through a door quite like it. There were no Mad Hatter's or March Hares, no Queen of Hearts, flamingo croquet mallets or little-big potions, only General Hammond's furrowed brow as he glared through the glass of the control room at the treacherous Stargate, and row upon row of muzzles pointed up at the iris as the first chevron popped and clamped into place with a flare of red. A disembodied voice echoed "*Unauthorized Off-World activation.*" The central dial rotated frantically, the urgency of its movement transferring to everyone in the gate room. It hit the second mark.

"Chevron two locked!"

The words sent a palpable chill down the ladder of Jack O'Neill's spine, bone by bone. He stared at the central dial as it hit the third co-ordinate and the chevron locked in place. Something felt wrong about this. He looked back up at the men in the control room and shrugged — the gesture was worth a thousand words. Hammond shook his head; there were no units scheduled to return and no one up there had any more of an idea what was happening than he did. It wasn't a reassuring exchange. He turned back to the gate as the forth co-ordinate locked in place.

"Chevron five locked!"

The guns came up, muscles tense. Safeties clicked off as

rounds were chambered. O'Neill walked toward the steel ramp. Airmen flanked him on either side. He didn't need a weapon; if need be they would open fire on any hostiles that stepped out through the wormhole. Still, he felt naked without one. Teal'c moved up to stand beside him. His face betrayed nothing, not even the slightest trace of curiosity. O'Neill had to smile. The big man was an enigma wrapped in a conundrum and tied off neatly with a big bow of mystery. Teal'c noted his scrutiny with a raised eyebrow. He held his staff weapon at ease but there was nothing nonchalant about the pose. In a split second it could be transformed into a tool of brutality and deliver deadly force. More than all of the rifles the sight of Teal'c with his staff weapon at his side put O'Neill at ease. Daniel and Carter stood two steps behind the Jaffa, their eyes fixed on the gate, expressions equally unreadable.

The disembodied voice continued its countdown, "Chevron six locked!"

"Open the iris," Hammond's order was met by the duel *hiss-grate* of the heavy-metal iris disengaging. "Jack, we're receiving a Tok'ra signature. It's a distress signal. Brace yourself people, there's no telling what's about to step through!" The tight concentric circle of impenetrable naqahdah recessed into the gate's frame as the final chevron locked. A glassy film of quicksilver appeared to puddle across the eye of the Stargate, the crystal blue surface agitated as the event horizon of the wormhole established itself at the destination. The surface agitation increased exponentially, the ripples surging and bulging outward as though the inner ring of the gate wrestled to contain the raw energy of the wormhole. In the space between heartbeats the quicksilver exploded outwards in an unstable vortex, a tidal surge erupting from the eye only to be sucked back in to the churning surface. Even after so long it was an awe-inspiring sight: so much pent up energy, the raw frisson of it, barely caged by the Stargate. It was elemental. O'Neill let out a slow, deeply held breath and stepped forward.

"Incoming traveler!"

The surface of the event horizon buckled, looking for a moment as though it might fail, and then someone began to emerge, one foot stepping down onto the ramp. A hideous ripping sound tore through the gate room. One of the riflemen squeezed off a single shot before he could stop himself. The report was lost beneath the screams of the traveler. The sound was terrible to hear.

"Something is wrong," Teal'c said, beside him. He shifted his position, bringing the staff weapon up.

He was right.

O'Neill watched as a trembling hand pressed against the skin of the event horizon, barely managing to break through. The gate room was gripped with the sudden chill of the tomb, the temperature dropping ten degrees in as many milliseconds. The rest of the poor soul failed to re-integrate. Their body remained, a shadow burned into the rippling skin of the wormhole, and then it was gone, as thoroughly and completely as that. The traveler ceased to be. Jack had seen wormholes fail before, and witnessed the catastrophic effects such a failure had upon the human body, but the wormhole hadn't failed — its skin still rippled, full of life. Without thinking, O'Neill ran up the ramp. Part of the man's hand remained, the wounds where it had been severed smoking, cauterized by the intense heat of the failed re-integration.

Charred shreds of ruined clothing smoldered at the foot of the Stargate. There was nothing else left of the man who had tried to step through.

"Carter, get up here, now!" O'Neill barked. "What the hell just happened here?"

"I don't know, sir," she said, visibly shaken. She knelt beside him, reluctant to look any more closely at the charred clothing. "Whoever it was didn't survive the re-integration process. I can't begin to guess why without seeing transcripts of the matter transferral. Anything might have happened."

"Anything?"

"I don't want to guess."

It took him a moment to realize why: a Tok'ra distress signal, an unidentifiable corpse. Sam was putting two and two together and leaping to the worst possible conclusion. He couldn't blame her, it was a soldier's mentality: expect the worst, hope for the nothing.

"It isn't Jacob," he promised her. It was one of those stupid rash promises he couldn't possibly keep but he made it just the same.

She looked up at him then, her eyes filled with fear and the need to believe him. She nodded once. "Close the iris," she told him, "we don't want whatever was chasing them to come through."

CHAPTER THREE

Flowers in the Desert

THE IRIS spiraled shut, breaking the link with whatever world the unfortunate traveler had come from.

For a long moment the gate room was eerily calm, everyone caught looking down at the severed hand and the peculiar dust it lay in. It was an ugly epitaph.

"Okay, enough standing around, people," Jack said, "Daniel, take the hand down to the medical bay, Jacob's files are still a matter of military record. Two minutes to run a match on his prints and you'll know for sure. No point getting worked up over nothing." He said it brusquely as though he wasn't even remotely willing to entertain the notion of it being Sam's father.

"With respect, sir, I'd like to be the one to take it down," Carter said.

"You sure?"

She nodded.

"Okay, Daniel, maybe you want to go down there anyway, keep Major Carter company. The rest of you, we're working on the assumption this isn't Jacob." He turned to Hammond. "General, we need to contact the Tok'ra. I would hope they'd know if one of their merry band are missing. Maybe they can shed some light on exactly what the hell is going on here. It'd make a pleasant change."

Hammond nodded.

"Colonel O'Neill, if I might suggest something," Teal'c said.

"Shoot..."

"Perhaps it would be wise to trace the point of origin before the wormhole is allowed to disengage. The Tok'ra have infiltrated many Goa'uld strongholds. Even knowing as little as the planet of origin will greatly reduce the likelihood of exposing other agents unnecessarily."

"Can we do that?"

Teal'c said nothing. His silence spoke volumes.

"Don't you ever listen during the briefings?" Daniel Jackson said, shaking his head. Jack couldn't tell if he was pulling his leg or not, so opted for the former.

"To be honest, when you guys start going on, it all kind of blurs together. What can I say? I have a short attention span. And you guys can *talk*. Why don't you just give me the edited highlights: can we do it, yes or no?"

"Yes."

"See, that's all I needed to know. You know what to do, so everyone get to it. Chop chop."

He followed the General up to the control room. Daniel went with Sam down to the medical bay. For a moment it crossed Jack's mind that they got their roles reversed and he should have been there for Carter if the wrong results came back. She would have been there for him. He knew that without even having to think about it. But Daniel would look after her. "He won't need to," O'Neill said, not realizing he had said it out loud. The declaration earned him a furrowed brow from Teal'c. "Talking to myself. First sign of madness."

"Indeed."

The steel steps clanged dully as the three of them ascended. The air had that curious subterranean quality to it; it was cold, and harder to breathe with a vaguely metallic tang, almost as though, despite the struggling air-conditioning, it was starved of oxygen.

Hammond opened the door.

The control room was a hive of frantic activity. Fingers rattled across keyboards searching for the protocols and routines that would track back the incoming co-ordinates.

The cramped confines were humid and rank with male perspiration. Schematics and blue-lines were spread out across every available surface, piled two and three deep. O'Neill went straight across to the computer. Thousands upon thousands of co-ordinates scrolled across the screen too quickly to read. The first identifier caught, drawn out of the array by the tracer program. By itself it told them nothing. It was almost a full thirty seconds before the second identifier was isolated. Before the third could lock down the screen went black and the airman at the controls slammed the flat of his hand off the side of the monitor's casing. They had lost the connection. With the wormhole disengaged there was no way to trace it.

"Lost it, sir."

"Okay, airman, I want you to treat me like I am a moron. How does this thing work? I don't want the techno babble, keep it simple, I am a moron, remember. Isn't it like the 'net? Does it have a history or something? A buffer that records every dial-in and dial-out? Seems to me a piece of kit like this ought to be advanced enough to save the most recent incoming co-ordinates. Doesn't that seem logical to you?"

"Something like that, sir. The buffer holds data from the last dialed connection, but as soon as another connection is established it's overwritten," the young airman explained. It was all Jack needed to know.

"So we take the gate off-line and nothing can dial in. Then transmit a message through to the Tok'ra. This is their mess, they can fix it."

"Yes, sir. The Tok'ra can send any response via the wormhole without having to dial-in to our gate. It should preserve any data in the buffer if they're not able to provide the answers we are looking for, sir."

"Good man. What do you think, General?"

"It's your call, Colonel. What do you think?"

O'Neill shook his head. "At times like these I like to ask

myself one simple question, 'what would Tyler Durden do?'"

Hammond glared at him.

"Sorry, General. What happens in the Fight Club stays in the Fight Club and all that."

"All right, Jack, I am just going to assume you know what in the blue blazes you are talking about."

"Sometimes, General. Let's send the call out to our friends in deep space. It strikes me they're the riddle at the heart of things, as usual. If anyone can tell us what's going on odds are it is them. Who else is off-world right now?"

"SG-3 and 7 are visiting the Vengari. They're attending a summit at the Library of Silence. They aren't due to report in for thirty-six hours."

"Good, that gives us a very definite workable window. We've got thirty-six hours to find out who our mystery visitor was, and more importantly, what they were running from."

"Or who," the airman offered.

"In my experience when it comes to running from aliens I think it's safer to think of them as a 'what'. Get a message encoded and sent out to the Tok'ra. We need to talk. Keep it simple but make sure they understand it is important. We need to know if they have lost an operative, and if they have, just what sort of trouble they could have brought to our door."

"Yes, sir."

"It's not Jacob's hand," Janet Frasier said. She hadn't run a single test. She did not need to. It wasn't an old man's hand. It wasn't a man's hand at all, come to that. "Unless he's undergone some major reconstructive surgery, and a major lifestyle choice, that is."

"What do you mean?"

"It's a woman's hand, Sam. Young, heavy-set, but very definitely female. Trust me."

Samantha Carter didn't know whether to laugh or cry. The

surge of relief she felt was overwhelming. In a few minutes her emotions had swung through every extreme from the ridiculous all the way to the sublime — and then the moment of realization that her good news was someone else's bad news and all the guilt that came with it. She thought of Jolinar and the gap she had left in her mate Lantash's life. There was no easy relief, good people were dying in this war with the Goa'uld, and the human cost was extortionate. Would any of them have willingly paid it if they had known what uncovering the gate at Giza really meant to the world? Part of her, the part that didn't dream of space and all of its wonders, sincerely doubted that they would. It was a faith-shaking confession, especially for the rational thinker inside her: Einstein had said that God didn't play dice with the universe. The Christians of the world took that as evidence of a supernatural entity controlling all things. Sam had long since come around to the Einsteinian way of thinking, her own personal god not some magical maker who answered prayers, but rather the very details of the world, the microcosm, the genius of nature and the random coalition of necessities that laid out the blueprint for life, and yet carrying the hand down to the lab she had said a prayer, bargained even with the faith-based God she did not believe in. That was the strength of fear. All it took was a single moment for it to root its way down into the psyche and all of the rationality could be undone.

"So who was she?"

"Well we can run the surviving prints and take a DNA sample, obviously," Fraiser said, "but barring a miracle that isn't going to tell us anything. Sorry, Sam."

"Don't be, you just gave me my dad back."

And took away someone else's wife or daughter in the process.

She felt Daniel squeeze her shoulder. She had completely forgotten he was there.

"Let's go and find Jack."

CHAPTER FOUR

Losing My Religion

THE GRAVE robber ghosted across the deserted Square.

It was midnight.

The twin moons of Krace and Banak hung traitorously in the sky, casting shadows across the cobbled streets. There was a chill to the night that bit bone deep. The man pulled his thick woolen cloak up around his throat. He clutched a hastily wrapped bundle to his chest, cradling it protectively. His breath wreathed up in corkscrews of steam in front of his face. The regular *tink* of the metal rim hammered into his boot heels meant that his footsteps were the only sound he heard until he reached the fountain.

In truth it wasn't much of a fountain. The water barely bubbled six inches high while the pump wheezed asthmatically. Blind windows looked down from all around. The buildings in this district were some of the oldest in the city, baroque and gothic monstrosities with intricate façades and leering gargoyles aplenty. None of them were in their prime; the cracks had begun to spread, undermining the foundations of the buildings and ruining their beauty. They were the perfect metaphor for Kumaran society. In the moonlight the sneers from the stone creatures stretched across the buildings they haunted.

The little thief cast a furtive look over his shoulder as he lingered by the fountain. He couldn't tell if he was being followed. Anxiety prickled the nape of his neck. He felt *something*. It's just paranoia, he told himself, and that was the truth — or part of it. That there was more than one truth was the nature of the game he played.

He looked up at the clock face of the Talon Tower as the huge hands juddered into place on the hour. The clock chimed the first stroke of thirteen. All was far from well. There was a satisfying solidity to the movement that set the puppeted dance into motion. On the left side of the old ceramic face hand-crafted devils crawled up a twisting pole while on the right distinctly human angels fell. On the third stroke, the old blackbird of Death emerged from the midnight window, and with one flap of its razor-sharp wings scythed through the immortal chain that tethered the angels to heaven, cutting them free to fall. The bell tolled twice more during the entire scene, those few seconds encapsulating so much of his people's fall from grace. It was the gift of the artists; they had a way of investing so much meaning in their art. No wonder Corvus Keen had declared their kind undesirable. Art was disgusting. It led to thought, and thought led to dissatisfaction, which in turn led to rebellion. That was the power of pretty pictures and sharp words. There would be no more art.

Of course, the Kelani were no angels, not in the sense of wings and scripture. But they were his people. The grave robber was under no delusions about that. His world was divided, and divided it would fall.

What price peace?

That was the question he had to come to terms with.

What was the value of a single life? The bullet that took it, the lifeless flesh it left behind, or the sum of all the acts that one life would never complete? What value did he place on his heritage? Was it worth clinging to, or best buried away and forgotten? Subservience was not enough, not any more. But neither was rebellion. He could stand in front of the wheels of Corvus Keen's tanks and be crushed as an example of how deviance was dealt with by the regime, or he could use his head and work a more subtle rebellion.

He had taken that road; the road more subtle.

But now his feet were well and truly set down on it, the doubts crowded in. What he was doing might damn millions. He had to believe that in the end it would save millions more. He needed to believe even though he knew the truth: he couldn't save anybody. He was damning himself to exile, shunned and vilified as a blood traitor.

It did not matter that he wasn't alone in his treachery.

Others like him had turned traitor in the hope of bringing about a lasting peace for the Kelani people. They wore the black crow of Corvus on their sleeve. That emblem that had come to signify so much suffering. It marked them as different from their own. The black crow told the world that they were loyal to Corvus Keen, the man who had inflicted peace on the various continents of Kumara. His own people were playing a long and ultimately tragic game: to end the slaughter they needed to get close to Corvus Keen and ingratiate themselves into the dictator's good graces. That meant becoming his soldiers and scientists, his assassins and thieves, his secret police and his relic hunters. That was the rationalization he clung to. Still, it was hard betraying his blood.

The first fat flakes of snow began to fall. For a moment they hung there in the dark sky like fallout ash, and then the wind spun them away.

He looked over his shoulder.

No one followed.

At least none that he could see.

That did not mean that he was alone. For every blind eye the city streets possessed there were a dozen more all-seeing ones in the forms of surveillance cameras. There were eyes everywhere. There could be no secrets in Corvus Keen's capital. Someone somewhere would be watching his passage from shadow to shadow across the old town, making a note of times and places, recording his journey for evidence that could and would be used as evidence against him should his treasure disappoint.

But it would not.

Not this time.

He was sure of that.

He felt the warmth of the stone tablet through the bundle of rags. It was impossibly hot against his chest. It was as though the stone were aware of his purpose and its role as betrayer of an entire species — and the notion excited it. He shook off the grim pessimism that settled with the snow. The paranoia engendered by this not so brave new world was akin to madness. He had borne the stone for hundreds of miles, never stopping, never daring to share his burden, for in his hands he clutched proof conclusive that the Corvani, Corvus Keen's elite, were everything the dictator demanded them to be.

They *were* the master race.

In one line of text carved deep into the bedrock everything he and his people held dear was undermined. His first instinct was to hide it. Its potential for pain was that great, but it was everything he needed to get close to Keen. He would have one chance to kill the dictator. One. He had carved away the stone and carried it all the way from Klozel, bearing it for over eight hundred miles. It was a treasure unlike any other. The dictator had bid the twelve of them to go, find him proof conclusive of divergent evolution.

He couldn't have known what he would find when he cracked the seal on the ancient tomb and heaved the funeral stone back. There had been nothing to mark it out as significant; it was just one of a thousand such tombs in the valley. Some were the final resting place of merchants and priests; others appeared to house petty princes and minor royalty, but this one, this miraculous place, was empty — well not quite empty — while there were no mummified corpses, no piles of rotten grave goods and tarnished treasures — there *was* another kind of treasure inside the tomb. And that was what made it so remarkable. A living history of the Kelani had been carved into the walls. He had found the final resting place of the Keepers.

He hadn't dared believe it at first; the Keepers were as much the stuff of legend as the secrets they protected.

Secrets worth murdering for, he knew now.

There had not been a Keeper for two hundred years.

Now he knew why: the last had been murdered even before the great tomb of knowledge could be completed, his precious wisdom spilled out with his blood before he could carve it into the stone. The murderer had almost certainly come before the Keeper could take an apprentice, meaning that there had been no one for him to school in the old ways of the Kelani, no one for him to entrust with the old stories and the even older truths.

The grave robber could only imagine the secrets that had been lost.

So now he came, a thief in the night running across the deserted town square as the snow fell, clutching one of those lost truths to his chest, ready to hand it over to the enemy. He made the sign of the Raven across his chest as one of the black birds ghosted through the silhouettes of both moons.

He forced himself to stop running, to regulate his breathing and simply be *calm* as he approached the ruin of the old cathedral. Once it might have been an awe-inspiring building but now it bled sadness and decay out into the night streets. The grave robber drew his cloak up tighter around his throat and shuffled up toward the door.

It was ajar.

With one lingering backward glance, he stepped through into the dusty interior. The acoustics of his footsteps changed immediately. Outside they had been solid, very much a part of the ground. In here each footstep echoed up into the fusty air, folding in on the next. The sound was as majestic as it was empty. The old cathedral was a relic to the age of the Redeemer, a better, vanished time. Beneath the vaulted dome it was easy to believe in divinity. It was ironic that Corvus Keen's man had chosen to make his home in the crypts. The grave robber walked down the aisle, eyes darting furtively left and right as he clutched his treasure to his chest. The huge ceiling cast a ripple of shadows over the lines of wooden pews. Blind statues stood sentinel, their faces turned away from the injustices of the world. Each one was a work of art. The craftsmanship that went into the sculpting was sublime but their beauty was marred where chisels had broken away the profile of noses and gouged into cheeks and eyes. That had been the first crime of the new regime — writing itself over the treasures of the old one. The thief shuddered, hurrying down the aisle toward the stairs that curved down into the crypts.

The oak on the handrail had silvered with age. The center of each step had been worn smooth by the passage of thousands of shuffling feet over the years. He went down. In the seconds before he knocked on the door his heavy breathing was the only sound in the place.

"Who is it?" the voice came from behind the door.

"Kelkus," the grave robber said. "I have brought you something."

"A treasure?" the old man said, opening the door a crack. Withered skin and the sharp angles of a nose peered through the narrow opening.

He nodded eagerly. "From the tomb of the Keepers," he said, still clutching the bundle to his chest possessively.

The nose twitched. "The Keepers, you say? Now that might be something worth disturbing my studies for. Come, show me this treasure of yours."

The huge door groaned inwards to reveal a crypt stripped of sarcophagi and the trappings of death. There was nothing holy or restful about the chamber. Where there ought to have been coffins stood a series of workbenches and crystal beakers bubbling on low flames. The grave robber had no notion what distillation was in the works; the various colors in the bell jars and beakers meant nothing to him. He was, after all, a historian, not an alchemist. He looked around the room, drinking it all in greedily. There was so much to see. Every angle and surface offered some peculiar delight or revulsion. It was impossible to take it all in at once, though he tried.

The chamber itself was big, stretching into the shadows where the eye could no longer see any details and everything was reduced to smudges of gray and darker gray. It was cold and poorly lit. Being subterranean, there was no natural light source. Instead, the chamber was illuminated by a dozen smaller ones, oil lamps and candles that guttered now in the draught that came through the open door. No single light lit more than a few square feet around it. Some overlapped, others didn't, leaving large dark patches. There was a row of metal footlockers that looked decidedly militaristic and functional, and very out of place lining the crypt wall, and bookshelves weighed down with manila folders stuffed to bursting with papers, some old and yellowed others still fresh and crisp white. On one of the tabletops he could see what looked to be a blue-line drawing of some description, but the inking was far too intricate for him to decipher without being able to study it properly. Glass-fronted display cabinets were crammed full of relics and treasures, some genuine, more fake. He had an eye for fraudulent bric-a-brac and Kelkus had hoarded a world's worth of it down here. There were broken fragments of weapons strewn haphazardly among the secular trophies from both the Corvani and Kelani heritage. The chamber was crammed with thousands of things the eye couldn't possibly comprehend in a moment's glance. Hundreds of thousands of things.

All the mundanity of the room kept his attention from the one truly spectacular — and equally revolting — scene that dominated the chamber. His stomach lurched. He stepped further into the room. The lights around him shifted and he saw them; four stone tablets identical to the one he carried. Each was suspended from the ceiling on a grid of chain. There was space for the fifth and final tablet to be hung. The centerpiece of the macabre display — he didn't know whether it was an experiment or a supposed piece of art — was a man.

He was strapped down to a huge wooden wheel-like table, canted on its side so he appeared to be suspended, head down on his chest, arms pulled up in a painful vee along the spokes of the wheel.

The hooks and barbs of the chains lashed him to the table.. IV lines snaked down toward him, intertwined with the chains. They were fed by clear plastic bags on stands — they could have been pumping anything into the wretched man's body, anesthetic, nutrition, unguents or life-giving antibiotics, it was impossible to tell. He wore a ventilation mask. The rasp of the respirator breathing for him filled the room. It hissed and blew with a slow, regular rhythm. In. Hiss. Out. Blow. In. Hiss. Out. Blow. The mask itself had filmed with moisture. It was a tiny detail, but it made the horror all the more human for the grave robber. He couldn't understand why the man was being kept alive — if that was what was happening here.

"Now, what of this treasure?" Kelkus asked.

He turned, grateful for something else to look at. Kelkus' voice was brittle but his flesh was anything but. He towered over the grave robber by almost a full twelve inches, and was twice as broad across the shoulders. He was a brute of a man with matted unwashed hair hanging down lankly across his face. It didn't mask the spider web of shrapnel scars that ruined the entire left side of his face.

"Here," the grave robber said.

"Give it to me."

He did.

Kelkus peeled back the rag-cloth wrap slowly, almost reverentially, corner by corner to expose the stone tablet. He studied the markings. The grave robber didn't need to look at them; he remembered precisely what was carved into the stone. The central image was a cross, a man being crucified in its cross-brace. It was a crude rendition of humanity, the face almost alien in its simplicity. Wrapped around the figure's left ankle was a serpent. Its tail coiled up around the man's leg to his waist, and seemed to emerge from a wound in his stomach. On each limb of the cross were representations of the elements, earth, wind, fire and water, and beyond them, more crude carvings, the words *lament, grief, mourning* and *suffering*, and a single symbol that marked eternity. The tablet encompassed the elements, time, and mortality all in one image. It was the final line of symbols that offered the proof Corvus Keen sought, the knowledge that this species came from beyond the stars.

Kelkus brushed his fingers over the tablet, feeling out every cranny carved into the stone as though he might somehow read its story in the language of the blind. He lingered over the image of the serpent.

"Now this *is* a treasure," he said. "You shall be rewarded, of course. First, though, help me hang this."

"Of course," the grave robber said, wondering how he could possibly help attach the tablet to the chains without having to see the man on the wheel. He couldn't. Together, they heaved the tablet into place. The hooks sank with surprising ease into the stone. As the first barb pierced the stone the grave robber felt a shiver of coldness thrill through his fingertips, almost as though the thing were alive. When the second barb pierced the stone it was worse.

"Oh yes, yes, yes, yes," Kelkus crooned. He turned about in a full circle, repeating each of the lines engraved upon the five stones one after another as though voicing an incantation. In between the words he heard a crack, a deep, stone-tearing noise that couldn't be anything else. The grave robber looked up, following the direction of the sound. He half expected to see the ceiling beginning to crumble and come down. A second later a fresh crack split through the heart of the fifth stone tablet, the fissure running through the center of the crucified man. A third rending crack cleaved the thing in two.

Something was moving. Coming out of the ruined stone. "What is it?" he gasped, stumbling back a step.

"Divinity," Kelkus said. "Bow down, little man, you are in the presence of the gods!"

He shook his head, denying the evidence of his own eyes. The thing Kelkus called a god slithered out of the ruined stone. It came an inch at a time, sinuous and sure, tasting the air. It took him a moment to realize what it was: a serpent. The serpent coiled around the iron chain suspended from the ceiling and climbed.

In a curious gesture that was almost tender, Kelkus pulled the breathing mask off the man and ran his fingers through his matted hair. Then all pretense at tenderness disappeared as he yanked the man's head back, forcing his mouth wide open in a scream that lacked only the *sound* of agony. Everything else was burned in the dying man's face.

As the serpent wound itself around the chains the grave robber backed away from the center of the circle, bumping into the table in his hurry to be out of the crypt. The ripple of motion along the iron links almost dislodged the snake. The creature hissed, opening its mouth impossibly wide. All he could think, staring at it, was that it had too many teeth. It was unlike any snake he had seen in his life.

And then it started to move again, coiling down the links until it reached the man's hand, and down the length of his forearm, leaving a mucus trail behind it.

Kelkus yanked on the man's hair again, forcing the wretch's mouth wider.

The serpent's tail lashed against his clavicle, and then with a sudden and shocking flurry of motion, reared up and plunged into the man's gaping mouth.

The grave robber stared, trapped in abject horror. His muscles refused to obey his mind. All he wanted to do was run but they wouldn't let him. The convulsions tore at the man's emaciated frame, and then his head came up, eyes blazing cold gold, a new found strength in his bones, and he surely heard the voice of the dead as the man rasped, "I am your God, worship me!" He pulled free from the chains and rose from the table. There was no pain in his face now, only strength. Glory.

The grave robber fell on his knees and wept.

Kelkus knelt beside him, eyes burning as he surrendered to the revelation.

"I live to serve," he said.

"Yes," the god said, "you do."

CHAPTER FIVE

One of Us

THE TOK'RA emissary came through the Stargate less than an hour later. She was grim-faced and wore her grief like a crown as she walked down the ramp. Her descent was slow and measured, her curiosity had her eyes darting across the room, taking it all in. O'Neill knew the routine, this one was a soldier. It was in her bearing, the way in which she carried herself and, most tellingly of all, the way with which she familiarized herself with possibly hostile territory. She was scoping out potential exits before she had even entered the room. The woman made no attempt to mask her annoyance at the muzzles aiming at her as she studied the faces of the Tau'ri watching her. "Which of you is Hammond of the Tau'ri?" Her voice had that brusque metallic echo of the symbiote talking through its host. The inhuman resonance never failed to unnerve him.

Hammond inclined his bald head slightly, almost deferentially, and stepped forward. He began to greet the woman but was cut off by her puzzled frown. "Ah, I was led to believe you were a great warrior… you do not look so great."

"Appearances can be deceptive," O'Neill said, putting himself between the general and the emissary. He couldn't help himself; something about the woman just irked him. "You, after all, look like a lady." The words were out of his mouth before he could stop himself.

"That is quite enough, Colonel O'Neill," Hammond said, cutting him off before he could talk himself into trouble.

"Quite," the woman said. Jack detected the hint of a self-deprecating smile. It took him a moment to realize that she was agreeing with him, not Hammond. It was enough to have Jack reassess his immediate dislike: perhaps she wasn't quite so irksome after all. "And you must be the one they call O'Neill."

He grinned. "Nice to see my reputation precedes me."

"Oh, it most certainly does. If you have accomplished half the things we are led to believe, you are most certainly a worthy ally."

"Thank you, I think. You seem to have the advantage here, what with us being so famous and all. You, on the other hand are?"

Her smile broadened slightly. "I am Jerichau of the Tok'ra, I share this body with Selina Ros, my host," she introduced herself. Jack pulled a face, making a show of trying to remember if he had heard of her. "We received your transmission, there is much we must talk about."

"Isn't there always?" Jack said.

"Can we talk somewhere..." Jerichau gestured toward the line of guns, "away from all of the weapons?"

"Of course. The briefing room," Hammond said. "Teal'c, Doctor Jackson, Major Carter, if you would care to join us? At ease, everyone."

The six of them adjourned to the solitude of the briefing room and settled themselves around the conference table. The lighting in the room was subdued. Jack pressed his palms down flat against the tabletop. He could feel the eddies of the air-conditioning blowing around them.

"Talk to us," he told Jerichau without looking up. There was no preamble. Now was not the time for it. The Tok'ra obviously knew more than they would let on. They played their little games of politics about as well as Daniel played poker. He tried to put aside his natural mistrust but as long as they were playing with a loaded deck he was going to be suspicious—it was thinking like that that kept him alive.

"We have reason to believe that your visitor was indeed

Tok'ra."

"Go on."

"Much is unknown and will remain so until we have the chance to examine the remains, but Nyren Var was working to recover a weapon of sorts. She has been out of contact for several cycles now. In her last transmission she reported that the Goa'uld were aware of the weapon and had sent Jaffa to hunt it down."

"I'm not sure I follow," Hammond interrupted. "Why would they need to hunt for a weapon? That's a peculiar choice of words, isn't it?"

"Indeed it is, General, but no less accurate for it. The weapon in question is a living thing. A creature known as Mujina."

"Okay, now you've got my attention," O'Neill said, looking up from his hands. "What are we talking about here? Big? Small? Breathes fire? Lay it on me."

"Mujina is an archetypal creature, O'Neill."

"And what's that supposed to mean?"

It was Daniel who answered, not the Tok'ra woman. He pushed his glasses back along his nose. "Archetypes are personality templates, Jack. Joseph Campbell identified them during his research into the monomyth, the single story that is at the root of all the others. There's the Mentor, the Hero, ah, others that are more obscure, like the threshold guardian, or the herald, then, more interestingly, the shadow, which is the embodiment of everything we would like to defeat, and the shapeshifter —"

"Now hold on a minute," O'Neill cut across Daniel. "Are you telling me this 'weapon' has the ability to change shape? That's a bit more than breathing fire…"

"Not physically, I doubt," Daniel said, and then turned to Jerichau for confirmation or denial. "Shapeshifting in this respect relates more to the fact that the shapeshifter is more of a catalyst, it makes things happen and you are never quite sure as to its allegiances."

"So it *can't* change shape?"

"Jerichau?"

"Doctor Jackson is quite right in his summation of the Mujina's gifts. It is an archetypal creature, a blank slate if you like, capable of being all things to all people, from hero to shadow, shapeshifter and trickster."

"So you're saying it isn't to be trusted."

"In the wrong hands nothing is, Colonel O'Neill," the Tok'ra said.

"And, let's be blunt, the wrong hands would be Goa'uld," Jack finished the thought for everyone around the table. Jerichau nodded. "Now, let me get this straight," he said, "this creature, whatever you call it, how many of them are there? I mean are we talking about mom and pop and baby Mujina makes three, or are we talking about a planetful of happy little shapeshifters?"

"There is only one Mujina, Colonel O'Neill, and the planet Nyren Var found it on, Vasaveda, was its prison."

"And there goes the other shoe," Jack said.

Teal'c raised a questioning eyebrow.

"Oh come on, you heard the weapon comment. A prison the size of a planet must make it one hell of a critter."

"Imagine the greatest evil of your time, that could be a reflection of Mujina, but conversely Mujina has the potential to be the greatest hero known to your people."

"All things to everyone," Daniel said. "The only place it is safe from the reflection of evil is away from everyone else. Can you imagine this in someone like Apophis' hands?" He looked at Teal'c. The Jaffa said nothing.

"I'd rather not."

"A dark and hungry god arises," Jerichau said. The metallic quality of her tone shifted, becoming immediately softer and more feminine. "That is why Nyren Var had to find the creature first, so it could never be turned fully into the weapon it has the potential to be. It needs people around it to define it."

"How did the Goa'uld find out about the Mujina?" Sam asked, speaking up for the first time.

"There is only one way," Selina Ros admitted. "The information must have come from within the Tok'ra; which means there is a traitor within our number." Her voice shifted, dopplering down to the metallic chill of the symbiote's filtered tone. Her face twisted in revulsion, her lips suddenly thin and blanched of color. "Which is impossible, so thinking about it serves no one," Jerichau finished for her host.

"So, to get back to the smoking hand," O'Neill said, making it quite plain that he didn't swallow Jerichau's protestations any more than Selina Ros did. It was interesting, seeing the host and symbiote openly disagree. He couldn't remember having seen it in any of the Tok'ra he had met before. "Your woman went to this prison, found the creature in all of its glory, but was compromised before she could exfiltrate?"

"I do not think, Colonel O'Neill, I fear, there is a difference. The planet of the Mujina lies in interdicted space, out far beyond the protection of the Asgard. It was banished centuries before, when all reason would have seen the creature put to death. Now we face the consequences of our predecessor's vacillation."

"You can't kill it because of its nature, that's inhumane," Daniel objected. "If what you say is right, it isn't inherently evil, not as we would understand it, and left alone it isn't dangerous. So by any conceivable measure that would be cold blooded murder."

"Which is precisely the argument they made, and yet by showing mercy and seeking to hide it, the Ancients have left us vulnerable. So which is the greater wisdom, Doctor Jackson? The death of one or the death of many? Which would your conscience prefer? What would appease your guilt? Perhaps you would sacrifice worlds?"

"That is enough, Jerichau," Hammond said, his voice every

bit as cold and alien as the Tok'ra's.

"As you say, Hammond of the Tau'ri," Jerichau ceded.

"There's still something you aren't saying," Jack said. It had been bothering him from the start.

"Does it really need saying?"

"I'd like to hear it anyway," O'Neill said.

"Very well. We cannot risk Mujina's unique gifts being twisted to the will of the Goa'uld."

"Which means you want us to go find it and clean up the mess your Neryn Var has left behind, right?"

"We do not have the resources to fight the Jaffa face to face, our strength is infiltration, working in the shadows. That is where we are best deployed in this long game. You, however, Colonel O'Neill, are very much soldiers. This is the side of the fight where your kind excel."

"Flattery will get you everywhere," Jack said wryly.

CHAPTER SIX

My Hero

THE CREATURE huddled up against the hot wall.

It was alone.

That was its curse.

It was always alone.

All it wanted — in this world or any other — was company. It had never needed more. Never wanted more. It craved nearness. It hungered for the proximity of thoughts and minds, the needs of hopes and dreams. But that was all. It had never harmed anyone. It was not evil.

It was not this thing they accused it of being when they passed down their judgment. They acted like gods of the galaxies lording it over the lesser species, claiming to protect those too weak to stand up to the aggressors, but that was the nature of survival, the galaxies were divided into two kinds of species, the predators and the prey. They judged it a predator, which was cruel, and the punishment they meted out was vile in its harshness.

It was no predator. All it ever wanted was to help, to serve the needs of those near it so that they might like it. Its needs were childish in their simplicity.

How could that ever be wrong?

But their words still echoed in its ears all these centuries later: *Vile. Evil. Corrupt. Dangerous. An abomination. A threat. Against the natural order.*

It pleaded and whimpered but they would not listen. They did not care. They would not look it in the eye as they sought to silence it, to stifle it, to lock it away alone in the dark and leave it to die.

But it would not die.

Not alone.

Not like this.

So it scavenged and it made a nest deep down in the dark out of the fire, down where the fungi and the lichen clung to the sticky wet heat of the stones, safe. It survived on the spores, for every mouthful it ate spreading another out so that more might grow in its place. It lost time — or the sense of it — day and night ceased to be of any importance. Instead it judged its place in the world by the rumbles of the lava and the gasses trapped deeper beneath the crust, venting their rage as the pressures built up beyond the ground's ability to cage them. At first it had counted the eruptions but when the numbers rose into the meaningless it gave up.

And through it all it was alone.

Until the woman came.

It had thought she was different. She didn't judge it. She didn't fear it. She had found it down here stumbling around in the darkness and followed it back to its nest. She had helped it. She had soothed it. She had shared herself with it willingly, letting it into her mind so that it could taste all she held dear, so that it could understand her losses and her pains, her hopes, fears, and the needs that drove her. And it did understand. They were kindred creatures for all their differences. They were cut from the same spiritual cloth. They sought to help, only ever to help.

It had sung to her, not with words because it had forgotten the shapes of so many of them, but with harmonics, resonances it found pleasing. She had smiled and, touching its rough cheek, promised that she would protect it, that it didn't have to be alone, and even as she lied to the Mujina and said it was safe, the others had come. Those she feared most in the world. It had sought them out, creeping closer so that it might taste their minds and learn their dreams and desires, but they were dark. The creature knew it could never be safe. Not with the others here. So it had tried to trick them for her, but one among them was stronger. It did not fall for the Mujina's mind games. With its power broken, the outsider had the others bind and gag it, robbing the Mujina of its sight and voice and effectively locking it out of their minds — and for once the Mujina did not want to help, it did not want the woman to come find it and save it, it wanted only to be left alone…

And was rewarded.

She had left it, like all of the others before her, all promises forgotten, broken. It was ever the same, the Mujina fated to be alone, it thought bitterly. But that was not fair. The others had hunted the woman to extinction. She had not left willingly. Her only crime was that she had not come back.

So it pressed its back up against the warm wet stones and rocked slowly forwards and back, forwards and back, each time a little further forward, a little harder back, until the rough points of the stone dug into its flesh. It needed to feel physical pain. Nothing else would block out the spiritual hurt.

It screamed out into the dark, a wretched, primal cry torn from its ragged lips.

It was alone.

Again.

How long would it be before others came through the dead eye looking for it? How many more eruptions would it count off before the eye lit up blue with its own fire? How much longer would it be before she came back to it?

It cried silent tears into the rough cloth covering its face, and sang again the song it had sung for her, hoping somehow she would hear the harmonics and come back to it.

It was never meant to be alone.

CHAPTER SEVEN

What Price Victory?

SG-1 KITTED up.

Daniel sat with Jerichau learning all he could about the prison planet. The woman was fascinating. Quite unlike many of the Tok'ra they had encountered. For one thing, she had a sense of humor. He had rather enjoyed seeing Jack squirm while she toyed with him. It was usually Daniel's role to play tongue-tied and twisted whereas Jack was always so together. It was part of that bad-boy charm of his. It was funny, with all this talk of archetypes, he couldn't help but think of them in the same vein. He had thought it would be easy to hang a label on each of them, Jack the hero, dynamic and strong, Teal'c the shapeshifter who had begun his time in the shadows only to come over to the light, Daniel himself as the mentor, offering knowledge instead of brawn, and Sam another aspect of the teacher, like Daniel but then so unlike him, but their roles weren't remotely so straightforward. Sometimes Teal'c wore the mantel of hero, at other times Sam, or Daniel himself. It was as though collectively they owned the attributes of the hero, the best and the worst, and together they were so much more than the sum of their parts.

But then that was what being a part of a team like SG-1 was all about, wasn't it?

Vasaveda lacked a breathable atmosphere: indeed if everything Jerichau said was the truth they were about to willingly enter a Miltonesque landscape of Paradise most certainly lost. She talked of a world so harsh it beggared belief; volcanic fissures venting steam, red lava leaking out of the ground as though the planet itself wept for the Hell it had become. She described wonders that resonated with the Christian iconography of that blasted place, the unending barren wasteland, the unbearable heat, the volatility of the oxygen in the air that caused the sky itself to ignite in flame and burn for days on end. He listened to it all and understood that no amount of planning or forethought could prepare them for Vasaveda. She was painting a picture of a place so wretched it was impossible to imagine finding it inhabited at all. The worst of it, though, was her contention that the Ancients had somehow made it that way, and that it had not always been so.

"We believe the Mujina has taken refuge in an elaborate subterranean network not far from the Stargate itself. Nyren Var's transmission was cryptic: see the world through the old man's eyes."

"Well that makes a lot of sense," Daniel said.

"It is all we have, but hopefully it will be clear when you arrive on the prison planet."

She wrote out seven symbols on the scrap of paper Daniel placed on the table between them. "The co-ordinates to hell," he said to himself as he studied them. He felt a thrill of fear chase down the ladder of his spine as he picked the paper up. It wasn't just that the place she described so vividly unnerved him, far from it actually — he'd been to hell and back before and it could hardly be worse than Ne'tu. No, it was the thought of bringing back the Mujina that placed a chill in his heart, because of all of them, Daniel Jackson understood the implications of a creature that could twist itself to represent all things to all people. History was riddled with examples of power corrupted. In each of those cases there was nothing *super*natural to amplify them. If mankind alone was capable of such darkness, what was it capable of with a creature like the Mujina at its side?

They were going into the Ninth Circle, fully intending to hunt the devil and, if they were lucky, drag him back out with them. It didn't bear thinking about, so of course it was all he could think about.

"It can't be allowed to fall into the hands of the Goa'uld, surely you understand that?" the softer voice of Selina Ros said. He had noticed the symbiote had a habit of allowing its host to rise to the surface when the conversation turned uncomfortably moral. But then, perhaps everything in its world was starkly black and white?

"I just can't help thinking it's a case of damned if we do, damned if we don't," Daniel said, surprising himself with his honesty.

"Isn't that always the way?" she said, sounding unerringly like Jack. It was precisely the sort of thing he would say.

"But it shouldn't be, should it?" he didn't know who he was trying to convince, himself or the Tok'ra. "Sometimes there should just be a right thing to do."

"It would make life simpler. But — "

"There's always a but," he finished for her, as though that were all she could possibly have to say on the matter. She nodded. Her faint smile didn't reach all the way to her eyes. "We need to join the others."

"You will do the right thing, Daniel Jackson," she said, as though that were meant to comfort him. It didn't.

"And that's where the problem lies."

He took the co-ordinates through to Hammond in the command room so that they could be input into the dialing computer. Jack and Teal'c were already there. The towering Jaffa gave him a curious look, his brow furrowing slightly around the gold glyph that marked him Jaffa. It left Daniel with the disconcerting feeling that his thoughts had been scoured, leaving his doubts red and raw on the surface. He tried to shrug it off. Now wasn't the time to unburden himself to the others. Selina Ros was right; the Mujina could not be allowed to fall into the hands of the Goa'uld. The implications did not bear thinking about.

"Something wrong?" Jack asked.

"No more than usual," Daniel said, managing a wry smile. "Jerichau has been telling me what to expect from this prison planet." He told them what she had said, skimming over some of the more colorful images but making damned sure he got the point across.

"As ideas go, this is sounding worse and worse," Jack commented, fastening one of the straps on the sleeve of his evac suit.

"Indeed," Teal'c said. "I have heard speak of such phenomena. I believe it is quite beautiful to see the sky aflame."

"I'm sure it's beautiful, T-man. I'm more worried about the practicalities than the aesthetics. Things like how much heat is going to be generated from the oxygen burn off and what, exactly, it's likely to do to us. The idea of being vaporized because I spent too long staring at the sun doesn't really appeal all that much. Not sure I want to go to my grave with a burning sky being the last thing I see, it's a little too biblical, if you get my meaning."

"You do not wish to die," Teal'c said flatly, his flair for stating the obvious not letting him down. It earned a smile from Jack.

"Atta boy, Teal'c. Daniel, go get suited up."

He nodded. Daniel walked toward the closed door, and then turned, as though pulled up by a sudden thought. "Jack?"

O'Neill turned to look at him. Daniel wanted nothing more than to take him to one side and share his misgivings about what they were getting involved in. "Something bothering you?"

Daniel shrugged. "Hard to say." Of course, it wasn't, it was easy to say, what was hard was to live with the consequences of what he had to say.

"Spit it out, Daniel."

"All right, here's the thing," Daniel said. "Are we sure we want to do this? I mean, have we thought through the implications of bringing this creature back with us? Are we talking about trying to keep it a prisoner here, trading one cell for another? And if we aren't, then what? It isn't as though we can drop it off at Disney World and tell it to go sightseeing. And the only other option I can come up with turns us into a death squad. So, what are we going to do? And don't say find it and worry about it later. The Ancients hid the Mujina for a reason: they understood the threat it posed."

"So what do you suggest, Daniel?"

"I don't know, Jack. I can't see any good coming out of this. The Tok'ra called it a weapon, but it's worse than that; you can choose not to detonate a bomb or put the safety on a gun, but how do you stop this creature from being what it is? How do you stop it from finding the one thing it knows you will respond to, and giving it to you? Kill it? That's not what we are, is it? Or did we become the Tok'ra's assassins when I wasn't looking?" Daniel screwed his face up. He'd said it. He hadn't intended to, but looking at his friend he'd not been able to stop himself. He owed it to Jack to speak up. Besides, of them all, Jack was surely the most likely to respond to the creature — after all, there was enough need in him to fuel an army of Mujinas.

"No one is killing anything," Jack said, and Daniel almost believed him, but Jack was a soldier — he had to know it came down to assessing a credible threat and removing that threat if there was no alternative. The Mujina could not be allowed to fall into Goa'uld hands, but neither could it be allowed fall into human hands. It didn't take a huge leap of the imagination to picture a Mayberry or a Kinsey with something like the Mujina by their side, and imagine the reflection their flawed humanity would conjure from the creature. Jack had to know full well that mankind was every bit as dangerous as anything the stars could bring down. And if he knew, then his promise had to be a lie. A well intentioned lie, but a lie just the same. "We're on a Search and Rescue, let's find this creature, extract it, and get back home. We can worry about the "What If's" when we've made sure it can't fall into Goa'uld hands. That's a promise, okay? But until then we have got our orders."

"All right, Jack," he said, closing the door of the command room behind him.

CHAPTER EIGHT

Jet Black Sunrise

IBLIS STRODE purposefully through the dank corridor. *This*, he thought, and not for the first time in the year since he had awoken, *is the hive of power? This filth-ridden place?* It was laughable. These Corvani had no class. They were like grubs crawling about in their own excreta. How they had risen above the Kelani amazed him. But then, the Kelani were hardly more developed than the average monkey. He looked back at Kelkus trailing along behind him, sniffing and sniveling in his footsteps. *Monkey, yes, that was an appropriate comparison.* Iblis was tired of the wretched human, but as long as he served a purpose he would allow the man to live. He needed a disciple, and Kelkus had proven just that. Willing to do anything to spread Iblis' influence in the Court of the Raven King without risk of exposing his nature, allowing Iblis to plant the seeds of unrest and greed he thrived upon. But it hurt him, all of this sneaking about. He battled with his ego, wanting to stride these corridors as god, as was his right. *In time,* he promised himself. *In time.* As it was, he had his own role to play and for the moment it was every bit as sycophantic as Kelkus's.

What have I become? he asked himself. He didn't know the answer.

He pushed open the door to the throne room. The light streamed down in bright unbroken beams from the dozen skylight windows around the high ceiling. Dust motes danced their dervish swirl, trapped in the beams. It was a solitary thing of beauty in a place of ugliness.

Iblis had no time for beauty.

Corvus Keen sat in the center on his chair of dead birds, his wolfhound at his feet. The man was a bloated slug, folds of fat oozing across the arms of his ostentatious chair. Iblis had to stifle the urge to laugh at the pomp with which the man dressed his world. From a distance it almost looked majestic but as he moved closer the grease and the fat stains became more noticeable. The throne was fashioned from the skulls and wings of hundreds upon hundreds of crushed and broken ravens. It was a vile construction and it stank as only carrion could. Keen sat there, drumming his fat fingers on the tiny skulls of the birds. He was surrounded on all sides by his cronies bowing and scraping and telling him what he wanted to hear. Behind them huge black velvet drapes were emblazoned with a silver sigil, Corvus Keen's wing-spread bird. He had taken to calling himself the Raven King recently. It was an aspect of the man's psychosis that Iblis nurtured. He seemed to truly believe that he was evolving into something greater than human. Keen wore a cloak of feathers. The gore still clung to the tips of some. It was decidedly primitive beside the crisply tailored black and silver uniforms of his soldiers.

The chamber was full. Iblis tasted tension in the air. This was good. Keen was nothing if not unpredictable, which made for curious entertainments in his domain. Iblis wondered what little delight the man had in mind for today? Torture probably. It usually was.

The crowd melted away from Iblis, allowing him to walk slowly toward the throne. He stopped at the foot of the dais and knelt, slowly, but without bowing his head, and rose. It pained him to pretend loyalty to any human. No, pain was too prosaic a term; it burned him to bend the knee. He was Goa'uld. He was no mere toady. But he could bury his nature a while longer and wear the mask of follower while it suited him. He had plans. Such plans. Keen owned these souls. Iblis owned Keen. He could live without their devotion for now.

The secret was in the game itself. Iblis was patient. He had laid out a long game. In the year since he had awoken and taken this host he had mapped out an immaculate strategy. He would not fail. When the time came he would snap Corvus Keen as easily as he would one of the human's brittle birds. There was no rush. At least not while Keen was useful to him.

The fat man was being entertained by a nervous juggler. Everything stopped as Iblis approached the fat man. Iblis inclined his head and smiled wryly. "Please, do carry on," he muttered, and all eyes turned on the sweating fool as he coughed slightly and shuffled his feet.

"What are you waiting for? You heard the man, entertain us."

The fool hurled his clubs up into the air above his head and scrabbled to catch them. Too high, and too hard, their arc took them out of easy reach. Sweat beaded on the fool's face. Iblis enjoyed the look of rapture on Keen's features as he watched the perspiration run into the fool's eyes. *It will all end in tears*, Iblis thought rather smugly, but then tears were Corvus Keen's preferred currency when it came to settling debts, so that was hardly surprising. A wooden club clattered on the marbled floor. As one, Corvus Keen's hungry court of vultures sucked in their breath. The huge wolfhound at Keen's feet looked up at the sudden absence of sound. Seeing nothing worthy of its attention it settled down to doze again. Like its master, the dog's fat jowls dribbled spittle as it breathed. Keen scratched the dog between the ears. It was curious how the man could look so much like the beast, and ever more so the longer they spent in each other's company.

Iblis looked at the juggler.

"You are a tedious man, Fool," Keen rasped. "What can you do that is more interesting? Watching you throw your clubs in the air is sending me to sleep. We have to make things more exciting. I know, you're going to juggle, Fool, but you are going to do it like your life depends on it. Between barks from Senisia here, you drop a club you lose a finger, understand? If you make it you walk away with your fingers and fifty Raqs for your trouble. Now, pick up your clubs."

Iblis watched the poor man gather his clubs with everyone staring at him, willing him to fail. A few fingers would put Keen in the right kind of mood to be amenable to the idea the Goa'uld was going to plant in his mind later.

Corvus Keen's hand snaked out and tugged at the wolfhound's ear, causing the dog to bark angrily as it looked around for the source of the unexpected attack.

The first club sailed into the air, followed along its arc by the second. The juggler caught the first in his left hand even as the he tossed the third with his right. It was a simple pattern but there was no need for anything elaborate, the threat of lost fingers added spice enough to the game as it was. The clubs flew hand over hand for six passes. He almost dropped one twice but recovered. Keen stared intently at the man. The sores around his lips and chin glistened with saliva.

The fool managed two more passes before he dropped the first club. He crumbled inward after that, whimpering and pleading for the dog to bark even as he fumbled another club and then another.

He dropped five clubs before the dog barked again.

"You owe me a hand, Fool," Keen said, picking at the dirt beneath his fingernail disinterestedly. "But I am in a good mood," Keen smiled gregariously. "I think I shall spare you."

Relief swept over the juggler's face.

It was short lived.

"I am a man of my word. I will just take the fingers; three from your right hand, two from your left, I think. Now get out of my sight before I change my mind and take both of your hands."

Two of Keen's loyal Raven Guard dragged the juggler away

kicking and screaming every step of the way. The court was silent for a moment, not shocked by the decree so much as savoring it. Of course, every one of them knew that but for the grace of Keen there they themselves went.

Iblis smiled at the cruelty of it. It was such a petty thing, this human condition, but there was much amusement to be had watching them play at being gods.

"Perhaps I might have a little of your time? In private," Iblis bent low and whispered into Corvus Keen's ear. The fat man nodded, and pushed his hefty bulk up out of the bird throne.

"Talk as we walk, my friend," Keen wheezed after barely three steps. His belly spilled out over the top of his bursting trousers.

Kelkus fell into step behind them, the shadow's shadow. The three swept through the corridors of Corvus Keen's Raven Tower, and up the three hundred and twenty-one winding steps to the privacy of the roof top aviary where Keen kept his birds.

Iblis took perverse delight in making the fat man huff and puff and struggle up the winding stair.

"Kelkus, make sure we are not overheard. My words are for the Great Keen alone. It would not do for pricked ears and wagging tongues to be party to our conversation."

"As you wish, my lord —" Iblis cut him off with a stare. It would not do for Kelkus to call him God before Keen. The corpulent tyrant's ego wouldn't stand for it. Kelkus bobbed his head and shuffled off, shooing the birds up into flight as he walked among them. Before he reached the tower door the air was a swirl with cawing ravens and cackling crows. There were so many more species up here in the aviary, but Keen's Raven Master kept them caged.

Iblis looked down upon the city.

There was a curious beauty to the sloping roofs and the twisting spires. They came together as a whole, like some great

tapestry of life laid out beneath him. Still, for every beautiful old spire there was a modern steel chimney belching factory smoke into the air. For every red clay rooftop there was
a corrugated iron one where function was more important
than form. Most noticeable of all though were the graveyards
and the crematorium fires that burned through the night.
These were Iblis' greatest achievement. The paranoia had
always festered away at the back of Keen's mind. The man
was a half-breed, that was his dark secret. He looked at the
Corvani and saw perfection; they were strong, the embodiment of the Divine Principle, angular, aquiline, beautiful. He
looked at the Kelani and saw a primate three rungs down the
evolutionary ladder.

Prejudice made him malleable.

It was a short step from being different to being demon-
ized.

"So why the secrecy, my friend?" Keen asked.

"Because this is for your ears only, Great Keen," Iblis said,
pandering to the man's vanity. It was a tricky game this flattery. Keen was no fool, and it would be a mistake to think of
him that way. The man was sharp. He had an uncanny gift
for knowing when he was being spoon-fed platitudes and had
a habit of playing the bluff incompetent when he wanted to
gauge the loyalty of those around him.

The idea of feigning weakness was alien to Iblis, but watching Corvus Keen he had begun to see just how advantageous
it could be, if played right. It took a certain finesse to pull it
off. It was all about playing up the clichéd expectancy of the
bloated greedy megalomaniac. The secret was to keep it as
close as possible to your true nature. Keen did crave power.
The man was corpulent but the slovenly manners were an act,
as was the unremitting cruelty. He enjoyed the air of blood-
lust his random acts of violence fostered among his followers
so he nurtured it and pretended at capriciousness.

Unlike so many humans Iblis had encountered throughout the galaxy, Keen's thirst for power was almost Goa'uld-like in its capacity and arrogance, but beyond that, the thing that had excited Iblis the most about this human monster was the guile and cunning he displayed on a daily basis in pursuit of it.

It went against Iblis' nature to lurk in the shadows, to lie, cheat, and steal, but being with Keen was teaching him that there was an entirely new way to wage a war. That was exciting. There was no other word for it. It opened up a slew of possibilities that promised to be amusing. And that, as far as Iblis was concerned, was the great fallacy of war. It wasn't merely about winning or losing, it was about playing the game with style. It was about the beauty of taking aim on a victim, not just about pulling the trigger. Anyone could kill, but genocide was an art form.

"Go on."

"Look up and tell me what you see."

"What foolishness is this?"

"Just do it."

"I see the sky. It is neither the night sky nor the day sky, simply the sky."

"Oh but it is so much more than that, Keen, so much more. That is just such a banal way of looking at the world. You aren't that simple, I don't believe it for a minute."

"Which is why you wanted this conversation alone. I understand."

"Indeed. What if I told you there were worlds out there, thousands upon thousands of them waiting to be conquered, what would you say then?"

"Then I would say I see opportunity," Keen said. "But you are talking absurdities, my friend. There is no life on other worlds. Life revolves around Banak and Thrace. The twin moons regulate the tides and provide the unique balance we need for life to flourish. That is just the way it is. Without them our world would wither and die. You might as well try and sell me the idea that the world is flat. Every rational thinking man knows it is not."

"And every rational thinking man is wrong, my friend. There are worlds out there. Humans like you are scattered across the galaxy."

"Like us," Keen corrected, absently.

"Like you," Iblis repeated.

"Are you trying to tell me you are not one of us?"

"I was not born under this sky, if that is what you are asking."

"Rubbish. Have you looked in the mirror, my friend? Your bone structure, your coloring, your eyes, even the aquiline shape of your nose is classical Corvani. There are a thousand statues that could have been sculpted with your face as their model. Stop playing foolish games. My patience is wearing thin. You wouldn't want to wear it through," he inclined his head meaningfully. Iblis followed the look, and the inference. It was a long way down.

"Humor me, Keen," he said, and then lowered his gaze. If Keen was half as aware as Iblis gave him credit for, the man would realize this was the first time since Iblis had come into his service that he had ever averted his gaze. When the Goa'uld raised his head again a peculiar golden tint suffused his eyes. His voice, when he spoke was different, too. Metallic. Cold. "I have such violent delights to show you if you have the strength to stand at my side, human. Such pains. I have walked a hundred worlds."

"But that's impossible," Keen said. He stumbled back a step, his certainty already eroded. Iblis smiled, the humorless smile of a man who delighted in unpinning the certainties that anchored the listener's world in all the realities he thought he knew.

"Is it? I could talk to you of the frozen gardens of Kabul, one of the wonders of the universe I am sure. Every plant, tree, every shrub there is frozen into an unchanging vista that catches the light and turns it into diamonds in the air. I could describe the still waters of Tania and its submerged city where the man-eating sharks swim through the crystal hive of tunnels that make up the sunken city. I could talk to you of Mitko or Paribas where evolution has twisted humanity in duals, where brother and sister inhabit the same flesh and war for dominance. There is so much you haven't seen or even dared imagine, Corvus Keen."

"Shut up, shut up, you are making this nonsense up. Shut up unless you want me to take your tongue, Iblis."

"These places all have one thing in common, Keen. They are places where my people once ruled. My people, Keen. The Goa'uld. We were your gods, Keen. Can you comprehend the power we had? We owned the suns and the moons and the stars. We oversaw the worlds and you worshipped us."

"Impossible. That is not how it was. The scripture says—"

"And who penned those precious scriptures? The humans my kith and kin scattered throughout the galaxies. Your people were slaves."

"Why tell me this?" Keen asked, shaken and obviously unwilling to believe.

"Because I can. Because it serves my purpose. Because I believe, finally, I have found a human worthy of the knowledge. Because the worlds are out there waiting for you to conquer. Because this world is yours and it is not enough, is it? Because you are not thinking."

As shocked as he was by Iblis's revelations, Keen bristled instinctively at the insult. Iblis could not help but smile.

"Then prove me wrong, man. Think. The Corvani and the Kelani *are* different. This is fundamental to your core beliefs, is it not? But ask yourself: why are they different? Because we brought you here from different worlds. That is your answer. Yes, you are both strains of humanity. Like vermin, humans flourish no matter how filthy the conditions of their existence."

"You brought us here?"

"Yes," Iblis said.

"But how?" Keen stared at him. Iblis could hear the thoughts running blindly through his mind. They all returned to the same one: but how? How when you appear so young? How could you colonize a world when it was young? How could we not know? And the truth was they did know. The deep-seated loathing that existed between the two species the Goa'uld had transplanted to this world ran deeper than anyone could explain, and went further back than any would have believed. It wasn't merely one man's fear of difference. And then something changed in Corvus Keen's expression, as though the servos powering the muscles had suddenly failed. The skin slipped. The brightness in the eyes failed. The sharpness of his cheeks softened and his jowls sagged. Each change was subtle, but seen all at once the effect was stunning.

It took a full minute for Keen to recover, but when he did he looked up at the sky, not at Iblis. "So where is this gateway to the stars?" It was the obvious question.

"In the arctic northlands."

"Why there? Why so far away from civilization? Why not here? Somewhere central where we could come and go at will? Why hide such a great treasure?"

"Because it was never meant for the humans we left behind," Iblis said. It was an answer that made sense. It didn't matter whether it was true or not.

"Do you know where it is?"

"It has been a long time since I traveled through the Chappa'ai, but before my people left this place they took measures to hide it. It is almost certainly not where it was the last time I traveled between worlds. So in answer to your question, I know where it is, but not *where* it is."

"Then we must find it!"

"Yes. I think we must."

"And," Keen said, the cunning sliding so gracefully back into his voice, "if the Kelani are not like us, we owe it to ourselves to understand their nature do we not? Their physiognomy, the stresses and strains their body might withstand in comparison to Corvani flesh. And not merely how they are different, but how they are the same."

"That would be wise," Iblis agreed. Yes, Corvus Keen was malleable. Pliant even. "We have the old factories out at Remoulade and Rabelais. I am thinking these might serve as facilities."

"Ah, so I see you have thought about this."

"No more than I consider any of your other interests, Great Keen," Iblis said smoothly.

"Then tell me what you have in mind."

"It is simple, really," Iblis began, outlining cruelties that alone even Corvus Keen could never have imagined.

CHAPTER NINE

Into The Fire

SAMANTHA CARTER was the last one through the gate.

She watched Teal'c's back as the event horizon swallowed him whole. Its skin rippled, and then he was gone. With one last backwards glance at the window of the control room, she stepped into the blue.

The sensation of stepping out into nothing, of becoming nothing, was every bit as ünnerving as it had been the first time she had traveled through the Stargate. It wasn't instantaneous; there was a lag as the wormhole carried her across vast expanses of empty space. The pull of forces on her mind was more distressing than the corresponding pull on her flesh. And then, even as her breathing came in harsh ragged gasps and her mind's eye swirled with the punishing kiss of the vortex, she finished that last step on earth and made her first in hell.

The heat hit her hard, even through the protective layers of the evac suit. In a matter of seconds, she felt the linen of the vest beneath the suit soak through with perspiration. The first trickle ran in a lazy curve along the line of her spine. Sam managed three uneasy steps before the sting of the fire in the sky burned through the helmet's visor. There was no way the suits could shield them from the intense heat for any length of time.

She closed her eyes, fumbling with the sensors on the helmet's cuff to activate the visor's tint. The filter glazed across the screen. It did nothing to reduce the painful brightness. Horizon to horizon the sky was ablaze, the firmament rippling with flares as pockets of oxygen ignited. It was all

Sam could do not to stare. O'Neill's voice crackled in her ear. "So I guess there is no point in telling everyone not to look at the sun."

For all the facetiousness, he was right, of course. Staring at the sky for even a few moments would be enough to damage their unprotected retinas irreparably. Even with the UV protection of the visor it hurt to look at the sky for more than a few moments at a time. She forced herself to look down at her feet. The earth was scorched black, the dirt like a fine dusting of charcoal scattered over the ground. Heat seared up through the soles of her boots. Sam took two more steps away from the gate and turned to look back at it. Black hills lined up on the horizon, too far away for them to possibly reach before the heat tore through their suits and burned them up.

"Nice place," she said.

Fissures ran red through the black earth where the rock beneath had smelted down to its core components.

"Okay, let's try and do this quickly. Send the drone up, let's see if we can find the needle in this flaming haystack."

It was easier said than done; the drone went up but even before it had climbed a dozen feet above their heads the fire wormed its way through the cracks in its shell, undermining its integrity. It began to smoke as its internal wirings melted, and by the time it was one hundred feet above them it was a ball of flame.

Sam shook her head. "Nothing. The drone burned up before it registered any signs of life."

"See the world through the old man's eyes," Daniel said.

"What?"

"It was something Selina Ros said: *see the world through the old man's eyes*. She said she hoped it would make sense to us when we came through the gate. Nyren Var's last transmission suggested she had located the Mujina in a subterranean grotto. I'm guessing that looking through the old man's eyes is how we're going to find our way down into the caves."

"Makes sense," Jack said. Then a moment later, "No, really, it does. I'd have preferred a GPS reference, but turn left at the old man's nose works for me. So can anyone see an old man?"

Sam scanned the horizon. There was nothing, no one. She had been doing nothing but look for the few minutes since they stepped through the gate. It was unlike any place she had visited. The reader from the drone registered nothing, not a single sign of life beyond their own biometrics. There was no way anything could survive in this place. It wasn't a prison. It was an execution chamber. The Ancients had banished the Mujina here knowing full well it could not possibly survive for any length of time — they had as good as murdered the creature but without getting their hands dirty. Yet it had survived, which meant there had to be signs — it needed food, water, shelter, and it left behind feces and other waste. Nothing could exist without leaving a trace, a sign that it had been there, so that was what they had to be looking for: signs.

"So much for that idea," Jack said. "Anyone else?"

She looked back at the gate and then down the steps toward the DHD. There had to be some sort of clue. The Tok'ra agent had found the creature, of that they were certain. There was no other reasonable explanation why she'd been forced to flee the planet. She had found the Mujina and the Goa'uld had in turn found her. Question was, had the Goa'uld found the creature or was it still hiding amid the fire and brimstone?

Sam shook her head. It took her a moment to realize that the gesture couldn't be seen through the tinted visor. "Maybe," she said over the comms channel.

"Good, because I don't need to work on my tan."

"If we were trapped here what's the first thing we'd have to do?" she asked Jack.

"Find shelter, somewhere out of the heat," Daniel said.

Sam nodded again. "Exactly. Now, let's extrapolate that onto a longer scale. Let's assume the creature has a similar basic physiognomy its going to have some fundamental needs, like water, food and a toilet."

Jack looked at her then, "Don't tell me you want to do a scan for crap?"

"It's not as stupid as it sounds, sir. There are going to be by-products in the fecal matter that our scanners could pick up."

"You're kidding me."

"On the contrary, O'Neill," Teal'c observed.

"Don't go there, big guy."

"Okay, quick recap. Daniel, what do we know about the creature?"

Daniel's shrug was lost in the bulk of his suit. "Not much really. If I understand things properly, the Mujina has no real identity of its own, it's a blank canvas that draws its form from those it encounters like some sort of doppelganger. It feeds off what they need, reflecting it back to them, and in turn they provide what it needs. It's self-sustaining in nature, really, and quite remarkable."

"But what that all means is that it must be a social creature, surely? Without someone to mirror it"'s empty."

"It's reasonable to assume so," Daniel said. "What are you driving at, Sam?"

"If you were a social creature and they stranded you here, what would you crave more than anything?"

"Contact," Daniel said.

Sam nodded again. "That being the case it's going to try to take shelter close to the gate. It's the one place it's encountered other life since its exile, the one place where it's made the kind of contact it craves. It isn't going to hide itself away. It wants to be found." It made a certain kind of sense but Sam was still unsure of her reasoning. "The surface is too hot, so I am thinking underground lakes, a cave network, anything that takes us beneath the surface and out of the hostile air. I'm thinking Robinson Crusoe here," she said, "when he was marooned the first thing he did was make a basic shelter, but the longer he stayed the more elaborate his construction became, not because he needed it but because it gave him something physical to do to ward off the madness. I think we're looking for an elaborate construction, something that sticks out like a sore thumb."

"Makes sense," Jack agreed, "You're thinking this might account for the old man's eyes?"

"I'm hoping it is more figurative than literal," Sam said. She pulled back the Velcro seal on one of the suit's pockets and fumbled about inside for the small handheld scanner. The fat fingers and thumbs of the suit's insulated gloves made it almost impossible to operate the device's finer controls. Twice the touch-screen responded with the wrong protocols because her touch overlapped with another command but eventually she succeeded in launching the geo-phys module. Flame reflected off the scanner's screen, and then the roiling patterns faded and the scanner came back with a string of geological data breaking down the component parts of the surrounding terrain, vegetable and mineral. None of the facts held her eye; Sam was looking at the sky. The fire had burned out. It was incredible to see, as though the night's black ate through the red, the flames rolling back toward their point of origin and snuffing out. It took a matter of seconds for the entire expanse of sky to clear. Suddenly they were gazing up at the stars.

"Kinda makes you wish we'd held off on launching that drone for, oh, five minutes, doesn't it?" Jack said.

The shift in temperature was immediate and surprising. The scanner read a concurrent drop of twenty-seven degrees within the next forty seconds. Still the temperature continued to fall, at almost a degree a second, and showed no sign of leveling out. A crystalline web of frost began to form across

Sam's visor. Spiders of white splintered in front of her eyes, a Mandelbrot Set of rime.

"What's happening?" Jack's voice sounded terse in her ear.

"It's an extreme temperature shift, sir. When the fire burned out, the surface temperature returned to its natural level—"

"Which just happens to be damned freezing," Jack said.

"Actually ten degrees below, sir. The moisture in the air has rimed into a frost, that's all."

"So we're good"

"Yes, sir," she assured him. The suits were designed to cope with hostile environments. Minus ten was well within acceptable thresholds. Minus thirty would have been comfortable. Her vision began to clear as the temperature settled. The frost evaporated slowly, leaving only the ghosts of its lines on her visor.

"Well that makes a change. So, ignoring Mister Frosty, what have we got?"

Sam studied the scanner results. They weren't what she had expected. She shook the scanner, as though that would fix what she was reading. It took her a moment to realize what was wrong with the numbers. She looked up from the handheld as though to contradict what the device was telling her; there was nothing out there but blasted terrain and scoured earth. The fact that the scanner had returned any vegetative results was curious to the point of being downright wrong.

She narrowed the range of the search. Again the device returned its curious numbers.

"This doesn't make sense."

"Which means precisely?"

"The scanner's returning various chemical composites which, taken at face value, would suggest plant life, but look around you, sir..."

"Did the heat fry the scanner?"

"I don't think so. Which means there's enough vegetation to sustain life here, we just can't see it."

"Which means we're back to looking for the 'old man's eyes'," O'Neill said.

"And the only way we're going to find them is to go for a walk, so eenie, meanie, miney or good old moe?" Jack pointed out the cardinals, north, south, east, west, and raised an eyebrow. "Which way do you want to go?"

"Hey Moe," Sam said, pointing what she assumed was west. There was a natural declivity cut into the ground that ran parallel to the distant mountains, as though a river had once run through it. Perhaps it had, before the sky started to burn and choked the life out of the planet.

They shouldered their equipment and headed off along the dry riverbed, looking for the old man's eyes. There were signs everywhere that this place hadn't always been hell. The further along the dry gulch they walked the more relics of civilization they noticed. At first they were limited to a few warped metal girders sprouting out of the dirt like grotesque wild flowers. Sam scuffed her feet through the dusting of sand that had settled over the ground, half-expecting to find a layer of black asphalt beneath from the road they were walking along. The few reminders quickly became more as they moved away from the gate. Some of the stones had broken away to reveal the steel rebar in their guts.

"Daniel," she said.

"I see it."

What looked like a needle of stone grew like an outcropping from the side of the valley. It was the lowest level of a building. The steel and glass had melted beneath the flaming sky but enough of the structure remained to betray its original purpose. It told them all they needed to know about the fall of Vasaveda. They were walking through a ruin where a town once stood. Sam closed her eyes, imagining for a moment that the circuits of her suit could somehow capture the residual energies of the long dead inhabitants. What would the dead say? Would they scream, aware of their downfall, or would they jibber and yammer on about the mundane stuff of the life that was no longer theirs? Or, worse, would their last words be locked on their lips? She shivered at the thought.

"O'Neill," Teal'c called out. Unlike the others, he had turned away from the detritus of civilization and was looking off to the south, seemingly fascinated by something he saw in the peaks of the black hills.

"What is it, Teal'c?"

"I do not believe the old man lies in this direction."

"And what makes you think that?"

"There is much we cannot see from this angle, meaning that the old man is hidden from us, but if we stand there," he gestured toward a slightly raised pedestal of red rock, "the rock formation presents itself quite differently. Do you see him now?" Teal'c pointed. Sam tried to follow the direction of his gaze. It wasn't until she came back to stand beside him that she could make out the curious rock formation he had seen. Through a trick of perspective it did indeed look like a crook-backed old man carved into the rock-face. He was huge, but like a geo-glyph could only be seen from certain vantage points, otherwise it looked just like any other pile of rocks.

"That's it," Sam said, squinting up at the shadowy face. She couldn't see any hollows that might have been eyes. "It's got to be."

"How far up do you think the old guy is?" Jack asked.

"It's hard to tell from here," Sam said. She tried to use the landscape to give her a sense of perspective but without any landmarks it was almost impossible. "A couple of hundred feet, maybe."

"And you say that like it's a good thing."

CHAPTER TEN

In The Kingdom of the Blind

A ROUGH STONE stair had been hewn into the mountain — and it was a mountain, Jack thought to himself, not a hill. Each stair was uncomfortably high, as though made for a man almost twice his height. It made the climb difficult but not impossible. The suit made him clumsy. He found himself clutching at the flaking rock, his gloves sliding across the surface as he struggled to get any kind of purchase.

"Remind me why we're doing this?" Jack grunted.

"We must pass through the eyes of the old man if we hope to find the home of the creature we seek," Teal'c's voice echoed in his ears. "We do not wish it to fall into the hands of the Goa'uld."

"You've got a nice way with the understatement, my compadre."

"If that is your way of saying thank you, O'Neill, you are most welcome."

Jack leaned out, craning his neck to peer upwards. The higher they climbed the more the center of the giant's steps had been worn smooth by the elements, making them progressively more treacherous. The wind whipped around him, blustering in his ears. The helmet amplified the noise, which only served to make it all the more disorientating. His foot slid out from beneath him. Grit grated and fell, spilling down into the faces of the others beneath him. Hand over hand, Jack hauled himself up. His world was reduced to finding the next handhold.

He didn't look down.

"You'd think whoever carved this staircase into the side of

the mountain could have made it a little bit easier to climb," Jack muttered to himself.

The wind worsened the higher he climbed, until it was almost fierce enough to pry his fingers off the rock-face. He clung on for dear life. Each new riser was one closer to the old man's face. He could make out the dark hollows of the eyes beneath the heavy overhanging brow. They were maybe twenty steps above him. The problem was that more than half of those steps had crumbled away and left a scar of raw stone across the old man's cheek.

"Houston, we have a problem."

"What is it, Jack?" Daniel sounded breathless.

"We've run out of ladder."

"How far are we from the top?"

"Far enough."

"Great."

"Can't say I am too thrilled about it myself." He couldn't see an alternative route — at least not an easy one. That meant at least fifty feet of free climbing with several hundred feet of free falling beneath them. "Still, onwards and upwards."

He gritted his teeth and reached up, trying to force his fingers into the stone. The last thing he wanted was for the suit to tear but, given the circumstances, he didn't have a lot of choice. "Up we go."

Jack managed four feet more before he ran out of hand holds altogether. Hanging there by the bloated fingertips of his gloves, he angled his body around so that he could draw the gun from the holster at his waist. He aimed up at the sheer rock and squeezed off a dozen shots in quick succession. Flakes of stone powdered as layers of rock broke away. By the time the dust cleared Jack could see a series of uneven handholds where the bullets had bitten into the face. He holstered the pistol and climbed quickly hand over hand.

The others came up behind him.

Five red spurs of oxidized iron rimmed the opening of the

old man's eye. Jack grasped one and heaved himself through. He wasn't sure what he had expected to find on the other side, other than an all-encompassing darkness. But it wasn't dark, not properly. A peculiar phosphorescence emanated from the lichen lining the passage as it twisted away down into the belly of the rock. The weird illumination was enough to light the way, but not enough to banish the hiding places offered by the shadows. Stalactites dripped down from the roof of the passage, in places meeting the stalagmites that had risen up beneath the steady drip, drip, drip.

"What do you make of this place?"

"I'd say it satisfies the basic needs of shelter," Carter said, "and if that fungus is edible, sustenance."

"If you're asking *me* what I think," said Daniel. "I'd say it's creepy."

"You think? Teal'c?"

"Major Carter is correct in her assumption that the cave offers the basic necessities of warmth and shelter," Teal'c agreed, looking around at the curious constructions.

"So we're talking possible Mujina refuge?"

"Possible," Sam said. "But there could be an entire planet of possible places."

"But not through the old man's eyes," Daniel disagreed.

"That's good enough for me. Okay boys and girls, in we go," Jack gave the order, indicating eyes right to Sam and Teal'c, eyes left to Daniel. He peered deeper into the darkness. He was sweltering within his suit despite the respite from the fluctuating freeze and burn extremes of the world above. The world below offered its own set of torments. Suffering wasn't unique to the surface.

"Would you look at this place," Jack marveled. He reached out, his fingers lingering over the crystalline base of one of the pillars. It was huge, more than double his arm-span in circumference, and appeared to be pitted with hundreds upon thousands of these intricate hexagonal flaws, like the facets of a diamond. He felt his words resonate through the structure, amplified by the crystals. "Weird."

It wasn't only the sound, it was the light as well; the phosphorescent lichen imbued the strange walls with an eerie glow all of their own. Jack peered at — into — the glassy surface, trying to make out what, if anything, was hidden beneath. The more he concentrated on a patch of the peculiar light the less he was able to actually focus on it until his vision became a complete blur and a strange ache took root behind his eyes. And still he stared at the wall until it looked as though life pulsed away deep within the crystals.

He felt a hand on his shoulder, the contact breaking the hypnotic lure of the light.

The deeper they went, the more remarkable the structures of the tunnel became. At first it looked as though the stalactites and stalagmites had simply fused together to form a honeycomb but it quickly became apparent that that wasn't the case. There was a damn sight more than nature's intelligence at work here — there was the grand design of madness to it all, to every fissure and join of rock.

"It's man-made, everything, every last detail. Amazing," Daniel breathed. "Well, not man, of course, but just look at it, it's incredible. I mean all of it, right down to the smallest manipulation of the existing strata. Every crystal has been shaped to reflect some bigger pattern. It's almost as though—"

"Spit it out, Daniel," Jack said.

"Don't you feel it?"

"Feel what?"

"There's something about the entire place, an atmosphere. It feels almost holy."

"Are you saying it's a temple?"

"Possibly," Daniel said, "I mean, look at it, if ever there was a case of a mind searching for some bigger meaning, some plan to it all, this would be it."

"You think the Mujina made this place?"

"Someone did," Daniel said. "And it's amazing, isn't it?"

"It's nuts is what it is," Jack said, trying to take it all in.

"It's so human, think about it, the mind on the verge of madness takes refuge in order and patterns, and what greater pattern is there than the one that gives order to the universe?" Daniel sounded like he was quoting one of his books.

"It is the secret of creation," Sam agreed. "Everything from bacteria through to plant life, mineral compositions, even something as random as beauty, has its roots in the symmetry of patterns. Break anything down to a quantum level and the pattern becomes obvious."

"But this? A church? Seriously?"

"Why not, Jack?" Daniel's smile became infectious as his enthusiasm for the idea increased. "Imagine yourself in the creature's place, ripped from your home, and transported here to rot. You're bound to ask why? And isn't that the fundamental question all religions ask of their deities? Why? It all comes down to how you interpret the notion of god. Listen and tell me this isn't a religious experience."

Daniel took a small device from the depths of his suit. It took Jack a moment to realize it was nothing more scientific than a long metal pin. Daniel bent it, fashioning a U out of the pin. Holding it lightly between thumb and forefinger, like a makeshift tuning fork. Daniel tapped it gently off the wall. Despite being muffled by his helmet O'Neill heard the note hang softly in the cavernous space. Then Daniel set the end of the tuning fork against the crystal wall and the nature of the harmonic changed completely as it became the longest and loudest single note he had ever heard. Each facet of the crystal wall played its part, absorbing the sound and then amplifying it all around him, the glass walls coming together to carry the note to a crescendo. The fragile sound hung there for what seemed like eternity and then it was simply gone.

"Acoustics like that can't be accidental. Listen to it, Jack...'"

Jack gave him a flat look. "I prefer the Stones."

"Funny."

"I try." He glanced at Sam. "Carter, is this thing here or not?"

She ran the scanner's routines again and this time she nodded.

"Now that's what I'm talking about," Jack said, with a grin. "Come out, come out, where ever you are."

"O'Neill?"

"Teal'c?"

"I do not know. Something is not right."

"Your Spidey sense tingling, huh?"

Teal'c said nothing, but studied their surroundings for a moment, then turned back to face him. "The Goa'uld are said to be hunting this Mujina, but I have not seen any sign of Goa'uld presence on this world. This concerns me greatly, O'Neill."

"Smells like a trap, you mean?" The same thing had been bothering him. Everything was just a little bit too convenient for his liking. "I'm right there with you, Big Guy. It stinks to high heaven. The idea of trusting the Tok'ra gives me the heebie-jeebies."

"There are dangers hidden here, O'Neill. Shadows. The Goa'uld are aware that we will come looking for the creature."

"And knowing that, they'll be waiting for us. You're preaching to the choir, Teal'c. It's a big old game of cosmic chess and they're at least three moves ahead. Which means we have to be careful."

Jack moved toward one of the larger pillars in the center of the vast chamber. It was covered with crude pictograms etched into the crystalline surface. He took one look at them and gave up trying to decipher what they were supposed to mean. He wasn't interested. Right then, something else entirely had captured his attention. A sound. It was instantly familiar but utterly out of place in the half-light. Jack moved around the pillar slowly, as though playing some peculiar game of hide and seek as he followed the sound to its source.

"Did you hear that?" Daniel asked.

Jack did and he knew the sound well enough; the slow wet rasp of despair.

They weren't alone.

CHAPTER ELEVEN

Karma Chameleon

JACK FOUND the Mujina huddled in a corner, hiding in the shadows. Naked, the creature lay on its side. It was badly burned and barely conscious, the cavities where meat ought to have been picked out by darker hollows of shade, as though in the grip of some vile wasting sickness. But that wasn't the worst of it. Someone had shackled it, and bound its mouth with primitive iron branks. The metal plate cut deep into its tongue so that blood trickled down the Mujina's chin as it whimpered. And then they had abandoned it here to die in its own filth.

"Doesn't look like Goa'uld tech," Jack observed, crouching down to examine the bolt mechanism of the medieval torture device. The bolt was oxidized with rust, as though it had been locked in place a long time ago.

"A scold's bridle," Daniel told him. "Used in medieval times to silence wagging tongues."

"So about as primitive as it gets then." O'Neill looked at the bolts that secured the headdress to the unfortunate creature's skull. It was barbaric.

"There's no end to a torturer's inventiveness," Daniel agreed.

"I advise proceeding with caution," Teal'c said, coming up to stand behind them.

A burlap rag had been bound across most of the creature's face, covering its features.

"We can't leave it like this," Daniel tugged at the bolt but couldn't wrangle it loose. "It's barbaric." The Mujina stirred fitfully and whimpered as he struggled with the mechanism.

"Have we got something that can cut through this? We've got to get this thing off."

He tugged at the bolt but only succeeded in drawing a desperate mewl from the Mujina's stuffed mouth.

"I'm not sure about this, Daniel," Jack said.

"What's not to be sure about, Jack? This isn't 1599."

"Fine, just hope I don't get the opportunity to say 'I told you so', eh?"

Sam came forward with the zat. She hunkered down beside Daniel, shuffling forward on her knees so she could get to the bolt mechanism, and fired a single pulse at the rusted iron.

The Mujina whimpered and twisted at the sound of the weapon so close to its face — it was an instinctive reaction to the auditory reminder of the torments already burned into its skin, Jack realized. He couldn't imagine the extent of the creature's suffering. Seeing the aftermath was more than enough. Sam fired again, drawing another mewling protest.

It was hard to imagine that this thing curled up on ground at his feet was the monstrous weapon the Tok'ra had warned them about. Surely it deserved their pity, not their fear? The thought lasted for as long as it took Carter to fire a third time, disintegrating the bolt, and pull the harness off. She cast it aside. Suppurating sores wept along the side of the Mujina's face. As tenderly as he could manage in the fat-fingered gloves, Daniel eased back the hessian blindfold.

For a moment the face that looked back up at him was utterly devoid of feature or expression, as though sheathed in a mask of flesh-toned plastic, and then as his hand came into contact with the blistered skin it began to change. It was an ugly metamorphosis. Images — faces — seemed to flicker across the mask, all of them familiar to Jack, some intimately so, some half-forgotten, others barely remembered. He saw the ghosts of his mother and father, the disapproving frown of his high school gym teacher, old sweethearts whose names he suddenly remembered even though he hadn't thought of

them since junior high: Sasha. Vicky. All these faces, all of
these memories, stirred by the single brief contact. He closed
his eyes when he saw Sarah looking up at him, and when he
opened them Charlie was there. O'Neill swallowed. He knew
it wasn't really his son. The likeness wasn't true; it was an
idealized recreation plucked from a father's need. Charlie's
eyes were too bright, his smile too fierce, but still it stole his
heart and he understood. The Mujina was giving him what
he needed most of all. It was giving him his son back — but
Charlie wasn't its' to give.

"Don't look at it," Jack said, but looking up he knew the
warning was already too late. They each of them had that
look of rapt need written in their eyes. He didn't know what
they were seeing, but he could guess. Daniel's lips moved,
just the slightest of twitches, but they seemed to form the
name Sha're. It was Teal'c's fervored expression that frightened him the most. There was something about it that went
beyond seeing old ghosts.

Moving quickly, Jack grabbed the hessian blindfold and
dragged it back into place over the Mujina's eyes and kept
pulling at it until it covered most of its stolen face. Even as he
did, he heard Charlie's borrowed voice inside his head. *"Why?
What have I done?"* It was all Jack could do to ignore it.

When he turned around he saw that Carter was crying
silent tears. She looked away from the Mujina, turning her
back on it, and walked away.

He didn't ask her who she had seen in the creature's face.
He didn't want to know. Some griefs still had the right to
remain private.

"Teal'c, give me a hand here," Jack said, snapping the Jaffa
out of the reverie that gripped him. Teal'c shook his head
once, briskly, and growled deep in his throat. It was not a
sound Jack ever wanted to hear again. Together they hauled
the shivering creature to its feet and carried it out of the cave.
No one said a word. Locked in thoughts of their own deep-

seated needs, they stood on the ridge of rock and looked down at the impossible climb.

"*I know a secret way down. I can show you,*" the Mujina said in Charlie's voice.

"Did you hear that?" Jack asked, but the way the others looked at him was enough to tell him they hadn't. He wondered what, if anything, the creature had said to them.

He rattled the side of his helmet, as though trying to dislodge Charlie's voice from inside his head. "Lead on, MacDuff."

"*I can't see the path. You need to remove the blindfold. I need to see or I'll fall.*"

"Not a prayer."

"*Please.*"

He never had been able to say no to Charlie.

CHAPTER TWELVE

The Last Temptation of Teal'c

KELNORIM OFFERED a refuge for his mind, tranquility. Emerging from the twin darknesses — of the cave and the Mujina's influence — he felt no such calm. The Mujina had shown its face to him, and in doing so had undermined everything the Jaffa held dear.

Could it be true? Could the acceptance of Apophis be the one thing he needed to be whole? The notion turned his blood cold. He had steeled himself in preparation for what he might see. He carried a world of guilts within him, but they were his to bear. He had thought the creature would test him with the ghosts of Chulak; the disappointment of Ro'nac, father of the Shol'vah; the melancholy sadness of his wife, Drey'auc, unable to understand why he had turned his back on them and thrown away all that they had worked so hard for; even the stubborn anger of his son, Rya'c, lashing out at everyone and everything in his abandonment. All of these travails and more he had expected, but nothing could have prepared him for the sight of that conceited smile blossoming across the creature's plain face. It had gazed at him with malign intelligence, its voice an insidious whisper inside his head.

"Come back to me, Teal'c. Stand at my side, my First Prime. That is where you belong. It is where you always belonged. You are no traitor. No Shol'vah! You are Jaffa, first among equals, the mighty Teal'c, favored of Apophis. Come back to me, my friend, and together we will stride through the galaxies. With our combined strength we can end this destructive conflict, we can bring order to the galaxies. The power to free your people is yours, all you have to do is join me."

Were these the words he most longed to hear?

If they were, what did that say about him?

Was this the promise that would make him whole once more?

If it was, what did that say about the man he had become?

He thought about it for a moment. It wasn't. The creature had read him wrong. He had no desire to stand beside Apophis or any of his kind. It had never been about power. It was always about peace. He wanted freedom for his people but not at any cost.

Above them, the sky caught fire again.

Teal'c grasped the creature tighter around the shoulders and refused to let it so much as wriggle as he carried it down the treacherous descent. The heat of the hellish surface rose up to engulf them. Teal'c welcomed it as though it might burn away the doubt that plagued him.

But deep within, Teal'c felt the discomfort of his symbiote. The larva was in turmoil, drawn by the Mujina's fork-tongued promise. Was it too hearing what the creature wanted it to hear? Was it being fed dreams of dominion? The symbiote's agitation inevitably transferred itself to Teal'c. He refused to believe the creature's words reflected his own desire; the possibility undermined the balance he had fought so hard to achieve. He felt his heart beating against his chest, the *dub dub-dub* becoming erratic as a renewed rush of dread rose up inside him.

Teal'c turned his immense will inward, breathing deeply as he sought to master the rhythms of his own flesh. His world boiled down to a single sound: the beating of his heart. He inhaled, held the breath, and then let it leak between his lips, again and again, and with each breath the tripping of his heart slowed. He erected barriers in his mind, fencing off the doubts that plagued him behind sheer indomitable willpower.

The creature's face belonged to the System Lord, as did the

voice, but the hands did not. Apophis' hands were delicate and fine-boned, the skin soft and supple, while the backs of Mujina's hands were marked with fine white scars and the palms bore rough calluses. It seemed that the creature's guise did not stretch as far as the hands, though perhaps with time the subsumption would become complete. As it was, the flaws were enough to weaken the temptation of the creature's impossible promise.

Still, the Mujina's insidious whispers touched his mind, promising forgiveness over and over again.

Teal'c looked at it squirming in his grasp and said simply: "You are not Apophis. Your forgiveness is worthless to me because I have no need of it. My soul is clean. Now leave my mind or I shall be forced to end your life to be free of you," his voice was soft, the threat implicit. The gentle tone made his message all the more chilling.

The wretched creature looked up at him, a desperate longing in its pupilless eyes as it shuffled forward, dragging its feet through the red dust scattered thinly across the rocks, and then he was alone. Teal'c sensed the Mujina physically withdraw from his mind. The silence was sudden and shocking — and the emptiness left behind dizzying. A last lingering urge to fight welled up within him, a need to strike out, but he crushed it.

The Mujina led them on a different path. It was narrow and precarious as it clung to the side of the huge hill, but even at its steepest the gradient was comfortably walkable even in the clumsy boots of the evac suit.

Something troubled Teal'c.

It was all too easy, this search and rescue. He looked at the others. Only O'Neill seemed tense. Teal'c had served long enough to know that if the Goa'uld had a foothold on this planet and were aware of the Mujina's unique gifts — and their true potential — they would not allow the Tau'ri to leave with their treasure. He did not believe that the Tok'ra operative had imprisoned the creature in such a cruel manner, which meant the creature had been left there to be found. And they had had no choice but to take the bait.

Teal'c scanned the horizon looking for the tell tale signs of the ambush he knew was waiting for them. Putting himself in the enemy's place he considered the opportunities the harsh landscape afforded. A normal foe would look to minimize their exposure to the worst of the elements, not wanting to weaken his hand, but the Jaffa were no normal enemy. Indeed, a certain breed of leader would take pride in exposing his men to the extremes Vasaveda offered, and consider it his duty to test them to the limits — meaning it was impossible to discount even the most unlikely hiding places.

There were six possibilities; one assumed that the Goa'uld would know the path the Mujina would use to lead them down the mountain; two relied upon the element of surprise, cutting them off even as they reached for the DHD. The other three were less obvious, and therefore more appealing to a cunning commander. It was these that concerned him most gravely. The dry gulch they had walked along afforded some measure of cover for a small war host, but it was not the only such crack through the desert-like plain between the Old Man and the Stargate. The ground was cratered like the skin of a septuagenarian. The fissures were deep and wide enough for the enemy to move unseen, like burrowers crawling beneath the surface only to rise up and strike when their prey least expected it.

Each fissure was marked by shadow.

Teal'c followed the shadows, reading the different paths they offered the shrewd warrior. Only one ran perpendicular to the gate, and at one point its shadow was less than fifty feet from the gate. The other two were more serpentine in nature, curving away from the gate, though at certain points the shadows encroached on the DHD. The second of these struck him as overly exposed, while the first offered just enough shelter to make any Jaffa advance virtually invisible. This was the trench he would have chosen had he been leading the attack on the Tau'ri as they retreated to the safety of the Stargate.

"Deliver the Tau'ri to your people, Teal'c," the Mujina's subtle insinuation returned to taunt him. *"Bring them to us and you will be rewarded, First Prime."*

Teal'c shook his head, as much in denial as to clear his thoughts from the temptation of betrayal. He learned something in that moment: the Mujina was mistaken. He was not looking for power, he was looking for freedom. They were not guilts he harbored; they were angers that simmered barely in check. That was his strength as well as his weakness. All that he had won, all that he had lost, all that he had been and all that he might have become, all of these things came together in the man that he was. The creature might be able to tap into aspects of his 'self', but not the whole. It pandered to the wants of the darker places, and perhaps in some those darker desires would subsume all others, but for Teal'c that darkness was where hope lay. That darkness was where he had first nurtured the belief that his masters were not gods, from where the strength to turn on them had come; it was not darkness at all but the first spark of light that pushed back the surrounding shadows. The creature had misjudged him.

"O'Neill, I believe the Goa'uld will strike from there." He pointed at the shadow-line. "If we move along this path," he gestured toward the second fissure cleaving a line through the red earth, "I believe we shall evade their ambush. We cannot allow them to look upon the creature. I fear that to do so would turn them murderous."

"Like they aren't already," O'Neill's voice was hollow in his ear.

"The creature has a way of influencing the mind."

"I hadn't noticed." Teal'c gave the colonel a puzzled look

through the helmet's tinted visor, and a moment later O'Neill said, "Doesn't Junior help you resist?"

He pushed the Mujina along the path in front of him. It stumbled but did not fall. "Perhaps, but I am not immune."

They covered the rest of the descent in silence.

Still there was no sign of Goa'uld presence.

Teal'c did not allow complacency to dull the edge of his unease. They were out there. He was certain. They were being watched even now. He could sense the scrutiny.

It was a peculiarly patient game this Goa'uld was playing. Time and again Goa'uld arrogance had been the Tau'ri salvation. Blind faith in their supremacy made the Goa'uld vulnerable. But that this Goa'uld held his forces back, instead of leading a rash charge across the open plains staff weapons blazing, augured ill for them all. Caution was anathema to the Goa'uld way of thinking, and yet clearly they were exercising exactly that.

Teal'c led them down into the ravine. The walls, blasted by the harshness of the sun and the sporadic burning skies, were charred black and high enough that they obscured them from plain sight as they crept back toward the Stargate.

He kept the Mujina at arm's length, ignoring its gentle testing around the fringes of his mind. It would slip into his consciousness again, that was its nature. Given time even separation wouldn't help.

He saw dust in the air. It took him a moment to realize its significance.

"Down," Teal'c rasped, holding up his fist. The others reacted instinctively, dropping to one knee, bringing their heads well below the sight-line across the plain. "They are close, O'Neill."

"Well that's not good. How many? Where?"

"There is a legion of Jaffa in the second ravine. Their presence is betrayed by dust. They move with great caution but sheer numbers causes the dust to rise."

"Crap." He set his back to the wall. "Options?"

"We cannot allow ourselves to be captured with this creature, O'Neill. We must use stealth."

"That would be the sensible thing to do. So I am thinking we do the exact opposite, because that's what they'll be expecting. Carter, any ideas?"

"Even if we follow the ravine we're going to have to break cover eventually. There's not a lot else we can do. Someone has to reach the DHD."

"I guess that's me then," Jack said, pushing himself to his feet. "I feel like the slow-motion version of Steve Austin in this get up — minus all the bionic parts. All right, wish me luck."

Before any of them could stop him, O'Neill broke cover. He went up over the top and sprinted for the DHD. The first blast of staff weapon sliced through the air before he was even half way across the killing ground. O'Neill ducked and rolled, going down hard. He labored back up to his feet, and looked around as though momentarily dazed. A second lance of energy speared the sky. Teal'c heard a distinct crackling followed by a pop and a sharp snap as a component within the staff blast reacted with the volatile atmosphere and the first bubble of flame ignited. The downdraft blast of heat bowled O'Neill off his feet and saved his life; the streams of three staff weapons crossed exactly where his head had been less than a second before.

"Whose bright idea was this again?" O'Neill's disgruntled voice sounded inside his helmet.

"It was yours, O'Neill," Teal'c told him helpfully.

Two things happened simultaneously; the flame silhouetted O'Neill, leaving him dangerously exposed, and the air above the second fissure ripped with flame, the oxygen in it igniting explosively. A series of detonations tore at the sky, each more savage than the last. Tongues of flame licked down at the red earth, burning the dust black. As the shockwave of the final explosion rippled out, dozens of Jaffa came out of their hiding places, aflame.

Teal'c watched in horror as they burned.

"Kill them," the Mujina's Apophis-voice crooned inside his head. *"Light up the sky, burn them all. They are nothing. They stand between you and the liberation of your people! Burn them, Teal'c. Set the sky on fire. Do what you have to do. Do what burns inside your soul, First Prime. Kill them. Let this be the beginning of your vengeance. Let this be the first triumph we share together! Burn them!"*

Teal'c had raised his own staff weapon before he realized what he was doing.

His shot went high over O'Neill's shoulder, igniting another wide expanse of sky. The Jaffa beneath it screamed as the flames snaked down to claim them.

Teal'c loosed a second shaft of lethal energy into the sky as O'Neill reached the DHD.

O'Neill stared at his friend and at the horror his two shots had created. Teal'c met his gaze with hard resolve. O'Neill looked away. Teal'c could see the shock and anger in O'Neill's face. It meant nothing to him. He raised his staff weapon and ignited another swathe of sky.

"Burn them!"

Beside Teal'c, Carter and the creature scrambled up out of the trench. There were a hundred blazing Jaffa between them and the gate. Teal'c felt nothing but pity for his people as they burned, but that did not slow him down. He ran, staff weapon blazing, toward the gate as O'Neill punched in the co-ordinates.

The sky was a brilliant burning sheet of flame. The heat coming off it was phenomenal. It scorched through the protective barrier of his evac suit. He felt his skin shriveling. He could only begin to imagine the damage the hostile fires were inflicting upon the Jaffa as they fell writing to the scorched earth.

In his peripheral vision Teal'c saw movement but he was too slow reacting to it. Twenty feet from O'Neill, a Goa'uld rose up, energy coruscating around him as he reached out with his dominant hand and brought the power of his ribbon device to bear. The gem in the heart of the latticework pulsed orange, and then flared, the center blazing red hot as its raw power gathered. The energy pulsed out from the Goa'uld's palm and across the distance, sending O'Neill down hard.

Teal'c swung around and fired, the shot taken too quickly for him to draw a proper aim. It fizzled wide of the Goa'uld commander, but the shock of it did enough to break his concentration.

Teal'c fired a second and a third shot, driving the Goa'uld back.

The System Lord looked across the killing ground at him. Teal'c could see the cruel malevolence plastered across the Goa'uld's face as he came striding out of the ravine. The ribbon device pulsed as he raised his hand.

"Go!" Teal'c yelled into the mouthpiece of his helmet. His voice crackled out over the airwaves. A heartbeat later Daniel Jackson and Samantha Carter were sprinting across No Man's Land toward the dubious safety of the unopened gate. Before it ran, the Mujina turned to look back at Teal'c.

"It is not too late to deliver them to your people, Shol'vah. Redemption is only a matter of minutes away."

"I do not seek absolution, creature. Now go!"

Teal'c racked another pulse and detonated the blast, blowing a crater in the red dust at the Mujina's feet. It ran then, all pretense of cunning abandoned in favor of flight. It was fleet of foot, moving faster over the uneven ground than the others, and quickly overhauled Jackson and Carter's lead.

Teal'c looked over its shoulder to see O'Neill dragging himself up on to his knees. Through the coms in his helmet, Teal'c heard him cursing and with a glance saw why: a staff weapon had ripped open a gaping hole in the leg of his evac suit and the strain from rising had torn it wider. With the integrity of the suit breached O'Neill was in trouble. Teal'c didn't hesitate. He went over the top and ran, bellowing a garbled war cry and loosing bolt after bolt from the staff weapon in his hands as he did. There was no rhyme or reason to the shots. They went high and wild, low and dirty, charring the red dust. Some scorched through the air, blistering more pockets of combustible gas and causing them to flame. It didn't matter. They bought O'Neill the precious seconds he needed to punch in the final co-ordinate and open the Stargate. The growls in Teal'c's ears were equal parts agony, desperation and determination. O'Neill wasn't about to fail them, even if it cost him his own life.

Teal'c roared.

Fifty feet from the gate the blue water of the event horizon ripped out of the aperture. The way home was open. O'Neill had done it. Teal'c saw the colonel go down again. The sucking silence that followed was hideous. Then both Carter and Daniel Jackson were yelling — this time the sound was primal and filled with fear for the fallen O'Neill.

Teal'c ducked beneath a wild burst of fire from a Jaffa weapon, and ran, hard, fast, keeping low, his arms and legs pumping. A burning man staggered across his path. The flames consumed him, turning his flesh to blistered sores. Teal'c fired once, putting the Jaffa out of his misery, and was past him. He ran to O'Neill's side and gathered him into his arms. The colonel shuddered once, violently, and opened his eyes. "Go!" he rasped.

"Indeed," Teal'c said, rising. He watched Daniel Jackson's back disappear through the gate and followed him. "We do not leave men behind, O'Neill. That is the law."

But O'Neill had lapsed into unconsciousness.

Teal'c gathered him into his arms.

The Mujina stood on the first of four steps leading up to the Stargate.

"Deliver him to your people, Teal'c. It is your duty."

"One more word and I shall silence you forever. Do you understand? Go through the Stargate."

The creature turned and scurried up the remaining steps, hesitated at the threshold, and then threw itself into the rippling blue wormhole.

Carrying O'Neill, Teal'c turned and cast one last lingering look back the way he had come before stepping through the gate. The killing field was littered with burning Jaffa, a hundred points of light, one for each dying warrior. It was a hellish sight that would burn forever within him.

CHAPTER THIRTEEN

Take the Long Way Home

"WE'VE GOT AN incoming wormhole, sir," Harriman's fingers rattled out a series of commands on the dialing computer. The screen flashed through a series of iconic images. They had become a second language to Walter Harriman. He back-calculated the point of origin as each new chevron encoded. "It's too early for it to be SG-1 or SG-12, Sir, they're not expected back for another twenty two hours."

General George Hammond looked up at the array of screens above their heads. The digital reads scrolled through at an alarming rate making it impossible to read any of the data they offered. Hammond drew in a deep breath. The waiting was the worst. The ninety seconds from the first contact through to the final chevron locking down. He traversed the gamut of emotions in that short space of time, from surprise to curiosity, anxiety, hope, all of them. He studied Harriman, reading the man because he couldn't hope to read the screens. Harriman was agitated, which was never a good sign.

"It's Colonel O'Neill's IDC."

"Open the iris, Sergeant. Let's bring our people home."

One of the white-coated gate technicians punched in the code to open the iris, and out in the gate room the huge naqahdah shield contracted smoothly into the Stargate's frame. A dozen soldiers wielding M16s lined up on either side of the ramp, their guns aimed solely on the eye of the wormhole. If anything other than O'Neill and his team came through the Stargate all hell would break loose down there, but it would be a cold day in the sun before they would establish a foothold on his watch. No matter how many times he had stood there and counted his men and women as they went out, and counted them coming home again, there was always that moment of doubt that this time would be the time something went wrong. Wormhole physics was hardly the most foolproof of disciplines. With Murphy always lurking just over his shoulder, there was always that element of 'whatever can go wrong will go wrong' about it.

"We're picking up five distinct travelers, sir."

"Looks like it is mission accomplished then, soldier," he leaned down to talk into the microphone. "SG-1 returning with a possibly hostile prisoner. Look sharp everyone. From what we know of this creature it poses a serious threat, so let's have no mistakes."

He held back the smile as he saw each of the men down there stand a little straighter.

"Sir, we're experiencing a weird sort of interference," Harriman told him.

"Weird in what way, Sergeant?"

"I'm not sure how to explain it, General." Harriman swiveled in his seat and pushed one of the two earpieces back so that he could talk and monitor the incoming traffic at the same time. "Once a connection is established, it's a solid signal," he moved his hand from left to right in a flat line, "but this one is more like a pulse." This time his finger peaked randomly as it moved across his chest, as though duplicating a tachycardic rhythm. "My guess is that the gate is struggling to hold the connection, sir."

"This isn't the place for guesses, Sergeant." Hammond's admonishment was harsher than he intended.

"No, sir."

And then the Stargate failed.

It was as sudden and shocking as that.

One moment the event horizon was open and SG-1 were coming home the next the aperture was empty and they were staring at the back wall, slack-jawed as the implication of what had just happened sank in.

"We've lost the incoming connection, sir." Harriman shook his head. "It's gone. There was a huge spike of energy, like an explosion or something, and then it was gone."

"Well get it back, soldier, SG-1 are out there."

He could see it in Harriman's face… The man didn't want to say it, but it was obvious what he was thinking: *not anymore.*

Hammond refused to believe it, even though he knew it was true. Harriman couldn't re-establish the connection anymore than he could order Mister Sulu to teleport the boys back home. A smooth stone of sickness settled in his gut.

This was it, the day he had always dreaded: the day they didn't come home.

CHAPTER FOURTEEN

To Seek the Sacred River Alph

THERE WAS no way home for SG-1.

Daniel Jackson stepped into the Vasaveda Stargate, expecting to emerge back in the gate room, safe and sound. He had made well over a hundred journeys since joining up with SG-1. That was a hundred times he had stepped into the gate only to finish that same step on the other side — wherever that may have been. But this time was different.

He felt it as he threw himself into the rippling blue meniscus, the sudden frission that surged throughout each and every cell of his body. He knew the science, or at least thought he did — the gate broke down every atom and neural relay that made up Daniel Jackson, translated it into a base signal that it fired out along the warp of the wormhole, only to be reassembled by the second Stargate almost instantaneously. There was a spiritual argument that the man who emerged couldn't possibly be the man who entered the wormhole, given that the nature of the matter transferal was to rebuild atom by atom, neuron by neuron... but that left no room in the equation for the soul. It had bothered him once, the idea that what emerged had to be a pale copy of the original: a facsimile. Yet the soul was supposed to be unique, a man's essence. It was one of those theological arguments that could be spun out every which way, but it didn't change the fact that he stepped in and stepped out, and bar a little light-headed travel sickness he never felt a thing.

This time, as he plunged through the gate, it felt as though his body were being stripped cell by cell down to the bone and down still into the marrow. He went blind with the agony.

Every ounce of his being burned. The thought that something was wrong barely had time to establish itself in his consciousness before he felt his mind tear asunder.

And a moment later the Stargate reformed it and he stepped out into darkness. Physically sick and reeling, Daniel fell to his knees and clutched at his stomach, retching. Without thinking he released the clasps sealing his helmet and barely managed to throw it aside before he dry heaved.

Sam came through a moment later, managed three awkward steps and collapsed at the bottom of the Stargate. He crawled over to where she lay and saw her clawing at her helmet. He helped work the clasps loose and pulled it off. She tried to speak but couldn't. Her mouth moved but she choked on the breath and the words, not managing either in her need to do both.

"It's all right," Daniel said, trying to calm her. "We're all right."

Sam stared up at him, wild-eyed. "What happened?" she managed before a brutal coughing fit wracked her body.

"I was going to ask you," Daniel said.

"Where are we?" Sam asked when she finally stopped coughing.

"That was another one I was kinda banking on you answering," Daniel said, looking around them. There wasn't a lot to see. Wherever they were, it wasn't Kansas — or Colorado Springs for that matter. Before she could answer, the Mujina came through the gate. It faired no better, managing four steps forward before it lurched off violently to the right, stumbled and fell. A pitiful whine escaped its lips as it lay there.

The gate provided the only source of light; it was enough to see the sheen of ice frosting the bare stone walls of the cavern. The walls were rough-hewn, blasted out of the ground with explosives — he could see the long thin drill lines where they had been planted. There were thirteen identical lines, each perfectly smooth, that seemed to be carved into the rock while all around them the stone was jagged from where it had been broken away by the blast. It suggested a basic level of technological development not dissimilar to Earth's, give or take a century or so. Daniel's breath misted in front of his face. Already the blonde tips of Sam's hair had whitened as the frost thickened. The ghostly blue light of the gate only served to make it feel colder still.

Teal'c was the last through the Stargate, carrying O'Neill in his arms. He walked resolutely forward, placing each footstep with exaggerated care, and then knelt to lay O'Neill down before he buckled and slumped against the wall. None of them said anything for the longest time. The confines of the chamber echoed with the sounds of their ragged breathing. O'Neill groaned but didn't move.

"This is not Stargate Command," Teal'c said, removing the clasps that fastened his helmet. He put it aside.

"What happened?" Daniel asked, crawling over to be beside O'Neill.

"The damage from the Goa'uld weapon tore open O'Neill's suit, exposing him to the worst of the sun's radiation and heat of the burning sky."

"Will he be all right?"

"I do not know, Daniel Jackson."

"I'm just toasty," Jack grunted. He still hadn't opened his eyes. "So stop talking about me like I am dead. Now would someone like to tell me where the hell we are?"

"We're in some sort of ice cavern, that's about as much as I've been able to work out," Daniel offered. "There's evidence that whoever excavated the cavern used explosives, which suggests we're talking about a society advanced enough to have mastered gunpowder and dynamite."

"Great. So let's hope they don't want to try out their flash bangs on us, shall we?" Jack struggled to sit up. Teal'c helped support him. "Carter, how are you doing?"

Sam lay on her side, looking up at them. She did her best

to smile. It was a weak effort. "I've been better, sir".

"Any idea what happened back there?"

"Something must have interfered with the wormhole," she suggested. "The gate must have lost its connection and leapt to the nearest possible alternative device, in other words we're very lucky we didn't just frazzle out of existence."

"Is that even possible?" O'Neill asked. "I mean for the wormhole to jump like that? I thought these things were locked in once a connection was established."

"I don't know, sir, until about ten minutes ago I would have said it couldn't happen, but that was ten minutes ago. Now I'm not so sure. It's theoretically possible that something might have interfered with the gate's link, I suppose. To put it crudely, if you think about the quantum 'road' between two gates being like a piece of string, it's conceivable that it could become tangled or simply twisted off true. That could theoretically have an impact on the quantum traveler, but while that impact would be enough to be measurable the kind of temporal shift would be so miniscule we'd barely notice it without some pretty sensitive equipment."

"So we're not talking about a black hole effect here?" Jack asked.

"I don't think so, sir. But..." Sam broke off as the gate closed and left them in darkness. "You might not be so far off there, sir. We know that the immense gravitational pull of a black hole can affect how time is experienced in its vicinity, its appetite is voracious, it's trying to consume everything around it."

"Like a hungry Pac Man," Jack agreed, nodding.

Daniel did his best to follow the leaps of logic, but Sam's understanding of the universe was so utterly alien to him she might as well have been speaking a different language. Of course, she was, in a way. She was talking about the building blocks of creation, using the language of the creator.

"Exactly. So what if the gravitational pull was so great it

could somehow drag the quantum 'road' off true, ripping the wormhole away from the gate that originally anchored it?"

"I don't like the sound of this," Daniel said.

"Teal'c," Sam said, "could the signal be bounced from one gate to another if the connection is lost?"

"I have not heard of such a thing, Major Carter."

"But that doesn't mean it couldn't happen," Sam finished, as much for her own benefit as for the others. She was growing more and more animated as the science unfolded for her. "It would take an incredible burst of energy along the quantum 'road' to cause the wormhole's path to deviate. But a strong enough gravitational pull could conceivably wrench the event horizon free of the gate. It would need to be incredible though. "

"How incredible?"

"A star going super nova, maybe," Carter offered.

"Right, that sort of incredible."

"Loose, I would imagine there's a fraction of time before the energy dissipates completely in which the quantum 'road' is lashing about like a garden hose on full power, and that's the window of opportunity for it to fasten on to another gate. Once the window's past, it's gone, the energy swarming down the wormhole loses its bond, and whatever was traveling down the wormhole is little more than dust on the wind."

Jack pushed himself up to his feet. He swayed awkwardly for a moment, before Daniel reached out to offer him a steadying hand, and then walked across to the DHD. "Can we get some light in here?"

Daniel obliged, taking a small mag-lite from his pocket and shining it down on the panel of the DHD. Jack punched in each of the seven co-ordinates to take them back home, but the last one refused to lock down. The gate lay stubbornly dormant. He punched in each of the symbols again. "I suppose that was always going to be too much to ask for," Jack said with a shrug. He knew it was a long shot that they'd stayed on Vasaveda. Unfortunately he didn't know where they were, and without the glyph for the point of origin they couldn't dial out. It was as simple as that. "So, Major Carter, how do we go about finding our way home?"

"Without the point of origin, we can't," she said, putting it succinctly.

It was like hearing the first nail being driven into their coffins.

"Then we need to find the point of origin. Simple," Jack said, knowing it was anything but.

CHAPTER FIFTEEN

Lost

IN THAT LONG sliding moment of terrible emptiness General George Hammond stared at the silent Stargate. He hadn't raised his voice. He had simply told the team around him to get his people back. It was the easiest thing to say and the hardest thing to do. He ground his teeth, a nervous habit. He could feel the adrenalin pounding in the room but it was deathly silent. That silence was only broken by the flutter of fingers over the keys of the many keyboards or the sudden impact of a fist being hammered off the workstation as a million to one chance went the way of the other nine hundred and ninety nine thousand, nine hundred and ninety nine and came to nothing. Failure was hard to take. The ground crew were stretched emotionally and physically, being pulled every which way by the demands of the machines and the impossibility of the task. It was hopeless and they knew it, but not one of them was prepared to admit it, even to themselves. It was the fundamental truth of the military ethic: no man gets left behind. They were clinging to one slim possibility: that the team hadn't been in transit when the gate went down. Anything else meant they weren't lost in any way that they could be found again. They needed to believe that SG-1 were still out there somewhere. That need ensured that there wasn't a single voice of dissent in the room.

Hammond watched his people — and they were his people every bit as much as any one of the SG teams — and knew he couldn't make the call. Not while there was still a chance.

The irony that the one woman smart enough to figure out what the hell had just happened was on the wrong end of the wormhole wasn't lost on Hammond.

He stared through the window at the gate. No matter how hard he willed the unstable vortex to rip out from its center he knew the reality of what that would mean: another incoming signal — and any trace of what was Jack and the others, gone.

General Hammond had looked at the artifact a thousand thousand times without seeing beyond the unearthly Naqahdah and the iconographic symbols of the Milky Way's constellations.

Part of him had always known that this day would come, but that didn't mean he was ready for it. It was strange; the program had lost men before. But this was different.

Hammond checked his watch. The iris had been open for a minute under three hours. It was a calculated risk but there had to be a point where risk outweighed reward. There were protocols in place that prevented him from leaving the Stargate open indefinitely, protocols he had every intention of following once the second hand completed its final circuit. They hadn't been able to re-establish contact and they didn't dare risk leaving the gate open much longer for fear of what might come through.

He picked up the intercom relay and stopped himself. He couldn't give the order.

He licked his lips. They were parched, rough and sore. It was as though all of the moisture had been sucked out of the air. Right then, at that moment as they hit the three hour mark, Hammond was engulfed by the overwhelming feeling that closing the iris meant giving up on O'Neill and the others, and he wasn't prepared to do that.

Not yet.

"One more hour," he said, thinking to hell with the protocols, O'Neill was one resourceful son of a bitch, he'd find a way home. Hammond needed to believe that, but that hour came and past. None of the ground staff had left their positions. None of them had given up hope or stopped trying to carry out that one simple order despite the obvious truth that it was always going to evade them. And it didn't matter; all of that stubbornness, all of that faith, didn't amount to a hill of beans. Hammond knew he was going to have to place the calls to next of kin because the threshold between rational risk and irrational hope had been crossed. SG-1 weren't coming home.

"Close the iris, soldier," he said.

He couldn't bring himself to watch the heavy metal shield lock into place over the gate. It didn't matter to him that the iris could be opened again the instant they picked up an incoming signal. Seeing it close was symbolic. It felt like he was giving up on them.

CHAPTER SIXTEEN

Hope Burns Infernal

THEY PERFORMED running repairs as they made ready to strike out from the cavern. Jack iced the burns on the back of his leg, using a large chip of ice he had broken away from the run-off. Daniel sat with the Mujina, seemingly captivated by it. Carter couldn't hear what, if anything, the creature said to him. She didn't need to. She remembered all too vividly the face it had chosen to show her.

The sadness in her eyes had been the sadness of a military wife, the warmth in her smile the warmth of a mother. The worst of it was that she knew she was beginning to forget what she looked like — little things at first, details becoming blurred and almost ghostly as she tried to remember them, and then bigger things. If she closed her eyes all sorts of faces blended in her memory, but each belonged to her mother at different points in her life, it was only when they came together that they fused into something that wasn't quite right. That was the tragedy of time — it healed wounds because it took away the sharpness of memory. Things lost their definition. Faces lost their shape. But there was one constant: her voice. It was almost as though auditory memory was somehow more faithful. Sam remembered exactly how her mother's voice sounded because it had never changed, never aged. It was the same the first time she heard it as it was the last.

So when the Mujina had spoken to her in her mother's voice, it had been exactly as she remembered it. The face had been wrong, mixing the features of the young mother with the more careworn frown of the frustrated soccer mom waiting outside the strip mall for Jacob to come and pick her up. It was like looking at one of those curious morphed pictures of a face through the filter of age, gradually and subtly changing to appear older and older — until it just stopped aging.

She had cried then.

She hadn't been able to stop herself.

And now the creature was working its distressing magic around Daniel. She understood why the Goa'uld had resorted to such primitive means of silencing it. Sam didn't know if it was simply the act of silencing its wagging tongue that protected them from the Mujina, or if there was more to it, but she was beginning to understand just what the Tok'ra, Selina Ros, meant when she called the creature a weapon.

She pushed herself up and walked slowly across to where Daniel sat, and crouched down beside him. There was an emptiness in his expression. No, that wasn't right, when she looked into his eyes she saw a ferocious need that frightened her. Without realizing what she was doing, Sam put her hands over his eyes and whispered, "Don't listen to it, Daniel."

"Sha're? Where are you? I can't feel you anymore. Don't leave me." It hurt to hear the desperation in his voice. The yearning. She realized again how lonely he was, and how much that loneliness had defined him of late. She soothed him, gentling her hand against his cheek until he calmed down.

"Colonel?" she whispered, not wanting to startle Daniel.

"Yes, Carter?"

"Sir, I don't think we can risk bringing the Mujina with us as long as it can alter our perceptions so easily. I've had it inside my head, sir. It made me see things that weren't there; things that I never want to see again. It could compromise us."

"Major Carter is right, O'Neill. The creature planted suggestions in my mind as we fled under Goa'uld gunfire. A weaker mind would have succumbed."

Carter didn't want to consider the implications of what Teal'c suggested. That the Mujina could exert some sort of hypnotic suggestion on a susceptible mind was obvious — and there was no telling just how compelling those suggestions might be, nor how far the intended victim of them might go. She looked down at Daniel and shivered. That shiver had nothing to do with the cold of the cavern.

"Well, I think that answers the question why the Goa'uld chose to use the branks, don't you? I'm guessing it's a case of stopping its tongue from working stops it from being able to plant ideas in our heads."

"But sir, strapping that thing on a helpless creature's head... well, doesn't that just make us torturers?"

"I'd say it makes us pragmatic, Major. Until I know differently I'm working under the impression that Old Silver Tongue here needs to be able to talk to mess with our minds so keeping him quiet is doing us all a favor."

"Maybe we could talk to it?" Carter offered. "Make a deal? We're talking about an intelligent life form here. Who's to say it can't turn the effect on and off?"

"It's a deal with the devil," Daniel said, looking up at the others for the first time since the Mujina let its influence on his mind slide. "Witchcraft. All of it. All of those superstitious things that were called magic and had people burned at the stake for believing them. It offered me my heart's desire, Jack. Can you imagine how potent that is?"

Daniel looked at him, and Sam realized how stupid the question was. The colonel had lost his son and blamed himself squarely for his death. Of course he could imagine. They all could. They had all lost things.

"Why do you think the Ancients wanted to hide the Mujina away from civilization?" Daniel said. "I can't believe it is capable of turning this thing on or off any more than we can switch off our pheromones. No, this is what the creature is, it's *raison d'être*. It doesn't make this thing happen, it is always happening. It's a defense mechanism, just like the chameleon's shifting colors that help it blend into its environment and become invisible. If there is no one around to react to its biology, there are no promises, no magic, if you like. It's only when you put a third party into the equation that things become dangerous. It's the way we react to it, rather than the other way round."

"And that helps us how?"

"It doesn't. But it pretty much guarantees it isn't the kind of creature that can keep any kind of bargains it makes. It isn't that kind of magic. And I hate to be a party pooper, but without a point of origin we aren't getting out of here, so it is all rather academic right now."

"You don't need to tell me," Jack began to take off his evac suit. "I'm all for getting off this rock, even if it means leaving the gate behind while we go find out where the hell we are. It's not like its going anywhere. Hey, you, yeah, come on over here," he called to the Mujina. The creature lay huddled in the corner furthest away from the gate. Sam couldn't see whether it looked up but it seemed as though the shadows back there shifted slightly. "Give me a hand with this, would you?"

"Not exactly how I imagined it in my head, sir," Sam grinned, helping him with the seals that he couldn't reach by himself.

"What are you thinking, Jack?" Daniel asked.

"We dress our new friend here in the full space suit get up, helmet and all, and keep the visor down. Maybe it'll help. It certainly can't hurt, can it?"

Teal'c said nothing. He merely raised an eyebrow at the notion. His silence spoke volumes.

He stripped the outer layer of the evac suit quickly. There was a tear behind the knee of his BDUs where the staff blast had smoldered through the fabric and burned into the skin. The wound was a mess. It needed treating or it would fester. Together they helped dress the Mujina. "No offense, pal, but the less people who see your ugly mug the better," Jack said, securing the helmet in place. He brought the smoky visor down over its face.

"I am infinite," the creature said through the helmet's speaker relay. "I contain multitudinous life. I am you and he and she. I am they and they are I. I am all your dreams. Your hopes. Desires. I am the song of your heart. I am all of these things and more. I am a reflection of you. What you see is what you are."

Daniel chuckled. "I think he's saying that you're just as ugly, Jack."

"Ah, nice, a sense of humor. Thanks Doctor Seuss, you'll fit right in. Okay, how about we get out of here? Daniel, the torch?" Jack held out his hand for the mag-lite. He spun his wrist, sending the thin beam roving all around the ice cave, high and low. The walls coruscated with an eerie inner glow as the torch's beam played over them. "This way."

They followed Jack as he led them through the darkness toward the surface. At every turn or fork in the subterranean passage he took the one that led upwards. It was a reasonable assumption to work from. Of course there had to be a reason for the gate being hidden away in the deep instead of up there, closer to the heavens. Sam kept the thought to herself.

It was almost like a game, following the bobbing light — a willow-the-wisp leading them on a merry dance through the dark. She hadn't quite regressed to the point of worshipping the light yet, but there was something fundamental about her need to see it. "Follow the light and everything will be all right," she said to herself. They walked in silence, each wrapped up with their own thoughts on their current predicament. Sam couldn't help but run the probabilities in her head as she walked. There was comfort in numbers. Sometimes she went so far as to dream in calculus, the numbers forging a connection between her and the infinite. Science was her truth. Unfortunately, that also meant she grasped the enormity of the problem they faced if they ever wanted to get home. Not only could they be anywhere in the universe, they could conceivably be any*when* as well.

A little while later she felt the gentle kiss of the slightest breeze against her cheek. It was the first sign that there might be a way out of this subterranean darkness. It was growing noticeably colder, too.

A minute later she saw the first chinks of day bright.

They started to run toward it, scrambling up the shale. Sam's feet slipped and skidded on the loose stones. She hit the light and stopped dead in the cave's mouth. The world, for as far as she could see, was white. Vast featureless expanses of snow stretched out beneath her. There was nothing but whiteness as far as the eye could see.

It was a heartbreaking vista — and not one she had ever wanted to see again, not after the last time when they had stumbled out of the second gate onto the polar ice. There was no sign of any cavalry coming to their rescue. She bit back the bitter disappointment. It wasn't the time for self-pity. Not if they wanted to find a way off the ice. Not if they wanted to find a way home. This was Fat Lady territory. Sam could hear her doing her vocal exercises.

"Okay, this isn't exactly what I was hoping for," O'Neill said. "I was thinking more like air cars and post-industrial cityscape. This is all rather… isolated. Carter, run a scan for life signs. I don't know whether to hope there's something out there, or really hope that there isn't."

"A yeti or two, maybe?" Daniel said.

Sam ran the bio-scanner. The results, for the second time since they set out from Earth, made next to no sense. "Sir? I'm not sure what to make of this. According to the scanner there's a small army virtually on top of us."

"They must be *really* small," O'Neill said, his sentence punctuated by the telltale snick of a round being chambered no more than a few feet behind them. Sam turned to see the muzzles of two old style service rifles pointing down at them from a ledge on either side of the cave's entrance.

"Now that's just rude," O'Neill muttered. He turned slowly, raising his hands above his head. "I am Colonel Jack O'Neill, of the United States Air Force. This is Major Samantha Carter, Doctor Daniel Jackson and Teal'c. We come in peace. Do you understand? Peace. No guns pointing. It's just not the done thing where we come from."

"The weapon is old, O'Neill. I do not believe it poses a threat to us."

"It's not polite to mock the people pointing guns at you, Teal'c. They might take offense."

"No offense was intended, O'Neill. I was merely stating a fact. The barrels show marked signs of wear. Statistically it is improbable that such a weapon could expel its projectile with any degree of accuracy."

"I don't think you need to worry about that," one of the four gunmen said, standing slowly. "Given that it would be really difficult to miss with the muzzle pressed up against the side of your pretty bald head."

"See what I mean, Teal'c," O'Neill said. "Upsetting the guy with the gun is a really dumb idea."

Sam watched as the rest of the gunmen rose. They moved with military precision. Each covered the other so at no point were there less than three guns aimed at their quarry. In a curious sort of way their discipline was reassuring. It meant they were less likely to get flustered or fire off a round accidentally — so the fact that they were at least organized meant the chances of making it out of this mess alive were greatly improved. The first man came down from the ledge. He was tall, maybe six inches taller than Jack, and broad shouldered like Teal'c, but with a markedly less defined musculature. He moved with a natural grace despite the treachery of the elements. Sam saw that he wore some sort of rubberized boot, designed no doubt for gripping the ice.

He was well protected from the elements with a fur-lined

animal-hide over his head and shoulders, and beneath what appeared to be a derivative of Arctic BDUs, white to blend in with the snows, and with enough padding to suggest some form of Kevlar lining or suchlike. He was blonde, blue-eyed, square-jawed and distressingly handsome. They all were, she realized, looking at them one at a time. They were beautiful people to the point of being almost comic-book idealizations of what the perfect man ought to look like. The sight of these perfect specimens of humanity coming down from the narrow ledge was unnerving. There was nothing sensual or erotic about them. On the contrary, the marked genetic similarity between each of them was enough for Sam's mind to leap to a certain set of inbred conclusions.

"You do not look prepared for the elements, which is puzzling, is it not, brothers?" The soldier said to his companions.

"Most puzzling," another one of their handsome captors said.

"It would suggest that they were not expecting this weather," the first man continued, "but that only posits another puzzler, does it not, brothers? Given that there is nothing but the ice of the tundra for more than two hundred klicks in any direction. Quite the conundrum, wouldn't you say? What is a boy to think?"

"Perhaps we parachuted in," O'Neill offered.

"I don't think so. You would have been seen. Believe me, with nothing to see for miles, even the slightest movement tends to draw the eye. Four parachutes in the sky are not going to go by unnoticed. Besides, no chutes," he pointed at their kit, and offered a wry smile. "So unless you were planning on bouncing I can't see you jumping out of a plane."

"Nice," O'Neill said appreciatively. "Good solid deductive reasoning and a smart mouth. I think I am going to like this kid."

"Aside from the whole pointing a gun in our faces," Daniel said.

"So, no parachutes," the soldier went on, ignoring the interplay between his captives, "and if I am not mistaken no tracks around the mouth of the cave here, so what am I to make of that? It isn't as though you could simply materialize out of thin air, is it?"

"That's a bit too *Star Trek*," O'Neill said.

That puzzled the man. He appeared to think about it for a moment, trying to work it out for himself, but eventually gave up.

"You do not fear our weapons, you appear in the middle of nowhere, out of nowhere, and you show absolutely no regard for the trouble you are in. I am Dragul of the Corvani, I do not believe you are either Corvani or Kelani, which means you are an enigma, O'Neill. You are clearly not one of us, yet how could you be anything other? You speak our tongue, wear the face of our people, though it is a good deal more haggard than is common. Perhaps you have escaped from the salt mines to the south?"

"Hold on a minute. Haggard?"

"But then I look at your companions, a mix blood with dark skin, a weak man better suited to books than hard labor and a woman. None of them would last a week in the mines, for very different reasons, so you cannot be escaped prisoners. The alternatives available to me are diminishing by the moment, you see, because the more I deduce, the less I know of you."

"Like you said, I'm an enigma," O'Neill said, wondering why they hadn't counted the Mujina amongst their number. Was it somehow invisible to them? Was that another talent the creature possessed? It was a question for later.

"Be quiet," Dragul said. The shift in his tone from amicable to sharp made it all the more unnerving. It was as though an aspect of his personality had simply been overridden. He wasn't their friend, neither was he interested in making small talk. They were his prisoners. He was evaluating the threat they posed, and what reward bringing them in might earn him. Sam looked at Teal'c. The big man raised a silent eyebrow and inclined his head. "Now, how did you come to be out in the middle of nowhere, utterly unprepared for the environment? And more to the point, what do you want here?"

"We're little green men," O'Neill smiled weakly.

"Little green men?" Dragul asked, obviously puzzled.

"Purple people eaters from out of space. Aliens. You know?"

"Ah, Off-Worlders? Perhaps you are at that," Dragul mused. "For all its implausibility, it is at least an answer that bears the semblance of truth about it. If I search will I find your rocket ship buried around here? The thing is, no matter how I look at it, there is no legitimate reason, or means, for your being here, which makes you interesting."

"I've been called worse."

Sam knew O'Neill well enough to know he was up to something. He played the fool well, but he had that look about him — in the military they called them 'tells' — facial ticks, twitches, or just shit-eating grins — things that give away the opponent's intentions without their even knowing it was happening. O'Neill liked to think of himself as inscrutable but Sam had him pretty much figured out.

"The thing about being people of interest, my new friend, is that more often than not you don't want to be noticed by the people to whom you are of interest."

"And that would be your people, I suppose?"

"My people? Oh, no. My people are the scum of the earth as far as Corvus Keen is concerned, but then, so am I. Being a traitor to the blood doesn't tend to go down well at the best of times."

Sam felt Teal'c stiffen beside her. This Dragul appeared to have a gift for saying the right thing to get a rise out of his captives. Perhaps it was all part of his diminishing calculations and traitors was the next logical assumption, or perhaps he was blessed with an uncanny ability to read people. She looked at Teal'c. He was obviously ill at ease, every muscle tense, ready to lash out explosively... Yes, traitor was a reasonable assumption, she realized, but the man couldn't possibly understand the connotations of the insult in the Jaffa's ears, nor how deep the hurt of the word ran.

"Which is your way of saying you're just doing your job and you are about to take us to your leader?" O'Neill said.

"Indeed," said Teal'c. "The alternative was almost certainly to shoot us where we stand."

"Your friend takes all the fun out of life."

"I've found that," O'Neill smiled. "So enough with the pleasantries, you've decided not to kill us, which I have to say is a good decision and should be commended. So how about we move on to stage two of your plan, the bit where you take us to meet your higher-ups because we might be of interest?"

"Are you always in such a hurry, O'Neill?"

O'Neill half-shrugged, half-nodded. Sam had seen the gesture a dozen times in the last week. It was trademark O'Neill dissembling.

"Follow me, and do not think about trying to run. Our weapons may be old, but our bullets bite just as hard as ones minted yesterday."

"I'll have to take your word for it," O'Neill said, falling into line behind the soldier. He winced at the sudden shooting pain that lanced up from his knee. "Besides, where, exactly, do you suppose we might run to?"

"No doubt that is what Jahamat will want to talk to you about."

"Jahamat being your superior officer?"

"Either that or his very hungry wolf hound." Dragul said with a chuckle. "I shall let you worry about which for a while."

They followed the four men back up the path to the ledge where they had lain in wait, and then up a concealed track worn into the ice by the shuffle of weary feet. Sam couldn't help but wonder why of all the places in this forsaken wilderness they'd chosen to make camp so close to the gate if they didn't know it was there? Was there something in them that responded to the gate's proximity? If nothing else puzzling it out would be something to keep her mind busy while she trudged through the snow. The sun beat down coldly on the white. Where it was thinnest the ice formed crystalline run-offs, like miniature frozen waterfalls that caught, reflected and refracted the light in a glory of colors. The sight of this simple nature was breathtaking. It was as though she were somehow being shown the very numen of the iced land, and coming in to contact with this luminous beauty how could she not be touched by it?

The narrow path took them over the top of the mountain, rising higher and becoming ever more treacherous before it slowly began to work its way down the other side. It was no wonder they hadn't been able to see this Jahamat's camp when they emerged from the tunnels. The place bore all the hallmarks of permanence she wouldn't have expected to find in some temporary bivvy in the middle of nowhere. The natural surroundings had been used to enhance the camouflage, blending the tents into the white where possible. More impressive though were the buildings she assumed had to be the command structure — these were built block by block with chiseled ice stacked one atop the other and canted slightly so that the weight of the structure was taken by the blocks from the other side, while the center of the roof itself was formed by thick skins. It was an ingenious twist on the basic igloo design. Each igloo appeared to be joined by low passages of more skins, each braced with an inner framework for support. Looking at the basic shape, Sam assumed the frame was constructed from various things they might have scavenged from the local area, including bones — after all the skins had to come from somewhere. Didn't they?

She counted thirty igloos and three times that many skin passages linking them.

Despite the sheer size of the camp she couldn't see anyone, but judging from the number of tents and the core building network she assumed they had stumbled into a small force, around two hundred to two hundred and fifty men, give or take.

From one of the igloos she saw smoke fires rising and felt her stomach contract with sudden hunger pangs as though the smoke reminded her how long it had been since any one of them had eaten real food, not those tasteless MREs.

"Sir," she whispered, trying to guide O'Neill with her eyes. He followed the direction of her slight nod, but she had no way of knowing if he could tell the furthest snow-laden tarp half-hid what appeared to be a serious piece of kit: a top-armored ATV with snow-tracks and a front-mounted cannon. It was incongruous with the almost antique rifles the men used, and that made it interesting. It suggested one of two alternatives to Sam; either the army was terminally under-resourced and the men were being forced to make do with whatever lay to hand, or this was such a remote unit that the expectation of them facing a combat scenario was virtually nil — meaning they didn't need the latest tech, only enough to make sure they weren't devoured by whatever this ice-planet's version of Wampa's were. Neither alternative was especially comforting.

Dragul held up his hand for them to stop walking. He knelt and planted something in the ice. A moment later the red glare of a flare burned out in the sky. It was obviously some sort of pre-arranged signal to make sure Tweedle Dum didn't shoot Tweedle Dumber on the way down into the encampment. It had the rather curious side effect of letting anyone within a fifty-mile radius know about their presence on the ice.

Eight more armed men met them at the bottom of the slope. These were better equipped, and dressed in the same black and silver arctic BDUs that Dragul and his team wore.

"Well, well, what have we here, soldier?" said the smallest of the men facing them. He had a weasely little face pitted with acne scars, the left side hanging slackly, mouth downturned, as though the result of some form of stroke. But it was his eyes that disturbed Sam. They blazed with the sort of fervor she associated with religious fanaticism.

"We found them on the other side of the mountain, Major Damorkand."

"And what were they doing there?" Damorkand asked without so much as acknowledging the possibility that any of them might have been able to answer for themselves, given the chance.

"We aren't sure, sir. "

"So you decided to bring them here, soldier?"

"I believe they will be of interest to Jahamat," Dragul said.

"It isn't your place to believe, soldier," Damorkand said with all the absurdity of a zealot locked into his dogma. Then he seemed to see the Mujina for the first time and everything changed. His head inclined a few inches to the side in quiet contemplation of whatever whisper he heard in his head. Sam had no liking for the expression that slipped so easily across his deformed face. Again, it was in his eyes. She shivered. There was nothing remotely pleasant about his scrutiny.

"Let me be the judge of that," another voice said. Sam turned to see a man emerge from the tunnel of skin. He straightened up, standing a full head taller than either Damorkand or Dragul.

"Jahamat," Damorkand said, his tone suddenly obsequious. "I was just reprimanding young Dragul for bringing a potential threat into our encampment. Once again he has shown a reckless disregard for the safety of the mission."

"On the contrary," the one called Jahamat said, "he has shown initiative, something sadly lacking around here, soldier. You are dismissed." He turned to Dragul. "Perhaps you would accompany me, soldier? I would be most interested in hearing the hows and wheres of your encounter with these intruders, and the reasoning behind bringing them into the encampment."

"But of course, sir. Might I suggest the one called O'Neill joins us? I believe a few minutes of his company will be more than enough to convince you that it was the right decision."

"Of course, and what of this one?" Jahamat gestured toward the helmeted Mujina. Like Damorkand he had seen something through the dark visor that intrigued him, but unlike the weasely little man, the hunger-lust hadn't immediately overcome his eyes. That made the newcomer even more interesting.

"It is unlike the rest of them," Dragul said. "But how much different I do not know yet, sir."

"Yes," Jahamat said. "I can feel something... Most interesting."

"Carter, look after things here," O'Neill said, deliberately cutting across Jahamat's train of thought. "I'm trusting you to keep Daniel out of trouble." Before Daniel could object O'Neill continued, "I'm serious, Daniel. I know you. I'm sure you could find some sort of cavity in the ice filled with the frozen remains of the missing link given enough time, so let's just try and stay out of trouble, shall we? No excitement."

Daniel looked wounded but he didn't say anything. Teal'c on the other hand looked at O'Neill with no small amount of consternation. "Am I to remain behind, O'Neill?"

"There's a good boy," O'Neill said.

"These strangers have given us no reason to trust them, O'Neill. I advise proceeding with caution."

"Wouldn't dream of doing it any other way, my friend."

O'Neill left with Dragul and Jahamat, leaving the rest of them in a curious sort of limbo between honored guests and prisoners. They were pushed and prodded toward one of the ice structures. It had been stripped of any creature comforts it might once have had. Five thick furs lay on blocks of ice to make beds and a small trough had been cut into the ground to form a latrine. It was dark but surprisingly warm inside, the ice walls somehow absorbing the heat of the sun and holding on to it without melting. No one spoke for the longest time, then Teal'c broke the silence: "There is much I do not understand here, Major Carter. Not least of which is the power the Mujina seems to wield over all that look upon it."

"Right there with you, Teal'c."

"Did you perhaps note the reaction of our guards to the creature?"

"If you mean the hunger that burned in their eyes, I did, yes."

"Indeed. It would seem that the creature's infiuence is extending beyond direct line of sight."

"You could be right." Sam remembered the way the men had stared at the helmet's dark visor. They hadn't been able to see through it but that no longer seemed to matter, they responded to the creature's presence just the same.

"Couldn't we use it to our advantage?" Daniel's voice sounded curiously strained in the dark. Sam wondered for a moment if it even was his voice and not some filtered need picked up on by the Mujina.

"Is this your idea of staying out of trouble?" she asked, only half-joking. Something about the notion of using the Mujina's gift disturbed her on a primal level.

"I'm not talking about raising an army and fighting our way out, Sam," Daniel said. "I was thinking more like having our charming new companion befriend one of the guards. Every good prison break movie seems to have a man on the inside. Maybe we can use him to smuggle in an ice pick or something?"

"Daniel Jackson's suggestion is not without merit," Teal'c agreed. "The creature does possess a curious gift for bonding with humans."

"It couldn't hurt," Daniel pressed. She heard him move in the darkness.

Sam wasn't so sure. She couldn't shake the feeling that it was a recipe for disaster just waiting to be unleashed.

"Sam?"

"I don't know, Daniel. There was something about the way it got inside my head that makes me reluctant to turn the Mujina loose."

"But —"

"I can see the advantages. I honestly can. But I don't know, I can't help thinking it would be like Pandora's Box. Once it's out there, there's no shutting the lid and I'm not quite sure I'm ready to deal with the consequences of that just yet."

"You all talk about me as though my mind is brittle and I am incapable of understanding what it is you are saying. I am not yours to use once and destroy." It was the first time the creature had spoken directly, and it was disconcerting to realize its level of understanding. It was more than a mimic. That changed things for Sam. "I know what you need and how desperate you are for desires you dare not voice, Major Carter. I know you better than you know yourself. There is love and fear in you, in equal amounts, though you never allow either to win. Do not for a minute think I know the guard outside any less intimately, nor that he knows his own desires any more clearly than you do. Few people know the secret yearnings of their hearts, and so often they are different to the desires of the mind. If I choose to use my gift in this situation it will be because I judge it necessary to save myself. Do you understand?"

She did. "But how come I hear you now, not the voice of my mother?"

"It is the darkness. For the moment it dulls the yearning because you cannot see her face in mine. Tomorrow it may not be so. It is difficult to tell, each mind succumbs at a different rate depending upon the force of the need driving it. You have a strong mind but you possess an equally strong need. I do not have the answer for you, but I will tell you this, I have seen the worlds inside your minds, all of them, and I would walk them all. I will not die here."

Something moved in the darkness. "Good for you," a disembodied voice rasped. It seemed to come from nowhere and everywhere at once. Those three words dripped with bitterness.

She hadn't seen anyone else in that brief moment when the light of outside had streamed into the prison — and she was under no illusion, that was exactly where they were. "Who's there?"

The only answer was a short bray of coughing. The sound was wet and thick with phlegm. She didn't need to be a doctor to know whoever shared the jail with them wasn't faring well. When the coughing finally stopped the prisoner said, "I said the same thing when they threw me in here a month ago. Now, I don't know, maybe I will die here," he broke off as another coughing fit wracked his body. "It's the blood. It is always about the blood."

"What do you mean?" Daniel asked, before Sam could.

She moved toward the corner where the prisoner huddled up against the ice wall. "My blood is impure. I am Kelani, not Corvani."

"I don't understand," Daniel said. Sam noticed the shift in his tone that always accompanied his curiosity being piqued. She thought back to O'Neill's warning. Did befriending an impure-blooded prisoner count as getting into trouble? She suspected it did. But she knew Daniel well enough to know he could never do anything else. His humanity burned brightest in dark places like this. It always had.

"Don't ever tell them that, not ever," the prisoner rasped, his voice suddenly intense, strong. "Because they'll know immediately that you aren't one of us. They already know you aren't one of them, and on Kumara it is always a case of them or us. That's how the world turns. You might just as well say you don't know the difference between Banak and Krace. And don't tell me you don't. I don't want to know. Ignorance marks you as an outsider. Being something else, well that ain't going to bode well for you, man. Because if you aren't from here it means you are from somewhere else, and Corvus Keen is going want to know where, exactly, and more importantly, how he can get there."

"I understand," Daniel said.

"What of the blood?" Teal'c asked.

"I am Kelani."

"What does that mean?"

"It means I am a sub-species, considered less than human, if the great Corvus Keen is to be believed."

"Ah."

"Such is Kumaran culture. My people are to blame for all the ills of the world simply because we are different. We are taught that different is wrong. They spray painted that slogan across my mother's house when I was barely knee-high. Different is wrong. It is burned in my soul."

"I'm sorry," Daniel said.

"You have no reason to be. It was not your doing, was it?"

"No, but still, difference should be celebrated," Daniel said. "Difference is what makes us special."

"That is what I believe, but the moment someone like me dares speak out against the norm, then we become a problem. Keen only has one way of dealing with problems: he removes them. That is why we are here in this place. Out of sight out of mind. We are good enough to toil away unseen, but heaven help us if we dance to the wrong tune. It's funny," the prisoner went on, the quality of his voice changing in the darkness as the bitterness faded into a more amused cynicism, "he's got us out here looking for his holy grail, proof that the Corvani are superior. We are out here looking for the evidence to prove once and for all that the Kelani are inferior. You have to laugh, how many people would willingly search for the means of their own subjugation? It's ironic if nothing else, and sums up the arrogance of the man."

There was something chillingly familiar about the scenario the unseen prisoner presented, a supposedly 'lesser' species being beaten down by a so-called master race, being mocked for their difference, and then finally turned into prisoners and being made to disappear. It made Sam's blood run cold. If she could draw the parallels she had no doubt Daniel could, just as easily.

"Corvus?" Daniel mused, "Is that an affectation or is it his name? Corvus, Corvani? It seems like a title, Emperor? God-King?"

"He took the name himself, another mark of his arrogance if you ask me. He claims it marks him as a man of the people, but really it does nothing more than serve to divide the two breeds, those of pure blood who bear *his* name, and the rest of us who are marked as less than human."

She knew Daniel well enough to realize he was already taking on this injustice as his own, and once it became personal there was no way they were going to be able to convince him it wasn't their fight — but it really wasn't. It wasn't their place to enforce their way of life on alien worlds; they weren't leaping about in space and time to put right what once went wrong, they weren't offering the American Dream to the cultures they encountered. It was difficult not to get involved sometimes, especially when things seemed so familiar — and so wrong — but it really wasn't their place to meddle.

But, with all that said, she heard a little Jiminy Cricket speaking with Daniel's voice in her head, *how can we not? How can we simply stand by and watch? How can we simply walk away?*

Knowing what she knew, it was difficult to argue against it. But societies had to be allowed to develop at their own pace, and that meant being left to make their own mistakes, and more importantly, to solve them.

Even if that means genocide?

That voice whispered again, and this time she realized it wasn't Daniel's at all, it was the Mujina toying with her. The way in which it could so effectively manipulate the more emotive heartstrings was terrifying. A few well-chosen words whispered into the deep-rooted core of her self, and all reason fled. Sam felt the cold seething anger it had intended to stir and swallowed it down. Every new hour spent in the creature's presence went a little further toward explaining what the Tok'ra meant when they called the Mujina a weapon.

"I can help you." She heard the words, but didn't know whether they belonged to the prisoner, or were another of the Mujina's promises. She suspected the latter, but before she could say anything there was a harsh grating sound followed by a chink of light as the door opened. She saw O'Neill's silhouette back-lit by the sun. "All right, ladies and gentlemen," the colonel clapped his hands, "out you come. Chop chop."

"Don't leave me!" The prisoner came scrabbling forward into the triangle of light cast on the frozen ground. He was a miserable wretch. The skin hung slackly about his face, leaving dark hollows where his eyes were hidden, barely more than slits, and sunken cheeks that elongated his face into a death mask. He was a thing of skin and bone, brittle and frail and too readily broken.

When he looked up at her Sam felt something inside break. Everything he had claimed came to life in the ruin of his body and she knew she wasn't seeing him through the filter of the Mujina's perceptions. The bones of his skull pressed out through his skin while every rib, every vertebrae, and every tiny bone between stood out starkly against bare leathery skin. She had only seen this kind of intimate death once before in her life, and that was in the pictures of the death camps, the gaunt look of surrender written all over the faces of the damned. And here it was now, in front of her, alive and begging for help. She was looking at a man very slowly and very deliberately being starved to death. And why?

Because his blood was different, she heard the Mujina whisper inside her head, and this time she allowed its indignation to inflame her.

"I can help you," the creature said again, and this time Sam believed it because she needed to.

She looked at every face in the cramped room and saw the same visceral response to the creature's promise echoed in the hope behind their eyes. Those four words had touched them all. They believed.

She stepped forward, into the light.

CHAPTER SEVENTEEN

The Fisher King

JACK O'NEILL caught Carter before she could get too close to the creature. He couldn't explain why he had done it beyond the fact that he knew he had to. He had seen her step into the triangle of light, and whether it was a trick of the light or the truth of his own eyes, a peculiar dullness appeared to take the luster from her eyes. It was unnerving and it was all the warning he got.

Jack had heard the Mujina's promise and knew there was more to it than the words. Something about the sentence jarred inside him and instead of being seductive it sounded repulsive. He always had been a contrary bastard, so it didn't surprise him that the siren's promise fell on deaf ears.

O'Neill matched Carter step for step, and as she began to lower herself he caught her arm and pulled her toward him. For the echoing silence between heartbeats it became a clinch. Then he pushed her away, toward the door.

"Come on, Major, we need to talk."

"I don't…" Carter mumbled. Then, as quickly as it had come over her, the fugue state seemed to lift and she said, "Sir."

"Outside, Major. Now. You too, Daniel, Teal'c." The Mujina made to follow them but Jack stopped it. "Not you. You stay here where you can't get into any trouble. Do we understand each other?"

"I mean you no harm, O'Neill," the creature said. He could feel it trying again with its saccharine tone and half-truths.

"Of course you don't." Jack bolted the door behind him. "But that's half the problem."

He ratcheted the final bolt home and turned his back on

the lonely mewling of the creature. It would survive. That was what it did.

Somewhere in the ice city a bugle sounded. It was an incongruous sound, a fanfare for the coming dusk.

"All right, people," Jack said. "I had an interesting chat with our host. Seems we've walked into the middle of what amounts to a civil war — but still we have one priority here, getting home. Everything else is window dressing."

"They're being segregated, tortured and murdered because of their blood, Jack. That's a little more than window dressing," Daniel said. "I'm sick of hearing the company line: it's not our place to intervene, we aren't here to meddle, everything's changed and nothing has changed. People are dying, Jack, and I don't know how many or why, but something about the whole thing sets my skin crawling."

"Teal'c?"

"I do not have enough knowledge of the situation to offer a considered opinion, O'Neill."

"Finally. Thank you, Teal'c. That's exactly my point. We don't know enough to make a decision on what side of the fence we fall. Who's to say we aren't being led a merry dance by the monsters of the piece? Right now we're fact finding, and the first fact we need to find out is where the hell we are."

"Ah, I think the planet's called Kumara by the locals," Daniel offered.

"Great. Teal'c, ring any bells?"

The big man shook his head. "I do not believe so. Once, perhaps, before I took the ritual of prim'tah and was apprenticed to Bra'tac, but the memory may not be my own so I cannot say with any certainty, O'Neill. One must surely question what is real and what the creature has manipulated. Though, I confess, I do not know why you would wish to know if I have ever rung a bell in this situation."

"Ah, not literal, a metaphorical bell, my friend, but thanks, you answered my question."

"I have never encountered a metaphorical bell, O'Neill. I can state with certainty that I have not rung one."

Sometimes there was a level of absurdity that accompanied a conversation with his team that beggared belief, but for all that he wouldn't change any one of them. Not now, not ever. Not willingly. They were his people. He trusted them with his life as readily as they trusted him. "So the mission's the same: we still need to identify the glyph that corresponds to Kumara on the Stargate."

The truth was the last half an hour had shaken him, but he wasn't about to let on. As far as he could tell, these people were out here looking for proof that, way back when, evolution had diverged, just as it had on earth with Neanderthal and Homo Sapiens. Only here, Neanderthal man had neither died out nor been assimilated into the second species, but rather co-existed.

He'd seen the same rationale applied to other races back home, seen the injustices of racism and prejudice first hand. It left a bitter taste in his mouth, but there wasn't a damn thing he could do about it.

They were here. They had to get home. The equation really was that simple. His responsibility was to his team, to the SGC, and to Earth, not to faceless thousands on an alien world. It was tough, but so was the damned universe.

And, hell, who knew how this was going to play out? Maybe the good guys — whoever they were — would win out in the end?

It didn't have to be the case of one species exterminating the other.

Unless…

Even from the little Jahamat had told him he knew it was only going to end one way if they discovered the Stargate. If ever there was proof to be had, the gate was it. The idea that these Corvani might have traveled the stars to arrive on this ice cube could only serve to reinforce the whole Master Race bullshit. So he'd lied to Jahamat when evasion wasn't enough to side-step the issue of where they'd come from. The man was no fool, but O'Neill knew he couldn't let them find the Stargate. Some things were better left hidden.

Outside, the bugle sounded again.

The blare masked a deeper rumbling. O'Neill felt it rather than heard it; the ice shivered beneath his feet. It was a peculiar sensation. The very stability of the ground was undermined by the pitch and yaw of the icequake. Moments later a second noise, less a rumble and more of a crack, echoed down through the ice and the entire ground tilted crazily beneath them. Jack reacted instinctively, pushing the others toward the mouth of the skin-lined tunnel while he threw himself at the brig door.

There was no way he was about to leave anyone locked up in there and he didn't care how much it might piss off the righteous 'Superior Race'.

"Go!" he barked, throwing back the top bolt. The lower one was blocked by a two-inch thick jag of ice that had been torn up from the ground with the heaving of the quake. He wrapped his hands around it and heaved but it wasn't giving an inch. He didn't have time or means to melt it, which meant he had to break it. He drew his Beretta M9 and squeezed off a single round into the center of the ice. It powdered beneath the impact, giving him plenty of room to reach the lower bolt. He drew it back and threw open the door. "Out! Come on!"

He turned and started to run back out through the hidebound tunnels, chasing the sting of the cold on his face even as another, deeper crack tore through the ice beneath him. He didn't look to see if the others were following him. He had to trust that they were.

A sudden seismic shift threw him sideways. O'Neill lost his footing as part of the ceiling came down, spilling snow into the passage. Light and the sudden bite of freezing air offered him another way out.

He took it.

He slipped and slid as he scrambled up out of the collapsing tunnel. Around him people were yelling. The bugle blared again. This time he understood; a watchman had seen the first fissure opening in the ice and had sounded the alarm. Even though he hadn't understood what it meant, the bugler had probably saved his life. O'Neill stumbled away from the ruin, dusting himself off. The Mujina emerged behind him, carrying the wizened husk of the other prisoner. O'Neill had no desire to see the abuse that had been inflicted upon the man but he couldn't in good conscience look away. Seeing it brought the evils home to him. He had no idea what the man's crime was, but whatever he had done, he didn't deserve to be starved to death. Not in any civilized world.

The Mujina laid its burden down by O'Neill's feet. He stayed there, crouched, head cocked slightly to one side as though hearing something O'Neill couldn't, and then he sprang. The creature bolted, haring over the unsteady ground, arms pumping furiously as it chased something Jack could neither see nor hear.

And then the ground opened up beneath its feet.

One moment it was there the next it was gone, swallowed by the ravine torn through the ice by the pressures being exerted from left and right.

The encampment exploded in panic. Soldiers ran toward the ravine while others ran away from it. Jack stopped running and became the one fixed point in the chaos as fear swirled all around him. He saw Carter and Daniel Jackson. There was no sign of Teal'c in the hysteria.

Another huge crack resonated through the ice. This time it was followed by an almost silken rush as the land pitched violently. It took O'Neill a moment to understand what he was seeing, so irrational was the sight of one of the igloos sliding toward the edge and then coming apart block by block as it disappeared into the ravine. Snow and screams swirled up into the air.

The first rescuers worked the edge, relaying back orders, demanding ropes and cages and anything else that could be used to bring survivors back up from the bottom of the fissure. The bravery of the men was obvious as they moved with incredible surety, traversing the jagged spurs of ice, making them safe.

And then came the horror.

With six of them working the ice face the edge broke away. They stood there for a sickening moment, betrayed by the ground beneath their feet, and then they fell.

O'Neill stared in mute denial.

He had just watched six men die in a heartbeat. It refused to register in his brain. He'd seen a lot of horrors in his life but this was somehow different. There was something elemental about it, something that took it out of the hands of the victims. There was nothing they could do about it. They couldn't fight back. They couldn't have done anything other than die. The brutality of it was grotesque. But soldiers died, it was their curse.

His initial impression of blind panic was wrong. The soldiers were moving with purpose, and what appeared to be hysteria was organized chaos as they swarmed quickly to limit the damage. It obviously wasn't the first time the ice had broken. Quickly, a second wave of men came toward the edge, working with brisk efficiency to lay down belay pins and anchor the rope that bound them together. This time there were three of them. They approached the edge cautiously, feeling out its stability with the teeth of the ice axes they swung. If one went over, they all went over, but hopefully the rope would save them from the fall.

Shouts chased down the line of workers, orders given and received.

The front man held up his hand. The others stopped. O'Neill found himself holding his breath along with the rest of the soldiers, and letting it out in a rush as the front man called back, "My God, he's climbing back up the side!"

O'Neill moved forward, compelled to see the drama unfold. He couldn't imagine how any of the men who had fallen could possibly have survived the drop, let alone have the strength left to claw their way back up the sheer side of ice. And yet another of the rescue workers at the edge confirmed it, "Come on, man, you can do it!"

He left the prisoner lying on a snow-laden animal skin; he was shivering but he was as safe as O'Neill could possibly make him. Others needed his help more.

"Carter! Daniel! Teal'c!" He yelled, cutting across the top of the frantic hubbub, waving them forward. He saw Carter nod her understanding and set off for the edge.

Before he made it half way Jack saw the hand come reaching up over the top.

The bloated fingers of the white gloves were shredded from where they had clung to the scars in the ice, and stained red with blood where it had opened up the flesh beneath. The second hand was followed by the Mujina's grimly determined face; the helmet had obviously been torn off in the fall, or taken off during the climb. The creature was not alone. One of the rescue workers that had gone over the edge clung grimly to its neck. The Mujina dragged itself up as far as it could, and even as its arms began to weaken and buckle two of the roped men pulled it up the rest of the way. A ragged cheer went up as people came forward to help the wounded man. His leg was in a bad way; the broken bone pierced through the skin and cloth. He had lost a lot of blood but thanks to the Mujina he now had a chance. Down at the bottom of the fissure his only hope had been to die quickly rather than slowly.

The Mujina stood, stretched, seeming to work out the kinks and twists in its bones from where the fall had battered its body, and before anyone could stop it, stepped off the edge in a dive.

An air of shocked silence swallowed every other sound until the *tick, tick, tick* of the stresses undermining the ice turned into a wrenching grumble. This time they heeded the warning. By the time the basso profundo *crack* of the landslide boomed out every one of the rescue workers was back fifty feet from the edge. Three more of the igloos were torn free by the collapse. They plunged into the ravine trailing animal skins like wings. O'Neill didn't move. His mind ran through the permutations and calculations and hit the same conclusion again and again — the Mujina was at the bottom of that lot, buried alive. But not for long. He felt an unexpected pang of loss, the last echo of Charlie's voice there at the back of his mind. It wasn't quite like losing his son all over again, but like everyone else staring down into the chasm he had just witnessed an incredible act of heroism snuffed out by the suddenness of the second landslide. Life once again made no sense.

"Nothing could have survived that." Daniel gave voice to what everyone else was thinking. Saying it made it all the more real. He was right. Nothing could have survived the crushing weight of the ice. It was almost funny that it should end like this, this so-called terrifying weapon crushed to death because, when it came down to it, the creature harbored a deep-seated need to be everyone's hero, even people it didn't know. That, O'Neill reasoned, was almost certainly the other side of the telescope — people might well see what they so desperately needed in the creature, but it needed to live up to those unreasonable expectations. It was a double-edged gift, for sure.

Jack saw Teal'c come striding out of the wreckage of one of the ice structures, a wounded man in his arms. With the wind kicking up the snow around him, O'Neill was struck by the similarity between the Jaffa and the fallen Mujina. But then it was hardly surprising that he would see the parallels, Teal'c was as close as he had ever come to meeting a genuine archetypal hero; the square-jawed comic book superhero figure capable of facing down any foe and walking away victorious through sheer unconquerable might. Right from that first moment he had turned his staff weapon on the guards inside the compound on Chulak he had embodied the very essence of his own name, Teal'c, strength.

Another soldier ran to his side to gather their injured brother. Teal'c refused to surrender his burden. Instead he carried the unconscious man to the makeshift first aid post the rescuers had begun setting up. He laid the man down on a bed of animal furs and walked back toward one of the collapsed buildings, pulling blocks of ice aside as he fought to find a way back into the screaming men inside. O'Neill joined him. Together they heaved aside the huge chunks of ice, moving with a sense of urgency as the cherry red sun began to slip from the sky.

For the next hour the survivors set about making the camp safe. Their position as prisoners was quickly forgotten as they labored side by side with the soldiers. Jack threw himself into the toil, going where he was most needed. The cold had the sweat freezing on his body. Exhausted and thirsty, he wandered across to where some of Jahamat's men had set up a refreshment station. A small fire burned beneath a metal vat, keeping the water from icing over. Jack joined the line. When it was his turn, he took a small metal cup and ladled a scoop of warm water into it. The metal pulled at his lip as he drank. "Anyone got some ice to go with this?"

One of the men beside him laughed. The sound was strained but it was the first glimpse of humanity any of them had shown since the Mujina had come up out of the ravine carrying their friend.

"Performing one night only, catch me while you can."

The laughing man said something but Jack missed it. Over beyond the broken ice houses he saw Jahamat giving orders. There was an economy about every movement the man made.

Each hand gesture was crisp and precise. O'Neill followed the direction of his hand. It didn't take a genius to realize what Jahamat was planning. He was taking advantage of the turmoil to send a small squad back up the hill to investigate the tunnels from which they'd emerged. There wasn't a lot he could do to stop them. Carter came up beside him. She wiped the cold sweat from her brow and held her face over the steaming mug she cupped in her hands. Corkscrews of steam coiled up lazily from the metal mug. He nodded toward where Jahamat was giving instructions. "I can't say I like the look of that."

Carter looked up from the steam. The clash of hot and cold brought out the startling blue of her eyes. She started to say something when a cry of alarm cut her short. O'Neill turned to see what all the commotion was about. Over by the jagged edge of the fissure the battered and bloody shape of the Mujina crawled hand over fist across the ice. The creature slumped forward, spilling its burden beside it. It took O'Neill a heartbeat to realize that not only had the creature clawed its way up through the debris of the landslide, somehow it had dragged another man up with it. "Well I'll be damned."

"Is that…?"

"Yep. That's one resourceful little bastard, that's for sure."

O'Neill finished off his warm water with one long swallow and wiped the wetness from his lips with the back of his hand. He put the metal cup down. "Come on, Carter. Let's go join the homecoming committee."

CHAPTER EIGHTEEN

True Colors

JAHAMAT WAS the first to the Mujina's side.

The leader of the Corvani expedition hunkered down beside the creature. When others tried to approach he waved them back. The creature spoke to him. He had to lean in so close that he could feel the warmth of the Mujina's shallow breath prickle his inner ear.

"*I can help you,*" the creature whispered, so faint the words might have been nothing more than the promise of the arctic wind.

"How?" Jahamat asked. He felt something stirring in his blood. He laid a hand on the creature's heaving chest and felt a palpable thrill surge up through his fingers. He licked at his lips. "Tell me."

"*I can show you the way to the stars... I can open up worlds to you... I can give you what you crave.*"

The words were in his head. He could see them with his mind.

"You? You can barely lift your head from the ice."

The creature moved then, with surprising strength. It came around beneath him, wriggling around on its back so that it looked up into his eyes. "*All is not as it seems, Jahamat. The eyes see what they want to. The mind interprets what it is shown, but the mind is influenced just as easily as the eye. It is all down to expectation.*"

It wasn't just the words that were inside his head; the creature was. He could feel its invasive presence rooting deeper and deeper, touching memories and emotions long since buried as it sought something else, something more profound. He understood then. The creature was hunting for his essence, the thing that made him *him*.

Jahamat knew fear then. Deep. Instinctive. Primal.

He looked down into the eyes of the creature and saw a blazing intelligence that shocked him, and in that moment of realization something of the creature's mask slipped and he saw the nothingness beneath. There was a flat plane where it ought to have worn a face. It had a ragged sucking hole for a mouth and black pits eyes. The folds of skin flapped as it breathed. And then, almost as quickly as it had been revealed, the truth slipped away behind another mask of need and he found himself looking down at the almond eyes of a woman.

"*I can be anything you want me to be,*" she said. It said. Jahamat found himself thinking of the woman in his arms as an 'it' not a 'he' or a 'she'; a sexless thing, despite its haunting beauty.

"I name you 'Monster of the Anima'," he breathed.

"*Isn't that where all monsters are born?*" the woman's smile was beguiling.

"Get out of my head, demon. Get out of my head now or I will cut your throat while you lie there crooning your sweet deceits."

His hand trembled against the Mujina's skin. He looked up. They were all looking at him. He saw the confusion in their faces. They were only party to half the conversation and the part they heard made no earthly sense.

"*Don't tell me you would walk away from the stars? I know you better than you know yourself, Jahamat. You question, you doubt but you would no more walk away than you would surrender me to my captors. Oh, yes, the people that brought me here are no friends of mine. They would snare me and chain me and parade me around as though I were a trophy they had claimed. They ripped me away from my homeworld and seek to use me, to transform me into a weapon to con-*

*quer galaxies. And I am that, Jahamat. I am an army. I am
death, eater of worlds. I am hope, breaker of dreams. I am
everything, from the beginning, the alpha, the zero point,
rushing through time to the end of days. I am it and it is I.
How can I bring you the stars? How? Because I am made
of the stars. Their dust hardens my veins. I do not bleed, I
crack and flake. I do not weep, I calcify. I am not of this
place. You know that to be true, don't you, Jahamat? You
can feel the alienness in my touch. Your blood sings with the
thrill of it. You understand even if you do not understand.
And you believe me."*

The words rushed around inside him. What they said,
what they promised, was so heady he did not dare believe,
and he wanted to deny it. He wanted to say: "I believe no
such thing." But it was a lie. He did. He believed. Instead,
ensnared, he breathed, "The stars? Truly? You can deliver
the heavens? How? Show me?"

*"There is a gate, beneath the ice. It opens to everywhere
you can imagine."*

"Show me," Jahamat said. He had been mistaken. The
woman's eyes weren't almond, they were hazel. Her skin
wasn't the flawless pale porcelain he had thought but
rough and pitted with the scars of acne and the first gray
of stubble. A man looked up at him now. A man with the
face of a fighter.

"Tell me you want it. I need to hear the words."

"I want the world," he said. And he meant it.

"More," the creature goaded.

"I want the heavens. I want the stars. I want it all."

"And I can help you, my hungry warrior," the Mujina
promised.

He liked the sound of that: the hungry warrior. That
was exactly what he was. He tasted the rightness of it in
his mind. "I don't even know what to call you."

"Oh, but you do. You already named me. But before the

world you may call me Mujina."

"Come then, Mujina," Jahamat said. "Show me this gate between worlds."

"Patience, my hungry warrior. Patience."

CHAPTER NINETEEN

Broken Circles

A HARD SUN beat down on the ice.

As the day wore into dusk a shallow film of melt still clung stubbornly to the surface. It would freeze again before the sun was out of the sky. The residual heat was never going to be enough to thaw the glacial mound beneath the camp, not all at once.

It had taken the better part of the day, but the camp was gradually beginning to show signs of returning to normal. What surprised Daniel was the seeming disregard for what had happened. It wasn't that the soldiers were untouched by the loss, but rather that they viewed it as just part of life. The human animal was remarkable like that; it was all part of that extraordinary resilience and tenacity that had allowed it to spread throughout the galaxy.

The camp illustrated it all on a microcosmic scale. He could see the triumph of spirit as the rescuers fought the elements to recover buried instrumentation from within one of the collapsed igloos. Six of them clawed away at the ice even as a second smaller tremor rippled through the heaving ground. It was a peculiar sensation. The horizon appeared to roll, all of the disorientation rising up from beneath Daniel Jackson's feet. All around him, men from the camp worked together without a word. There was an almost hive-like mentality to it, with Jahamat as the queen bee in the center of it all.

Jack threw himself into the heart of it, risking his own safety without so much as a second thought, which was so like him. But Daniel noticed the way he seemed to gravitate toward Jahamat as the need for help moved across the temporary settlement. That almost certainly meant O'Neill's efforts were far from selfless acts of heroism. He was ingratiating himself, being seen to be at least one man's savior. Daniel watched Jack a little while longer. There was a lot to be admired in the man. Indeed he was not dissimilar to the Mujina in the way that he inspired those around him to want to please him. The notion of Jack O'Neill as an ancient mystical creature brought a smile to Daniel's face. Jack was about as *un*mystical as they came.

And yet the Asgard had named an ill-fated ship after the man.

The more Daniel thought about it, the more he realized what a fair comparison it actually was.

Across the camp, Sam and Teal'c labored hard and with no less disregard for the risk. Rather than join them, Daniel hung back slightly from the rescue efforts, watching the others watching the Mujina. There was something Messianic in the way they responded to the creature, even Teal'c.

It was fascinating to see.

Daniel turned his attention from the worshippers to the worshipped for a moment, and again felt that haunting sense of the Messianic. He thought of all the charismatic leaders he had ever encountered, from the icons on the silver screen to the demagogues who owned their people heart and soul. All of them, he reasoned, possessed that same Svengali-like surety and owned that same connection with their subjects.

The memory of Orwell's Oceania was not one he wanted to live out in reality.

He could all too easily imagine John the Baptist on the beaches, making his impassioned speeches to crowds hungry to understand his new message of hope; or, at the other end of time, Kennedy promising to end the escalation of the Cold War on the balcony of Berlin's Rathaus Schöneberg. Omar al-Bashir, Kim Jong-Il, Ríos Montt and so many of the world's oppressive regimes, Batista and Stroessner, Pol Pot and Nikolai Chauchescu, Ho Chi Minh and Bin Laden, and even Saddam Hussein; men with the power to coerce men to kill for them, or die for them and what they believed in. It was all too easy to transfer the Mujina's charismatic magic to them, and understand the implications of what was already happening here in the few hours since their capture.

"He's not the Messiah," Daniel muttered beneath his breath, holding off on the obvious Pythonesque end of the quote. None of the others were close enough to appreciate it anyway.

Down in the heart of it O'Neill turned, shading his eyes against the sun. Daniel did likewise, following the direction of his gaze. Behind him, through a deep vee slashed into the ice-mountain, he saw a lone man silhouetted against the sky. It was impossible to see his face from this distance, but his excitement was almost palpable, even from so far away. He came running down the mountain.

Daniel knew precisely what it meant: they had found the Stargate.

The echoes of the blasting caps had finally silenced. Jahamat's men had blasted open the cave network but they didn't have the heavy machinery to lift the naquadah ring so for now, at least, it was still anchored in place. Jahamat assured them they would be back, with the machinery, when the time came. In the mean time they were ensuring that the cave wouldn't remain hidden any longer. Even now, away from the gate, the look of almost reverential awe on each of their faces made it appear as though they were in the grip of some holy revelation. Rapture. Daniel wondered if they had even the slightest idea of what the Stargate represented, what it actually *was*, or if they simply thought they had discovered some ancient artifact.

Both Jahamat and the Mujina walked toward them. Daniel had no liking for the way the creature had attached itself to

the Corvani leader. It leaned in and whispered something in
the man's ear. Daniel had heard those same whispers himself
and knew just how seductive they could be. The Mujina was
no doubt telling Jahamat exactly what he wanted to hear — but
in a way that served the Mujina and the Mujina alone.

The way the Corvani's smile spread across his face sent a
shiver of trepidation down the ladder of Daniel's spine. There
was nothing even remotely healthy about the expression.

O'Neill followed the pair of them, a few paces behind, as
though he expected to be challenged every step of the way but
intended to get as close as he could before that happened.

And then, seeing the gate and the look of absolute rapture on Jahamat's face, Daniel began to understand what the
Mujina was promising him. He didn't need to read the creature's lips. It was an obvious promise given the usual dreams
of a military man. Words of conquest. Promises of glory. All
of that and more. To abuse the cliché, the Mujina was offering power beyond imagining, untold worlds and the kind of
triumphs reserved only for the greatest generals of history.

And the Stargate was the key to all of it.

Thanks to the Mujina's treachery, they had found it after
all the centuries it had lay hidden in the caves beneath the
ice. All sorts of scenarios played out across Daniel's imagination in the time it took him to walk a dozen steps forward,
none of them happy.

They hadn't recovered the DHD, Daniel realized, and
from that he reasoned that the creature didn't actually know
how to use the gate, or if he did, he didn't know the glyph
for his prison planet. Which, of course, made sense. Surely
it would have used the Stargate on Vasaveda to escape if it
had known how? The creature had been inside their heads,
sifting through their thoughts. There was nothing to say it
hadn't found the glyph for Earth there along with the one for
Vasaveda. He didn't want to think about the implications of
that. The thought placed a chill in Daniel's heart.

He heard the soft crunch on the ice behind him.

Daniel turned, expecting to see Sam or Teal'c. The blow took him on the side of the head, hard. Because he wasn't expecting it, he didn't even begin to try and fend the attack off. He saw his blood on the wrench as the man looked down at him. The world swam out of focus. He hadn't realized he had fallen until he felt the welcoming chill of the melt on his check.

It was too cold to be blood, he thought, as he lost consciousness.

CHAPTER TWENTY

The Beautiful South

O'NEILL CURSED himself for a fool as he came around.

The world above his face lacked any kind of focus or clarity. The last thing he remembered was seeing Jahamat's men retrieving the Stargate. After that, blank. He screwed his eyes shut again, trying to force his brain into seeing clearly but it wasn't just his vision that was blurred. Nausea brewed in his guts. He groaned as he opened his eyes a second time. This was more than just the after effect of a blow to the head, he realized, trying to sit. He couldn't. It wasn't just that he lacked the strength — he had been chained down to the flat wooden bed.

"Carter?" It sounded more like *ca thur* as it slurred off his swollen tongue. He'd been drugged. That explained his brain's refusal to really wake and the languid torpor that clung like melted marshmallow to his thoughts. O'Neill twisted, but the shackles at his ankles and wrists had him effectively trussed up like a turkey. "Daniel?" *Da null?*

It took him a moment to realize that the cell where they had him prisoner was moving. The occasional and sudden lurch was disconcerting.

"Teal'c?" *The ulk?*

"Yes, O'Neill?" Teal'c's voice came back to him. It was the most welcoming sound in the world.

"Buddy…" *buth he…* It was pointless, his lips refused to obey him. It was good to know that he wasn't alone.

"The creature betrayed us to the Corvani, O'Neill," Teal'c said, filling in the first of the blanks in his memory. Knowing it didn't make him feel any better.

"The gate?" *thuh gathe?*

"They have the Stargate," Teal'c said. There was a quality to the Jaffa's voice that sounded so wrong in O'Neill's ears. It took him a moment to realize what it was: defeat. He had never heard the big man sound so utterly devoid of hope. He couldn't begin to imagine what had happened to Teal'c while he had been unconscious for the Jaffa to give up hope.

But then, he felt the bite of iron at hand and foot and something inside him twisted; even as he pulled at the pin anchoring his right hand down he knew it was pointless. It was all pointless. The sudden swell of black that accompanied the thought wasn't his — at least he didn't want to believe it was. O'Neill felt the anxiety gnaw away at him, like an addict's cravings. Part of him understood what was happening; he was coming down off 'the hit' of the Mujina's nearness. It had withdrawn from his mind. He could feel the emptiness where it had been. He was alone inside his own mind, and it was the first time he could remember the feeling since they had found the creature. Almost as soon as he realized, his stomach cramped. He twisted his head violently and retched, dry heaving. The emptiness churned inside his gut and clawed up his craw.

Seconds, minutes, hours, days, weeks, months, all of those comforting things lost all meaning in the dark of the rolling cell. O'Neill's world was reduced to absolutes — the cravings of withdrawal, the tremors of need, and the warm fullness of the sedatives. He couldn't remember eating, but he felt no real pangs of hunger so he assumed in the delirium of the drugs they forced some sort of nutrition down his throat.

He remembered fragments of conversation and recalled snatches of memory, including the look on Jahamat's face as he saw the Stargate for the first time. That wouldn't leave him, even as the sedatives took him under. His body stank. Sweat clung to his skin feverishly. He moaned, or thought he did. He was long past being able to tell.

They came with their needles. He even started to welcome them because they brought the blackness with them.

He heard the others occasionally — often enough to know that they were still alive, though their words were every bit as inchoate as his thoughts.

He dreamed Jahamat visited him. At least the meeting had all the dreamlike qualities of his imagination haunting him. The Corvani's voice was seductive, compelling with its questions about the stars and the worlds beyond, about the Stargates and their creators, about the Asgard and the Goa'uld and all of the other human races he had encountered from Abydos to Vasaveda. And still, even when he thought he was empty of knowledge, the dream dug away into some secret hidden in the depths of memory and betrayed him that little bit more to his enemy.

"Where are you taking us?" he asked the dream Jahamat.

"Karelea," the enemy said, or might have said, or might not. The word made no sense to O'Neill beyond the shape the syllables made in his mind. "I believe you, and your gateway to the stars, will be of considerable interest to Corvus Keen."

Keen… he'd heard that name before. He knew he had, but it slipped away from him and he slipped away from consciousness.

When he woke again, the world had stopped moving.

CHAPTER TWENTY-ONE

Secret Garden

THEY TRADED one prison for another.

The haze of the sedatives gradually cleared, but Teal'c felt no better for it. The Jaffa tested his bonds. There was no give in the iron. He felt naked without his staff weapon. For much of the journey south to the capitol, Karelea, they had pumped drugs into his body to subdue him. They were ineffective. His symbiote processed much of the toxins rendering the sedatives harmless. Teal'c did not allow his captors to realize he was effectively immune. Instead, he feigned grogginess when they came in to the rolling prison and watched as they sedated the others, and listened to the one called Jahamat as he ingratiated himself into O'Neill's drug-addled subconscious with his questions. It was well done. The man might have used more direct methods, cracking O'Neill's psyche open like the shell of a nut, but instead he teased the information out one secret at a time.

It took time, but so did the journey south.

The gradually increasing warmth through the cell's thin walls was the only proof that they were actually moving away from the arctic north to more bearable climes.

It was not only the Corvani that learned secrets through deception. Jahamat and the Mujina were careless with their tongues, confident that none of their prisoners were lucid enough to understand even if they heard. Teal'c listened, content in his silence, as the Mujina filled Jahamat's head with all the secrets of the Stargates and the lies of possibility. More than once he wondered if the creature was aware he faked unconsciousness. If it was, it gave no indication of it. In return for the Mujina's promises, the Corvani shared all that he knew of his own society and his hopes that the Stargate would once and for all prove that his people were indeed above the cursed Kelani in terms of their evolution.

How could that be argued, now that he could prove they had come to Kumara from the stars? It couldn't, surely? And once they opened the gate for Keen, every belief he held would be vindicated. It would be the dawning of a new age, and Jahamat would stand right at the very heart of it, the most important man in the world for a few minutes at least.

Keen would reward him.

Teal'c hid his skepticism behind a veneer of sleep. He had served enough men to know that the messenger was never truly important, no matter how much he might crave the acclaim. Keen would accept Jahamat's proof and then he would send the man off on another fool's mission. That was the nature of men like Corvus Keen; they were never content, and they never kept anyone capable of posing a threat close enough to hurt them. If they opened the gate, Teal'c knew, Jahamat would be among the first to go off world, and none of those he left behind would shed any tears if he did not return.

Listening in the dark, Teal'c came to understand the creature more and more as it goaded the man on. It was obvious it viewed Jahamat as a means to an end, not the end itself. It wanted to be taken to the capitol, Karelea, for one reason and one reason alone — because that was where the greatest concentration of people lay, and it needed to be in the center, at the heart of everything if it was going to replace Keen. It needed people to feed it and feed off it, much as Teal'c needed his symbiote and his symbiote needed him. So for a while they served a commonality of purpose, but as soon as that mutual need was sated, the creature would move on to another who would better serve it, and then another and another, until it was as close to Corvus Keen as it could come, and then, perhaps, it would even replace the man himself. Would the creature make a beneficent ruler? Would it present itself as a pontiff, a holy figure to be worshipped? Or would it stand before the people as a warrior worthy of mens' bended knee?

The answer was that it would be all these things, of course.

When the talk wasn't about the stars it was about much more earthly concerns: the weapons that had been confiscated from the visitors. Jahamat had never seen such controlled killing power. Teal'c lay on his pallet listening to the staccato rattle of gunfire as the Corvani tried out a gun. He had no way of knowing whether the man aimed at a live target, not for sure, but occasionally the quality of sound changed. That was when his rounds found their mark. There were no accompanying screams but that didn't mean anything.

Jahamat seemed happy when he came into the rolling cell that night.

"Almost there," he told O'Neill. The colonel was too far gone to appreciate what that meant. Teal'c was not. They neared journey's end. Soon they would have two choices, escape or execution. That was what it always came down to with men of power. There was no moral ambiguity; their world was one of absolutes, the known and the unknown. The known was conquered, tamed, the unknown neutralized so that it could not pose a threat. Teal'c had come to understand that much about humanity — it was governed by an overbearing fear of the unknown. As a result it was kill first, study, analyze and ask questions later. With the weapons it would be easy enough to back-engineer similar mechanisms, updating their hopelessly archaic low-caliber bolt-action rifles with genuine weapons of war.

With the men it was always going to be different once the information they needed had been prized out of their heads.

Teal'c was a man of war. He had no desire to lie to himself. For now they were being kept alive — it was a practicality, they had secrets still to be unlocked, things that Jahamat believed he could barter for greater influence with Keen. When they reached their destination everything would change. They would be handed over to Corvus Keen himself. For a while they would be a curiosity, and like Jahamat, Keen would bleed them, but only for so long because he would instinctively suspect treachery. Men like him always did. After that they would pass some invisible threshold where they would once again become a threat and their hours would be numbered. Teal'c had lived his life fighting every day for as long as he could remember, and not once in that time had he encountered an enemy foolish enough to leave the proverbial teeth in the snake so that it might bite him. Men of Corvus Keen's ilk, tyrants, did not survive by being foolish. Power was amassed with an almost predatory cunning. When they had outlived their usefulness they would be dealt with. It would be clean and efficient. Practical.

"Tell me all about this wonderful weapon of yours," Jahamat crooned, so close to Teal'c's ear the Jaffa felt his foul breath prickle his skin. He suppressed the shiver of distaste even as it started. "I have seen the future of death... I have held it in my hands... and it is glorious." The lust in the man's voice was barely restrained. He leaned in closer still so that his lips brushed against Teal'c's ear. "Is this a promise of what awaits through the Stargate? Have all these worlds refined death to such an art?" The man grunted. "I know you are not asleep, Teal'c. I have been watching you. It is truly remarkable how little the drugs affect you. I suspect it is a secret of your physiognomy. You are not like the others are you? Like a woman you carry a second life within you. Oh yes, the Mujina has told me all of your secrets. I will hear them from your own lips sooner or later. I hope later. I should like to hear you beg and plead first, Jaffa. Oh yes, I know *what* you are. Now tell me about this weapon of yours before we reach the city. I can hide you from Keen's men," Jahamat promised. "I can protect you. Or I can turn you over to his freak, Iblis, and let him carry out one of his vile experiments on you. It is up to you, Teal'c. What's it going to be?"

Teal'c said nothing. He did not need to. The name Iblis was a Goa'uld name.

Had he not been chained, he would have reached around and snapped the man's neck.

It was an unknown dawn when they came for them.

Teal'c rose groggily and shuffled toward the light docilely. His skin crawled with the grime of the cell. Six men stood guard at the door. Teal'c appraised them quickly. They were big men, overly muscular which meant that they would be slow if it came to a fight. They carried weapons — batons. Teal'c assumed that they must deliver some sort of charge, rather like a zat'ni'katel, otherwise they would be almost useless even in close combat. The shortest of the six bore the worst scars. Teal'c narrowed his eyes, trying to discern some sort of tribal pattern to the wounds, but they appeared both random and sadistic in nature. He had been cut for the sake of pleasing. The guard saw his scrutiny and grinned viciously. Light streamed in as they pulled the tarpaulins back to reveal the bars of their cage. He looked at the faces of his friends. They were frightened but alive.

Samantha Carter looked the worst. Her face was waxen, the luster gone. She tried to smile as she looked back at him with bloodshot eyes but there was nothing to smile about. She had lost a lot of weight. Her bones stood out starkly beneath the skin. Teal'c counted the meals in his head, judging that they had been prisoners in the dark for a month, maybe more, kept drugged up and undernourished. Being kept in captivity like that was obviously going to take its toll on the humans. Perhaps, as a woman, Carter's metabolism functioned differently to O'Neill and Daniel Jackson's? He nodded slightly in Carter's direction. The others were not much better. Indeed all of them stank of sickness and from being cooped up in the prison wagon for so long. There was no surprise in that.

He saw Jahamat through the bars of the cage. The man looked inordinately pleased with himself. The Mujina stood beside him, no longer dressed in the remains of the evac suit. Now the creature wore a crisp black uniform, closely cut to follow the lines of its body. There was a single silver embellishment on the chest, a silver spread-winged bird.

"Bring them out here," Jahamat ordered.

The guards responded with unnecessary vigor, grabbing the prisoners and pushing them bodily out of the cage. Daniel Jackson stumbled and almost fell, his legs buckling from disuse. After a month or more of drugged-up captivity the muscles had no doubt begun to atrophy. Again Teal'c appreciated the ruthless efficacy of the Corvani's leadership. He had effectively neutralized them all without lifting so much as a finger. There had been no beatings, no brutality, only weeks of inertia. It was incredible what evils time alone could work on the flesh.

Teal'c moved cautiously down the steps to the gravel. He took a moment to look around him, fixing landmarks in his mind. There was not much to look at. They appeared to have been brought in to some sort of monastic cloister. He saw the pitted stone of a bell tower. The climbing ivy had reached within grasping distance of the lowest gargoyle. The stone demons were a peculiar detail that didn't really fit with the rest of the architecture. Indeed their stone appeared to be considerably newer — less weathered, the pitting hadn't had a chance to work itself deeply into the leering faces or crack away parts of the furled wings. He followed the line of the tower down, and then swept his gaze across the red clay tiles of the roof. He counted twenty-one windows. There was no uniformity in either shape or size. How many eyes looked down silently on them while they stood there, exposed? None or a hundred, it did not matter.

There were a dozen arches, and hidden in the shadows they cast a dozen more. Behind them, almost invisible in the shade, were four doors. One almost certainly led up to the bell, while another was actually two huge double doors twice Teal'c's height and more than twice the span of his arms across. It dwarfed the remaining doors into insignificance. The cloister was actually a horseshoe in shape, though trees walled the open end of the shoe. He counted a dozen genuses, none of them familiar. The verdant wall was comprised of so many hues of green it was impossible to differentiate them.

There was a fountain in the middle of the square, at its center an idealized sculpture wrought in bronze. It was the usual heroic lies of rippling muscles and strong features. The kind of face that a hero ought to wear, not one of the thousand other real guises they more often did. Water rippled over the bronze muscles, lending them the sheen of sweat and the illusion of action. The artist had added dozens of small birds in various stages of flight around the base of the fountain. There was something dynamic about them that truly did suggest the illusion of flight. The man standing proud in the center was no doubt a rendition of Corvus Keen, Teal'c surmised.

A second wagon and a third pulled up, and more prisoners were dragged from them.

"Line up, and think yourself damned lucky the Great Keen has taken an interest in you personally," Jahamat barked, walking the line. He stopped in front of Teal'c, a slow smile of cunning spreading across his lips as he looked the Jaffa up and down. "If you were not of interest to the master you would already be on your way to one of the facilities. As it is, there is a chance yet that you might find a place within our new bright and bountiful empire."

Teal'c caught the fact that he said 'our', not 'his'. Already the lackey's rebellion had taken on such a level of arrogance that he dared flaunt it in front of all of these men loyal to Keen. *Or are they loyal to Keen?* It was an obvious question, given the nature of the creature; perhaps the Mujina had already bought their souls for Jahamat?

The prisoners shuffled listlessly into line. Most moved with a drugged lethargy, their heads bowed so that the only thing they saw were their scuffing feet. Teal'c kept his head stubbornly held high. One of the guards walked up behind him. He heard the crunch of footsteps on the gravel, and then felt the sudden crippling surge of electricity lance through every muscle and tendon right down into the bone as the man delivered the charge with cruel precision. "Head down," the guard rasped. Teal'c complied. He had seen enough and this wasn't a fight he needed to win.

They were led in single file, not toward the great double doors, but toward one of the smaller ones. It opened into what could only be termed a secret garden — a garden hidden within the cloister's courtyard. The trees were the first thing he saw. They had been sculpted to resemble tears. It was a curious inversion of what he had expected. Teal'c heard the raucous caw of a blackbird somewhere in the weeping leaves of the downcast trees. Ahead of them, he saw the high topiaries of a hedge maze. In the corners more of those ugly faced demons had been carved — this time in the leaves. The motif was as chilling as it was curious, with the wind stirring their leaves and lending the illusion of movement as it sighed through them.

"Time to play a game," a bloated ball of a man called out as he waddled toward them. "Try to think of it as fun." Teal'c wondered if this was the man, Keen, that Jahamat was so eager to topple. He heard barking. "Those are my precious dogs," the fat man said, inclining his head slightly. A look of beatific calm spread across his face. "They are hungry. Can you hear it in their voices? They haven't been fed for two days. Now all they want to do is eat. They will, soon enough. What's going to happen is this: you are going to run the maze. There are a number of secret passageways and tunnels out, for the more industrious of you. For the less, ah, shall we say, intelligent? Yes, why not. For the less intelligent of you, well your role is purely to feed my hungry dogs. I shall be up there," he pointed toward a veranda overlooking the maze. "Enjoying the spectacle. Those of you that escape; we shall meet again. Those of you that don't; die knowing that you are doing a good and noble thing, sacrificing yourself so that my dogs can grow fat." He laughed at that, as though it were quite the funniest thing in the world.

It was a pointless cruelty that spoke volumes about their captor.

Teal'c tried to catch O'Neill's eye but the man was not inside his own head. He saw Daniel Jackson shuffle his feet. When he looked up he too was gone. The overzealous guard walked over to Daniel and with an ugly sort of tenderness applied his taser. The shock of the electro-muscular disruption drove Doctor Jackson down to his knees. His head went down but he didn't cry out. When he looked up again Teal'c saw the thin ribbon of blood dribble down his chin where he had bitten through his lip.

"Separate them," Jahamat told his guards. Carter and O'Neill were dragged off toward different entrances into the maze. Jahamat looked at Teal'c then, and saw through his feigned weakness. "You cannot save them all," he promised. "You do realize that don't you, Jaffa?"

Teal'c said nothing.

"It does not matter. Throw them into the maze."

Rough hands grabbed the prisoners and propelled them forward. Teal'c saw more than a dozen openings in the hedge maze; each no doubt followed its own possible path toward the middle. The walls that divided them had grown to more than twice his height, cutting out much of the light and transforming the cramped passageways into murky alleys of leaf and branch that seemed to be collapsing in on themselves.

"Now run."

Corvus Keen braced his hands on the granite rail, digging his fingers into the stone as he stared down at the Kelani dying in the maze.

Some had the strength and wherewithal to run, others simply stumbled into the dogs and fell as though begging at their sharp teeth. The animals fed with delighted savagery. One though, one did not bow down. Keen watched with fascination as the black skinned warrior faced two of his wolfhounds with his bare hands. "Kill him, my children," he whispered, the words barely making a sound. Stone flaked from the railing as he dug his fingers in deeper, worrying them into the weaknesses in the hard granite.

Beside him, Iblis watched with grim fascination as the hounds attacked. The warrior's balance was impressive. No, it was more than impressive. It was familiar. The Goa'uld recognized the precision of the open-hand fighting technique the man used: Lok'Nel, one of the ancient Jaffa martial arts. *Where would he have learned such a thing?* Iblis wondered. The man appeared to sway as the first of the beasts launched itself, the movement subtle enough to shift him away from the momentum of the attack without causing the dog to realize what was happening. He reached around with shocking speed and snapped the creature's neck, tossing the carcass aside.

Keen howled as though it had been his own bones that had been broken by the man.

The black warrior turned to face them, the sun glinting gold on his forehead. Iblis recognized the First Prime's glyph immediately. It answered one of the questions he had, but presented countless more. Iblis watched the second dog die with the same economy of movement and effort, the Jaffa channeling the attacker's aggression into its own downfall. It was almost artistic, like watching a ballet of brutality being played out for them. He followed the Jaffa as he fought his way through the maze with calm efficiency. While others screamed and stumbled and fell into the hedges and tried desperately to claw their way through them, the Jaffa simply walked the maze, looking left and right, listening and calling out and listening again for any response to his shouts.

What Iblis had not expected was to see the Jaffa risk everything to save a human female, but that was exactly what he did. He found her lying on her side, one of Keen's wolfhounds slavering over her as it prowled around her, backwards and forwards, backwards and forwards. He brought his hand down on the animal's spine, driving its legs out from under it, then scooped up the woman and carried her in his arms toward one of the bolt holes out of the maze. It was almost touching to see such tenderness amid all of that pain and suffering and fear.

The Jaffa did not leave the maze.

Instead he turned and went in search of another of the Tau'ri. Even from this far away Iblis could hear the Jaffa shouting: "O'Neill? Daniel Jackson? O'Neill?" over and over again.

"Tell me, Great Keen, are these perhaps the prisoners brought to us from the arctic expedition?"

"I suppose so," the fat man said, quite disinterested in where his amusements came from, only that they died for him. Watching his precious dogs die was obviously taking the edge off all of the suffering he was inflicting. The irony that the ultimate proof the human craved was right there in front of him, stalking his damned dogs through his death maze, appealed to Iblis. It was every bit as twisted as the tortures Corvus Keen dreamed up. The man's ignorance merely sharpened Iblis' own amusement.

"This makes things more interesting," he said to himself. A Jaffa fighting side by side with the humans? A First Prime turned Shol'vah no less. It had to be. There could be no other rationalization of what he saw. Such curious things came through the Chappa'ai.

"No. No it doesn't," Keen disagreed, thinking the Goa'uld was talking to him. "This makes things anything but interesting. I am bored now. Kill them all, Iblis," he turned his back on the maze and walked away.

"As you wish, Great Keen," the Goa'uld said. He *would* kill them, certainly, but not quite yet.

Iblis found Kelkus lurking in the doorway. The man had a disturbing habit of skulking, no doubt learned from his years spent sneaking around in the dark in search of his 'great discovery'. He was a broken man in many ways, but what hadn't broken was stronger now, the cracks in his psyche papered over with the satisfaction that he had succeeded in bringing his god back into the world. His reward for finding a worthy vessel for the Goa'uld was to stand a step behind him as first disciple. He was no mere lackey though. Much of what the Goa'uld was doing here depended upon the madness of Kelkus. The man was a genius — of sorts. Twisted and depraved but brilliant all the same.

He had a scientist's curiosity and a murderer's cruelty to go with it.

Things occurred to Kelkus that just would never have crossed the mind of any dozen of Corvus Keen's supposed 'great minds'. It was men like Kelkus who discovered the true potential of the world for pain — who found black powder and turned it into guns; who split the atoms and turned that genius into bombs that shredded skin and melted flesh; who took weed killer and turned it into flesh-eating poison; who sought to propagate a universal language across the globe and turned it into a means of spying on each and every man woman and child hooked up to their machine. Kelkus was one of these geniuses worlds could happily live without.

That was why he had seen to it that Kelkus was placed in charge of the Rabelais Facility.

Under the mask of proving divergent evolution, Kelkus had taken it upon himself to go so much further than Keen or any of his kind could have imagined. His fascination began when the first twins were brought for him to experiment on. Iblis had watched with delight as the man began with blind tests, flash cards and such meant to prove the existence of a telepathic link. Only as pain was introduced into the equation did the girls begin predicting each other's cards. It was fascinating to think that pain might somehow open the mind, make it more receptive, but as Kelkus went on to show, the greater the pain the less the accuracy in prediction became. There was a fine balance where the hurt was conducive to the link, but beneath that threshold or beyond it, it was useless. Of course, reading flash cards was hardly the summit of the man's ambition. If they could link minds, could they share pains? Cut off a finger, did the sister suffer ghost pains, that sort of thing? There was no end to the man's ingenuity when it came to pain.

"Are the survivors ready for inspection?"

Kelkus nodded.

"Good. Good. How many?"

"Of the ninety Kelani released into the maze only thirty made it out. Most curiously, one, a black skinned man bearing an ugly tribal tattoo on his forehead, succeeded in killing seven of the hounds. He rescued four of the others before we prevented him from going back into the maze. It would not do to have all of the Great Keen's hounds put down by a single slave."

"No. I trust he has been dealt with?"

"Oh yes, my lord Iblis. He is in no fit state to offer any resistance."

"Good. I want him kept away from the others; especially those he rescued. Take him to Rabelais with you when you leave. He is dangerous, Kelkus. More dangerous than any man you have ever encountered."

"Is he one of your kind, master?" the man said, almost reverentially.

"No. He is not a god." Iblis thought about it for a moment. "You might consider him an angel of sorts, if you have room for such things in your philosophy. The ideal best describes what he is: a vengeful warrior of his god." *Or was,* Iblis mused, considering the Jaffa's fall. It was peculiar and wrong to see such a great warrior stand side by side with the vermin of the Tau'ri. If ever there were a 'lesser' species it was that human animal. Let Keen play his games of segregating rat from mouse from vole, as far as Iblis was concerned they were all vermin whether they were called Corvani, Kelani or Tau'ri.

"As I am to you, Iblis."

The juxtaposition of the assertion against the spoken word and the silent thought made the Goa'uld smile. Such a simple statement, so filled with devotion, and so absolutely true on both levels. "Indeed, as you are to me, Kelkus."

"I shall enjoy cleaving the wings from this angel personally, master. Thou shalt worship no other gods," the scientist said with an utterly straight face. "He shall pay for his blasphemy."

"That is as it should be. Tell me, Kelkus, how go your experiments? I am eager to hear of some successes to appease the Great Keen's restlessness."

"Ah," the scientist said, wringing his hands together as though washing the filth of the Kelani out of them with lye. "There is so much to tell, master. So much."

"Then tell me, Kelkus. Share your genius with me. It would please me greatly to hear of your successes."

"Yes, yes, of course, my lord. Of course. I do not know what, precisely, you know of the Facility and how I have divided its operations?"

"I know enough, believe me."

"Good, yes, of course. The Kelani are sorted by age and sex as they arrive. At first we were not interested in the women or the young, so they were sent for treatment." That was the scientist's euphemism for being disposed of. It was rather interesting the way his mind rationalized the slaughter, turning it into simply another function of his studies. "The men we divided according to age and body type, endomorphic, ectomorphic and mesomorphic, to better study the effects of certain things. The unique specimens are sorted out, the twins, the midgets, those with startling genetic differences are sent to the experimental blocks. There is much to be learned. We have performed a number of live autopsies, for instance, studying the effects of stress and pain on the heart. One thing of interest, given the nature of the world, is the effect of extremes on the body — of heat and cold. Did you know a body can be chilled into unconsciousness and then revived by warmth? No? That is interesting, no?"

"Fascinating, I am sure," Iblis agreed.

"The average body temperature is thirty-seven degrees. Kelani only seem to die when their body temperature is reduced to around twenty-five. That is a drop of twelve degrees."

"That does not seem overly much," Iblis agreed. "It would suggest that these humans freeze to death rather easily. That may well be something worth remembering, Kelkus."

"Thank you, master. I believed it would prove an interesting fact. Curiously, the temperature also affects a woman's ability to ovulate. This was not something we had originally considered, but it has helped us greatly to develop a technology that effectively renders the Kelani sterile."

"Oh, Keen will be pleased," Iblis said, barely masking his distaste for the notion.

"This of course has opened many other avenues of investigation — for instance, it set me to wondering if we are superior, are we actually perfect, or are there perfections that can be refined?"

"What do you mean?" Iblis asked, but he knew all too well what the scientist meant. He could see the light of madness in the man's eyes.

"If one is to assume that there is a blueprint encoded in our flesh, something that separates Corvani from Kelani, is that blueprint complete and perfect, or are there still impurities? After all, if a Kelani woman ruts with a Corvani male, what of their offspring? She merely provides the egg, it is the Corvani seed that fertilizes it, so is the genetic purity of the species diminished or can the stronger Corvani genetic encoding override the impurities and prevail?"

"So tell me, can it?" Iblis knew of the room in Rabelais that Kelkus had set up with its women and children subjected to endless tests and experiments before inevitably their tiny innocent bodies failed them. Neither Keen nor Kelkus cared, obviously, because as half-breeds they were less than human. The sickness of the human monster was endlessly fascinating to Iblis. With them he could create an army of demons far more lethal than anything the System Lords could harness. If only they understood the human race's capacity for cruelty...

"No. The genetic coding does not appear to work that way."

"A pity."

"Indeed, but other studies have proven that it is possible to alter the general coding before birth."

"Truly? That is fascinating. Are you saying you have the key to weed out the weak from the strong, the clever from the retarded?"

"That would be something, would it not?"

"Indeed. So do you have that knowledge?"

"Not yet, but to my understanding this genetic code is

rather like a set of building blocks. We are coming to understand what makes a person's eyes blue or their hair brown, and as we do so, we can refine the process of winnowing out the undesirables."

"Keen will be pleased."

"But are you, master?" the scientist asked, desperate for his god's approval. Iblis smiled indulgently.

"More than you could possibly imagine. You are indeed worthy of being called my disciple, Kelkus. When I rise up and take my position at the forefront of this society and reshape it in my image there will be a seat for you at my right hand."

"You honor me, my lord."

"Yes, I do."

"And what of your failures?"

"Those that do not fit the ideal can be cleansed easily enough," the scientist said with such detachment it sent a thrill of delight the length of the Goa'uld's spine. "At the moment we are investigating the possibility that the secret might actually be in the blood itself, not in the flesh at all."

"An interesting extrapolation of the facts," Iblis said. It wasn't, it was a dullard's way of thinking but he had no intention of dampening his disciple's enthusiasm for the task at hand.

"Thank you, master. I am glad you approve. It is vital that we collect living data. Only so much can be learned from the dead."

"Indeed. I trust you will use all of your resourcefulness on this fallen angel that has wandered into our midst."

"Oh most certainly, master. I am sure there is much that can be learned from his living tissue."

"I am sure there is," Iblis agreed. "I shall report the good news to the Great Keen, I trust it shall improve his humor. You have done well, Kelkus."

"Thank you, my lord god Iblis."

Iblis walked away, then stopped at the doorway, his hand

on the huge iron handle. He appeared to think for a moment, and then turned. "Tell me," Iblis said, making it seem almost an afterthought, "do the Corvani respond to your experiments in the same manner? Does the cold render them unconscious, for instance?"

"We have not carried out any experiments upon the Corvani, master."

"Ah, but perhaps you should? In the name of science and understanding, of course. What better way would there be to prove Corvani superiority than to demonstrate it empirically?"

Kelkus nodded emphatically. "Yes, yes, of course. Of course. It shall be as you suggest, master." His eyes lit up with obvious glee. "For every experiment we carry out upon the Kelani, we shall duplicate it on a Corvani test case."

"As it should be," Iblis said. "I look forward to learning more of your results, Kelkus." He closed the door behind him.

CHAPTER TWENTY-TWO

Fear of Daylight

THEY WERE surrounded on all sides by thousands upon thousands of terrified Kelani being herded like cattle. Indeed, the analogy was distressingly appropriate, Daniel thought, seeing another black and silver clad soldier walk forward and taser a frightened woman. There was something utterly reprehensible about the man's calm. Daniel bristled but before he could do anything stupid O'Neill rested a steadying hand on his shoulder.

"Pick your fights, Daniel."

Daniel wanted to argue but there was absolutely no point, O'Neill was right.

There was something soulless about the Kelani. It was as though every last ounce of spirit and resistance had been stripped from them. They milled about like ghosts consigned to Purgatory. Beside him a young girl clawed at her father's arm. She had cried all the tears she had inside her. She wasn't even afraid, she was just hungry. He could see it in her bones as they pressed out through her skin. Her father drew her close to his side as though he could somehow absorb her so that she need not suffer any more than she already had. It was a tender moment in a crowd of desperation. People pushed and shoved, but without any real spirit. The fight had been leeched out of them.

He had talked to a few families, their stories had all been the same. The Raven Guard had come at night and dragged them out of their beds. It was all about fear. Come in the dark, batter down the doors, use fire and noise and anything else at their disposal to instill fear. Nothing broke the spirit as effectively as the unknown — and that was what they had been subjected to. They stumbled into the streets, frightened and disorientated, clinging to each other. Family became the only thing they could hold on to as more and more of the Kelani were dragged into the streets, branded filth, spat at and beaten. It was almost a science, intimidation and hate. It was all about striking hard and fast, not giving the people time to understand what was happening to them. Inevitably some of the Kelani must have died from the beatings, and not only by accident as the Raven Guard flexed their muscles.

It was every bit as effective as heads on spikes and other medieval tortures — it worked the same way, after all. Fear.

And now they were here, huddled up in their familial groups, the fear no less dulled for the hours they had been forced to sit and wait, not knowing if they were going to be separated and given all the time in the world for the reality of their situation to sink in.

They were never going home again.

Daniel listened sickly as one father told a story of the last few months in the city that broke his heart. It had started with the simplest of discriminations, children in the classrooms segregated according to race, the Kelani picked out for 'special classes'. This had moved into other sectors of life until Kelani men were being sent home from work suddenly surplus to requirements and women on their way to market were being sworn at and spat on for being filthy. None of it made any sense to the man but it made far too much sense to Daniel. He could imagine the diagrams on the classroom walls showing the difference between the shape of a Kelani skull and a Corvani one and the lists of measurements about eye placement and shape of nose and all of these other spurious differences. The evils of man repeated themselves from planet to planet, they dressed themselves in different colors and sported different flags and badges, but they were all the same when stripped down to basic evils.

Daniel's stomach churned; it felt like the drum of a washing machine tumbling around inside him, wringing his insides out. The next stage would be the shakes. They were classic withdrawal symptoms. He had no idea what they had been pumping into his body but he felt every hair follicle and every nerve ending creeping and crawling like they wanted to come out through his skin. He knew all it would take was one more hit to make the pain go away, but that kind of thinking wasn't going to help any of them.

A woman walked among the crowd carrying a pitcher of water. She gave out barely a mouthful at a time, and only to the children and the old. Beside her walked two men with a huge platter of moldy cheese chopped down into cubes less than the size of a fingernail in any dimension. They rationed it out one piece of cheese per person. Desperate people pawed at them trying to get a second mouthful. One of the men kicked out, his booted foot catching the Kelani under the chin and snapping his head back. He lay sprawled in the dirt unmoving. More Kelani just climbed over him reaching out hungrily. Before they could pull the cheese man down a gunshot rang out. A second and third were fired into the air. Everyone in the square froze, eyes darting, frightened. Daniel half expected to see a blood-red rose flower in the side of someone's temple but the bullets had been fired into the air — this time.

Sam sat beside him, her back pressed up against the wall. She was shivering. It wasn't cold. He scooted up closer to her and put his arm around her. The gesture made them look like any other Kelani family frightened of being torn apart. She scratched at her arm where they had hooked the drip into her. He wanted to sooth her but he barely had the strength to hold himself together. She looked like hell. Her hair, lank and unwashed, had begun to clump into greasy ringlets. Her eyes had taken on a dark sunken look and her skin was flaking. She was living with ghosts. But then so were the others.

He couldn't remember the last time he had eaten a proper meal. He knew he wasn't alone. The hunger showed in each and every haunted face in the crowd. There was something utterly desperate about all of them. They didn't know what was happening to them or why.

He must have looked at a thousand faces, but none of them were Teal'c's. They hadn't seen the big Jaffa since he had rescued them from the maze. It had taken eight of the guard to bring him down, and even then he had maimed more than half of them with his bare hands. Teal'c was the immovable object being bombarded by the irresistible force. And for a moment it had looked as though he might hold his own forever, battering them back even as they threw themselves forward. And then a tranquilizer dart fired from long range had buried itself in the Jaffa's open palm as he went to swat it away. He weakened heartbeat by heartbeat as the sedative mingled with his blood, his symbiote fighting to neutralize the drug. Still he didn't fall until a crushing blow struck the side of his head. There was nothing any of them could do to stop the guard from taking him away. Jahamat had come to taunt them after that, goading and kicking O'Neill as he delighted in telling them that they would never see the Jaffa alive again because Iblis had chosen him.

Iblis.

It had taken a little while for the significance of the name to register.

Iblis. It that causes despair. The enemy of man.

According to the Qu'ran, Iblis was the name of an Islamic demon prince with an army of fiery demons at his beck and call. "The Companions of Fire," he said softly, trying to remember everything that he had heard in relation to the demon. Sam looked up at him, not understanding. In four years they had encountered enough so-called gods and devils across the galaxy to know any such mythic resonance was no coincidence. Daniel hoped beyond hope that he was wrong, even as he became more certain he was right — Iblis had to be a Goa'uld. Had to be. It was an essential part of their psychology: the aggrandizement, the fraud, it was all part of their psychosis, and Iblis was no different.

Islam was outside of Daniel's comfort zone, he was much more familiar with ancient Egypt, the Sumerian myths, Babylon and Mesopotamia and such, but he knew enough without having to go back to the books. The story went that Iblis had refused to bow the knee to Adam because he was formed of clay, a lesser being, and had been cast out of heaven for it. Fallen, he had been given the name Shaitan for his hubris and set to wandering the world as penance. The Arabic epithet Shaitan translated roughly into 'evil' or 'devil'. Indeed, the role of Iblis in the Qur'an bore some startling similarities to the devil figure of Judeo-Christian faith, Iblis being the tempter of both of God's first children to eat the apple, earning their expulsion from Eden. Part of the demon prince's vengeance on God was a promise to corrupt as many of Adam's descendants with lies and half-truths as he could before judgment day.

Lies and half-truths. It was hardly the Goa'uld way; it suggested subtlety and cunning as opposed to braggadocio and arrogance. But then, perhaps this Iblis was a different monster, being that he chose to hide himself behind Corvus Keen, opting for the shadows over sunlight?

Daniel used the distraction to take his mind from the hunger. He ran through the pantheon of gods the Goa'uld were known to have drawn upon, trying to find parallels to the demons and angels of Islam. Oddly, perhaps, Shaitan was almost completely analogous to the Christian concept of Satan: a whisperer who urged men and women to commit sin. What that meant in terms of this Iblis, Daniel shuddered to think.

Around the square he saw the occasional muzzle flash as the sun caught the sniper's steel, reminding them that all around them guns were aimed silently at their heads and chests. At the first sign of trouble death would rain down from on high. It was a far cry from the world any of them had been born into. At every corner stood a dozen or more of Corvus Keen's black and silver Raven Guard, ostensibly to keep order and see the refugees were railroaded onto the trains that would take them to the Facility.

Daniel shuddered, his head racing with all of the parallels. Over the heads of the prisoners he saw the funnel of steam and heard the clash and hiss of a huge old train rolling in. Everything about this sent a murmur of trepidation through the Kelani packed into the square. A few stood, craning their necks trying to see, more seemed to sink into themselves as though they hoped they might somehow become invisible inside the crowd.

Guards came forward and slammed back the rusted iron bolts holding the drop-down sides on the carriages in place, and stepped back as the wooden panels fell with a bang. The sound rang out across the square, as deafening and more damning than any retort of gunfire.

The segregation was as quick as it was ruthless, soldiers walking through the clusters of tired and frightened people, picking out one or two from each group and dragging them toward the train. They took young and old. Something about the selections disturbed Daniel. On the surface it appeared as though there were no rhyme or reason behind the choices but it was so random it had to be deliberate. A few minutes of watching them and he knew what it was that bothered him about it — they were weeding out the weaker ones, the youngest of the kids, the older men, the women, anyone lacking the physical strength they would need to survive a labor camp. And with that realization came a second one: he was looking at a death train. These grandfathers, mothers and sons were being culled.

To his left a blonde haired woman played airplanes with

her baby son. She was a pretty young thing with a scarf tied in her hair and no make-up that he could see. She smiled and made burbling noises as she held the boy up to the sun and then brought him back to her breast and hugged him tightly. She knew. Daniel wept quietly then for all of them.

Whistles blew sharply; the piercing sound cut above the hubbub of the prisoners. Guards grabbed more bodies — they weren't people to them — not caring now as men pleaded to be taken with their wives and sons. For a minute he thought that the Kelani might fight back. By sheer weight of numbers they could have turned their callous execution into a blood-bath and taken more than a few of the Corvani with them, but they didn't fight. They allowed themselves to be separated and stood weeping and reaching out as the carriage sidings were lifted and the bolts slammed into place. Tiny slits no more than an inch wide had been cut into the wooden sides. Fingers reached through desperately clawing at the air and in the darkness behind them eyes without hope stared out at everything that had been taken from them.

A different kind of whistle sounded then. The train engine vented a raft of steam as it lurched backwards. Pistons pump-ing, the iron wheels began slowly to roll and as they did more and more steam curled up around the base of the engine, wreathing the entire underside of the train. When it finally moved away the train looked disturbingly like some kind of mythological beast, an iron and wood dragon. It was every bit as lethal as any imaginary creature that had bubbled up from mankind's subconscious fear of the dark, because the death it was transporting them to was real and final and not fairy tale at all.

With the crowd thinned the last of the resistance seemed to bleed out of the Kelani. Guards changed shifts. The sun fell and rose and fell again, the bite of the night cold almost blessed relief as it reminded them they were alive. Not that many of the left behind wanted reminding.

With his strength returned, at least as far as it could with so little food to fuel it, O'Neill had taken to going out amongst the prisoners, talking to them. At first Daniel had thought it so utterly out of character for the Airman he had followed him. Unlike Daniel, Jack wasn't interested in their stories or their grief, he was interested in what little strength remained inside them. Some of the Kelani took to calling him "the steel man", possibly because of his graying hair but more likely because he simply refused to be broken. He planted a few words here, a few there, and let them grow inside the men. They were simple words. The message was all about hope. He didn't lie to them and tell them everything was going to be all right; no one would have believed him if he had. Instead he told them simply that they would have a chance, and when it came they had to be ready to seize it. Daniel knew O'Neill well enough to know at least part of the message was no more profound than that these men would get a chance, somewhere between here and the Facility, to own their own deaths and not meekly be herded along to the experimental laboratories, the shower blocks, or whatever other hideous fate awaited them. It didn't need to be profound. It needed to be truthful. These men needed to hear the truth because lies couldn't help them run away from what was happening to them. Only the truth could set them free — even if that freedom meant accepting the reality of the genocide going on all around them. He didn't promise them that they could save their loved ones or that their wives and sons would be fine. Far from it, in the most subtle of ways O'Neill planted the seeds of revenge.

Daniel saw the Mujina twice over the coming days. The effect the creature had on the crowd was fascinating and horrific both at the same time. The Kelani looked to it as salvation. Daniel saw only death's hungry eyes looking back at him. The first time, the Mujina stood at Jahamat's side, though for its second visit it stood beside a bloated slug of a man in black and silver who treated everything as his domain. This had to be Corvus Keen, Daniel reasoned, struck by the way the man embodied every cliché of corrupt incompetence. Of course, logic dictated that the man did everything in his power to nurture that misconception — truly incompetent men rarely rose to hold such power and they certainly didn't hold on to it for any length of time. The fat slovenly embodiment of greed and excess was nothing more than a layer of cunning used by Keen to lull both friend and foe into underestimating him.

Both visits seemed to serve the same purpose, for the man with the creature to gloat.

Each time the Mujina left them something died within the Kelani.

That something was hope.

It was a brutal game the creature played, lifting them up and then crushing them. It took a certain kind of malice to be capable of it.

They would never look at Jack in the same way that they looked at the creature from the flames of Vasaveda. He was a leader but he wasn't a beacon. He didn't blaze in the same way. But, Daniel knew, he would never fail them. That was O'Neill. He was a genuine hero in a world of false Messiahs.

In the darkest part of the night, Daniel heard something. It was no owl, no matter how much it wanted to be. Beside him O'Neill cupped his hands over his mouth and loosed a wolfish howl. A guard came up behind them and gave the colonel a savage kicking. O'Neill lay on his side, taking it. No amount of blows could rob the smile from his face.

Another train rolled in that morning, and two more during the course of the day. The guards were every bit as ruthless as before as they weeded out their selections. There were two kinds of train servicing the station. There was no telling whether the train that rolled was meant to transport the soon-to-be-dead or the damned that were destined for the Facility.

Finally they were chosen.

CHAPTER TWENTY-THREE

Master and Servant

TEAL'C WAS alone.

The Mujina had seen to that. The black and silver clad soldiers stood lined up against the wall like a firing squad, watching him without so much as a twitching eye. The old rifles were held almost carelessly. Did they think so little of the threat he posed? They did, Teal'c realized. He considered his options. He could make a stand here—their body language betrayed their arrogance; these people were not used to their captives making a stand. It was all about controlled aggression. A burst of pent up fury. He could break free of his guards and in three steps ram the flat of his hand into the face of one, taking him down, and before the second could react have him lying on the floor bleeding out of his ear, larynx crushed from the force of his elbow. Then in another two seconds he could almost break two or three more before a single gun came up to aim at him, but what would be the point? There were a dozen more. These soldiers were lazy because they could afford to be. In the turrets along the high walls the dead eyes of trigger-happy sharp shooters followed him. He could feel how much they wanted him to try it, to make a move. Losing five men was nothing to them. But for the Jaffa to die here was not glorious; far from it, it was nothing short of foolish. So he would let them live, for now, even if it meant taking their pokes and prods and abiding the scorn and distaste of lesser men. It was not a fight for now.

"You! Forward! Move!" barked a split-faced man with snow-white hair. Teal'c watched the spittle froth up over his lower lip. The split in his face was more than a trick of the light. The Jaffa had almost mistaken the birthmark for shadow but as the shove in the back staggered him forward he saw it for what it was, a big angry raw welt that covered more than half of the man's face. "Take him to Kelkus!" the guard barked, turning on his heel. He was gone before Teal'c was halfway across the gravel.

Another shove prodded him forward.

They drove him toward a small facility annexed to the main building. There were bars on the windows but no glass. Glass offered some indication of the technological advancement of a society — if it was fine blown and clear they had learned certain purification techniques, if it ran with streaks and was impossible to see through, it was a reasonable assumption that they were still technologically stunted. The rusted bars gave nothing away. Teal'c looked around, taking stock of the soldiers on the walls and the muzzles aiming down from the turrets as much as he did the men policing the square.

Servants in rags shuffled about their business. At the door of the facility he saw stick-thin women forming a line. They clutched tin bowls and wooden spoons and wore the same beaten-down sadness. They might have been pretty in another life. Teal'c smelled the abuse on their skin. He looked at them one at a time, committing their faces to memory. There would be a reckoning before he left this place. He promised himself and he promised them.

"In here. Kelkus is expecting you."

"Old rat-face has taken an interest in you, man," his guard gloated. "He picked you out from all of the new arrivals. You should be flattered."

Teal'c said nothing.

He did not need to.

He walked with his head high, hoping the women saw his silent defiance and drew some little solace from it. He had been both guard and prisoner often enough to know strength was found in the little things.

The room they left him in was empty. They slammed and

bolted the door behind him. Teal'c paced the room once then settled in the far corner, back pressed up against the wall. It was no more than five paces across, seven long. The floor was scuffed hardwood, the walls smeared with some sort of lime composite that smelled of old death. Teal'c was in no doubt that the room had been used for both torture and murder in its time. Death rooms had a certain ambiance. This was a death room. He noticed a series of scratches around the base of the wall. Names. He crouched down low and looked. Some were so old and faded he could barely read them others could have been carved that morning. There were thousands of them. Tiny names scratched into the lime, the only proof that the prisoners had ever been here, and for many the only proof they had ever lived. Using his thumbnail Teal'c scratched his own name into the soft lime, adding it to the wall of remembrance for the next prisoner to read. It was another one of those little things. There was strength in a name.

But there was so much pain in a thousand of them, and all the untold stories trapped in the stone.

He was still on his knees when the door opened.

The rat-faced newcomer smiled as he closed the door behind him. He did not bolt it. Teal'c had no doubt that he could kill the man. He decided not to. Later perhaps, if the need arose, but for now it served no purpose other than to vent his mounting anger. He looked up.

"No need to worship me," the man said, his nose twitching ferally as he offered Teal'c his hand. "Oh, okay, but only if you must."

Teal'c's right hand snaked out and snatched the man's arm. His grip was merciless. He pulled Kelkus down until they were eye to eye. "You are presumptuous, old man. I do not worship anyone."

The man's smile was disgusting. "But you will, you will." There was no fear in his eyes.

Teal'c pushed him away.

"Perhaps now that the anger is out of your system we can get on with things?"

"What do you want from me?"

"You interest me. You are plainly neither Kelani nor Corvani, so the logical extrapolation of that thought is that you are by necessity something else. I know only one 'other' so I am trying to decide whether you are a god like him, or something else entirely. I do not believe you are a god—"

"And I do not believe he is a god," Teal'c said matter-of-factly.

"—so that makes you something else again. A treasure, of sorts, no? Perhaps Iblis will reward me if I deliver you to him... what do you think?"

"I am no treasure," Teal'c said.

Kelkus smiled his wretched smile again. "No, perhaps not. But that makes you a problem, my tattooed friend. Because that means you came from beyond the stars. Tell me, how did you come to be here? Why this place of all the worlds?"

Teal'c stared at the little man, but said nothing.

"Oh, come on, there is nothing to be gained by being inscrutable. Talk to me."

Teal'c merely furrowed his eyebrows.

"Fine. I had hoped you would see reason, but it is not something I shall worry myself over. You present me with a problem, stranger. Perhaps I should just kill you and have done with it? What do you think?"

"You are not strong enough to kill me."

"Ah, death does not require brawn my thick-necked friend. Sometimes all it requires is a tiny little pin-prick." He mimed delivering a lethal injection.

"Then perhaps you are suitably equipped."

Kelkus burst out laughing at the insult.

"I like you, it would be a pity to have to kill you."

Teal'c looked around the room, "There is no pity in death."

With that, Kelkus left him. The bars on the door weren't pulled back for another day. He sat with his face turned to the stars. They were yesterday's confetti in the sky, thrown away by a billion careless lovers. Dawn came slow and red. Who would remember the coming day, Teal'c wondered to himself, because for so many there would be nothing remotely memorable about it. He would remember it though, he had decided that already.

Kelkus came to him a little after dawn, before the small cell was filled with light. There were six black and silver clad soldiers with him. "Help him up," Kelkus told them. And to Teal'c, "It's time for you to meet your new god, my talkative friend."

Teal'c rose slowly. Judging the relative strength of his captors was instinctive: these few were more formidable than yesterday's men, but still barely a match for his explosive aggression should he choose to unleash it upon them. The thrill of anticipation itched through his right hand. He clenched his fist. Smiled. "There are no gods, only lies. I do not believe in lies."

"Ah, but there are truths as well. Glorious truths. Come with me and I will show you."

As they walked through the narrow passageways, rifle muzzles prodding him in the back, Teal'c looked at these so called truths and saw more lies barely concealed beneath the flaking concrete. They reached a set of stairs that led up. Kelkus nodded. Teal'c climbed slowly, counting each one. One hundred and twenty seven steps later they reached the first and only door. It was a humble gateway — that was the only way the Jaffa could describe it. Where other doors in this place had been banded with iron or decorated with unnecessary ornamentation, this single door was bare blond wood. There was no knocker and no handle. No, Teal'c realized quickly, there was a pressure sensitive plate set into the stone beside the door. Kelkus pressed his hand flat to it, allowing the device to scan his print. The door opened. Teal'c frowned.

The simple act of opening the door changed everything.

The hand sensor wasn't homogenous technology — it had been brought in from outside. It could have been a leftover from the time of the Goa'uld, but he doubted it.

Kelkus pushed him inside.

"Here he is, master," the man fawned, scraping his sandaled feet across the floor as he shuffled in to the room. Ever the warrior, Teal'c's instinct was to take stock of this new environment. The room seemed disproportionately large given the narrowness of the stairs. It was a curiously clinical chamber, all sharp angles and sterile surfaces that were not in keeping with the rest of the rooms in Corvus Keen's folly — it wasn't a castle or a keep or palace or dungeon, municipal block or any other kind of habitat. It was just a sprawl of adjoining rooms with no rhyme or reason to the build. Teal'c tried to place this new room according to the impression of the interior he had pieced together in his mind, but the place was a sprawling mess of architecture of which there was no sense to be made.

He could guess the general vicinity in terms of towers and the annexed prison, but there was no way of knowing where he was for sure without looking out of the chamber's single window.

The light was almost radiant as it filtered through the flawless glass, so pure he could see the dust motes hanging in the air.

Wearing a medical face-mask that covered all but his black eyes, the creature that called itself Iblis stood in the center of the room. He leaned forward, hands braced on the side of a steel-topped bench. Blood dripped down a steel tube beside his head. Teal'c heard the buzzing of flies. He did not know what he had expected to find up in the tower room, but a Goa'uld surrounded by medicinal drips and monitors was not it.

"Bow down in the presence of your god," Iblis said, that

cold metallic arrogance rusting through his voice as his eyes flared silver.

"I would rather die," Teal'c said.

Kelkus rammed a fist into the base of his spine, meaning to drive him to his knees. Teal'c did not flinch. He turned slowly to face the weasel-faced man, arching his eyebrow. Kelkus stumbled back a step, his hands coming up instinctively to ward off the anticipated blow. Teal'c did not give him the satisfaction. He turned back to Iblis.

"Is this your doing?"

The white linen mask hid the Goa'uld's expression but not the delight in his eyes. He took a delicious moment before answering. Teal'c did not know whether he could believe Iblis or not when he promised: "No, no, no, this is all their doing. Humans are so creative when it comes to hurting each other. Have you not learned that in your servitude, Jaffa? Leave them alone and they will drive themselves to extinction. It is their way. I am merely an observer, a set of eyes off the stage watching this Grotesque Theater unfold. It is fascinating, though. Beyond that, it is rewarding. Only the fool believes he knows all the pain there is to know. These cattle are opening my eyes to suffering I could never have imagined. So tell me, First Prime, what brings you to my world? Are you looking to serve a new master?"

"That is no secret, Goa'uld. I came here to kill you," Teal'c lied, thinking of O'Neill. It was the kind of thing the Colonel would say to throw his opponent off balance. The words came easily to him.

"Have I become so legendary that Apophis would send his First Prime to dispatch me?" There was genuine amusement in his voice at the prospect. Iblis shook his head. Teal'c could tell he was smiling beneath the mask. It was a curious thing for a Goa'uld to wear.

"Apophis is dead." As always, Teal'c took immense satisfaction in the declaration — and in the brief shock Iblis could not mask.

"You do not lie well, Jaffa. I shall consider the fact that you are capable of deceiving your god, but now is not the time for that punishment. The truth this time?"

Teal'c said nothing.

Iblis waited.

"Silence will not save you, Jaffa. I can make you talk, and believe me, I will not be gentle." Iblis raised his right hand. The jewel in the heart of his palm glowed a dull red then turned angry as Iblis spread his fingers wide. "Do you enjoy pain, Jaffa? Do you think there is nobility in suffering? Let me assure you, there is not. But if you wish to suffer as atonement for your failure, pain is the very least I can offer you."

The pulse of raw energy slammed into Teal'c's chest and hurled him across the floor. He hit the edge of the doorframe and sprawled whorishly in the center of the doorway as the blazing light sizzled its way up over the muscles of his chest before fastening on his face. In seconds a mask of crackling energy engulfed his gasping lips. The bright energy bristled with a life all of its own, splinters of angrier scarlet darting into Teal'c's eyes and up through his flared nostrils, invading and invasive.

In a supreme feat of will, Teal'c bit down on the screams, refusing to give the Goa'uld the satisfaction of seeing his pain.

That only served to infuriate Iblis, and intensify the fury spitting fire from his palm. The Goa'uld stood over him, the smile completely removed from his eyes as he drove the rage of the hand device deeper into the Jaffa's skull.

Blood dribbled from Teal'c's mouth as he forced his head forward.

His eyes rolled up inside his skull but Iblis would not allow him to collapse.

"The truth, Jaffa."

"Apophis is dead," Teal'c spat through the pain, baring his teeth. "I betrayed him. To the Tau'ri."

The Goa'uld stood over him, pulling the white linen mask down so that Teal'c could see him properly for the first time. Iblis' face was as much a mask as the white cloth. His eyes blazed with intolerable cruelty. "You sicken me, Jaffa. Do you really believe someone as weak as you could kill Apophis? You are not worthy of the air you breathe. I should tear the symbiote from your gut and leave you to rot in regret as you mourn yourself, the life leaking out of your limbs hour by hour until there is only betrayal to cling to as you slide slowly into that endless winter night where your god will be waiting for you to torture you throughout the afterlife."

The mask of energy writhed across Teal'c's face, turning the world violent red. Pain blazed behind his eyes as the Goa'uld's will dug deeper, churning through his grief and guilt and leaving him raw.

"It is your Tau'ri friends who are dead, Shol'vah. How does it feel to know that there will be no salvation for them now?" Iblis smiled cruelly, and then, as though the notion had just struck him, asked: "Do you know where they are?"

Teal'c said nothing.

"No? Well, shall I tell you? Yes, yes, I think I should. These humans of yours are on their way to one of our facilities. Shall I tell you what happens there? Yes, yes, of course you are curious. They will be stripped, tortured, experimented upon, and in the end they will be destroyed along with the other cattle. That is the fate that awaits your friends. Ah, I see the curiosity in your eyes, Shol'vah! You are worried about yourself. And well you should be. Believe me when I say yours will be a fate worse than death. That is my promise to you, traitor. I shall kill you, and raise you, and kill you and bring back again and again until all traces of rebellion in your soul are purged, and you are a hollow thing devoid of mind or spirit. Your friends will not save you, just as you will not save them. Consider it my gift to the memory of Apophis."

CHAPTER TWENTY-FOUR

Skin and Bones

"LET ME HAVE him, master," Kelkus said, fawning at the feet of Iblis.

The Goa'uld looked at his apostle. "I think not."

"Please, master."

"Why?"

Kelkus thought about his answer, choosing his words carefully. "I would do you honor, my god."

"Explain."

"I would turn his flesh into an instrument of your will, master," Kelkus said, slowly, relishing the notion unfolding in his mind. "I would cure his skin and fashion a book to record your wisdom for the ages. I would turn this traitor of the divine into a testimony of your power, master."

"Indeed?" Iblis looked down at the Shol'vah's unconscious body. "And you would record all of my triumphs on his body?"

"I would make it my life's work: The Living Book of The Lord God, Iblis," Kelkus promised. "I would record every moment from your resurrection. I would chronicle the glories of your will, the triumphs of your might, every word, and every righteous death. The brilliance, the beauty and wonder, all of it, writ on sheets cured from the traitor's body. I would make you immortal, master."

"I am a god, Kelkus, I have no need of words to make me immortal, but I will admit there is a delicious irony to the thought of the Shol'vah's corpse being used to draw new followers to my side."

"It is fitting, master. The Apostate betrayed your brother

god, but by turning his flesh into a holy relic you rob him of his victory and forever make him a fundamental part of yours."

"Your words please me, Kelkus, and you are right, again. Make it so. Turn the traitor into my scripture. I would write the first testament in tribute to my brother god, Apophis. The remainder of his flesh is yours. The future is waiting to be written on the bodies of the faithless."

"Very well, master." The little man tried to lift the Jaffa, wrestling his hands beneath his bulk, but try as he might, he would not move.

"Perhaps you should cut the brute down into more manageable pieces," Iblis suggested as he stepped over the body. "I am taking the transporter to the Rabelais facility. I do not wish to be disturbed. See that I am not." With that the Goa'uld walked out through the door.

It took all of Kelkus' strength to man-handle the Jaffa's deadweight up into a sitting position. Teal'c's head lolled forward and his arms hung slackly at his side as he lurched forward into the little man's embrace. Kelkus grunted. He braced his back against the doorway to give him the extra leverage he needed to haul Teal'c up onto his knees, and then gasping and panting, all the way across the floor to the steel table.

Teal'c lifted his head groggily.

Without thinking, Kelkus drove his knee into the side of the Jaffa's head with as much force as he could muster. The noise was sickening as bone crunched bone. For a moment Kelkus stood there, horrified by what he had just done, and then Teal'c fell, crashing face first into the side of the operating table. The collision pushed the table into the line of drips and monitors, and began the chain reaction that brought everything down.

Scalpels and scissors scattered across the tiles. One of the drips bled out saline across the floor, the puddle swelling around the unconscious Jaffa as it swallowed the surgical implements.

Giving up on trying to get Teal'c onto the slab, Kelkus fumbled about in the saline for one of the blades, determined to please his god.

He watched the shallow rise and fall of the Jaffa's chest.

Kelkus took Teal'c's arm, found a vein and worked the needle of one of the drips into it, and then set the liquid to stream into Teal'c's blood. He waited a full five minutes, believing that the chemical was taking his victim deeper and deeper into drugged oblivion. Each minute's patience bought him that little bit more safety. He poked at the peculiar cross-wise wound in the center of the Jaffa's stomach, sinking his finger into it all the way up to the second knuckle. Kelkus felt something squirming beneath his touch. "Curious," he mumbled, probing deeper, and then instead of a slight shift he felt whatever it was suddenly lash out — and then he screamed and flinched as teeth sank into him. The slender white symbiote came wriggling out, suckling at the blood leaking from the bite. The slurping turned his stomach. Kelkus reeled away, stumbling as he tripped over the fallen instruments. Still the white worm clung to him, gnawing deep to the bone as he tried to shake it loose.

Kelkus shook his arm more and more violently, desperately trying to dislodge the thing, until finally the skin of his finger shredded and the worm flew across the room.

He fell to his knees, gagging.

Sickness clawed up through his gut into his throat.

He looked around, frantically trying to see where the worm had fallen, but he couldn't see it for the mess he had made trying to get Teal'c up onto the operating table. Kelkus flailed about frantically, pushing aside the fallen drips and kidney trays, and scrabbled back, kicking out left and right as he did so until his back was pressed up against the wall. His eyes darted everywhere but there was no sign of the worm.

He didn't dare move. There was a small metal dish just

within reach, if he stretched. He couldn't see beyond it. Tentatively, Kelkus reached out, turning it over with his fingers. Relief whistled between his lips. A cold anxious sweat trickled down the side of his neck. He looked down at his ruined finger and saw the blood already clotting around him on the floor. There was so much blood. More than he could afford to spill. He wrapped his good hand around his ruined one, the blood still leaking between his fingers. He needed to fashion some sort of wadding for it to leak into or he'd simply bleed and bleed until there was nothing left. Nausea and dizziness both swarmed up inside him. Kelkus pressed his back against the wall. He needed to focus. Think. He couldn't see the worm so he had to forget about it, as simple as that. He had to concentrate. Think. Clearly. Think.

He watched the shallow rise and fall of the Jaffa's chest.

Think.

Think.

He could cut away the Jaffa's uniform and fashion a dressing from the cloth. Yes. That made sense.

Kelkus crawled across on his hands and knees, cradling the wounded one to his chest as the blood kept coming. He picked up the scalpel and held it there, poised above the Jaffa's chest waiting for it to settle before he cut away the layers of Teal'c's clothes. Moving quickly and clumsily, he wrapped the cloth around his hand, making a makeshift bandage, and then, still on his hands and knees, bent forward and rested the tip of the blade on the hardness of the bone where Teal'c's throat met his breast.

"One last chance to tell me your secrets, star man," Kelkus said, his voice ragged with pain. He looked around, half-expecting to see the worm slithering across the floor toward him. He held off on making the incision for a full minute, silently urging Teal'c to open his eyes and spill everything, all of the secrets in his head, the worlds beyond the Stargate, the cultures, the lost and found civilizations, all of it. The thought set a thrill of excitement through him. He could feel himself weakening and couldn't afford to collapse without first ending the Jaffa's life. "Talk to me. Tell me all of it," he virtually pleaded, and then when the Jaffa said nothing, he gave a final shrug. "Suit yourself then."

Gritting his teeth, Kelkus pressed down, hard enough to draw blood, opening his prisoner up with a single swift slice.

CHAPTER TWENTY-FIVE

Shine

TEAL'C OPENED his eyes as the scalpel's blade sliced into his chest.

Instinctively, his hand snaked out and clamped around Kelkus' wrist, preventing the blade from biting deep. Without the symbiote he was weaker, and his head swam with the narcotic the man had pumped into his veins. Kelkus almost succeeded in wrenching his arm free, but Teal'c drew him closer, pulling him down until they were eye to eye, and with a single savage twist he snapped the man's wrist. The scalpel fell through his fingers as the bones cracked, digging into Teal'c's pectoral. Kelkus screamed. Teal'c launched himself straight up, arching his back and driving the gold tattoo into Kelkus' face. The impact was sickening. Kelkus reeled back, spitting blood as he flailed about for balance. Teal'c pushed himself up but fell, his body betraying him. He slipped and fell back, cracking his head against the floor. The world spun around him and he heard mocking laughter ringing in his ears. It was a galling sound. With blood dripping from his broken nose and cradling his broken wrist, Kelkus still managed to laugh. It was a mad burst of relief escaping him but that didn't make it any less galling.

Stupidly, the man leaned closer.

"Not so strong now, are you, star man? Oh no, not so strong at all."

Teal'c closed his eyes and let the rage of frustration fuel one colossal effort: without opening his eyes, Teal'c roared up at him, fists flying. Three blows hit Kelkus, face, throat and sternum. The man stopped laughing. He fell back, clawing at his neck and sucking at the air, unable to swallow any of it.

And then his eyes flared wide and he was dead. Teal'c fell back onto the cold tiles, spent. His vision swam, everything in the room losing its solidity and morphing into something else — none of it made any sense to his drug addled brain. He struggled to force his eyes to focus, but the world was having none of it. Every sharp line seemed to bleed into another shape or form.

It was only as the symbiote crawled back out through the dead man's mouth that Teal'c understood what had happened. The symbiote slithered down Kelkus' bloody chin. It looked weak and sickly, as though the few moments out of its incubator had drained it badly. Teal'c knew it had killed the man for one reason — to protect its incubator. Had it been able to take a host it would have been him lying on the floor, and not Kelkus. Teal'c gathered it up and fed it back into the breeding pouch in his stomach. He knelt over the dead man, able to see now the wound where the symbiote had entered him. He didn't dwell on it; death was death no matter how it was delivered. He stepped over the corpse and out of the room without looking either down or back. He had to get out of this place and find the others. The time had come to make it his fight.

Teal'c' rationalized what was happening. His head was fogged with the anesthetic Kelkus had pumped into his veins. It slowed the world down and leant it soft edges. He stumbled tangle-footed five times as he lurched down the winding stair, needing the wall to stop himself from falling. Every twist of the spiral stair had the world shift another fraction beneath his feet. He struggled to maintain his focus. He tried to think. He needed to find his staff weapon if he was going to have a chance of getting out of this place, and then he needed to purge the drugs from his system and clear his head. The symbiote was sick. It would take a long time for it to be strong enough to cleanse his blood and for him to feel focused and strong. He reached the door at the bottom of the stairs and stopped, listening for sounds, movement. Left or right? Teal'c drew in a single deep breath and held it. Right. He moved away from the door and stumbled as he started running. He reached out with his left hand to steady himself but didn't slow down.

The corridor presented him with more choices: left, right, or straight on? He had no way of knowing how many men Corvus Keen had garrisoned in the complex — but even accounting for their slovenly behavior in the drill yard, it was surely more than Teal'c could handle. But he had promised those slaves a reckoning. Guilt held him in place a moment longer than was safe.

Two of Corvus Keen's Raven Guard came around the corner and stopped dead in their tracks. The look of surprise on their faces lasted as long as their grip on consciousness. Teal'c swept the feet out from beneath the first and drove his elbow down hard into the man's temple as the second man raised his gun. In the time it took for him to squeeze off a single round Teal'c drove his fist hard up between the soldier's legs, hammering the blow right the way through to his gut. The gun misfired twice as the man fell. Teal'c rose cautiously, keeping his eyes fixed on the groaning soldier. The man rolled onto his back and looked up at him, still trying to reach out for his gun. Left with no choice, Teal'c leaned in and delivered an incapacitating blow. He had no way of knowing if the man was alive or dead when he left him. He didn't have the luxury of caring.

With the echo of gunshots still hanging in the air, he started to run again.

He had to make a choice, but it was no kind of choice at all — staggering around like some blind man looking for a weapon that could be anywhere, risking being found and brought back to face the madness of the Goa'uld, or running toward the light, and finding any possible way out of there.

He chose the light — which was easier said than done. With bare bulbs buzzing and sizzling in the chill of the windowless corridors the secret geography of the place was impenetrable. He took the lack of windows to mean he had come down one level too far and was underground. Which meant he must have missed the door onto the level above, which in turn meant he needed to retreat back to the spiral stair — but before he could back track he heard shouts of alarm and booted feet charging up behind him.

Teal'c didn't wait, and didn't look back. He ran, knowing even as he did that the trail of bodies he left behind would tell them exactly which way he had gone. There was nothing he could do about that. With each step the fog clouding his brain parted a little more, his symbiote starting to neutralize the narcotic. All he had to do was keep on moving and stay out of their way, eventually he would find a window and then he would be out of there.

He hit three locked doors and what appeared to be a garbage chute. Banging his fist off a fourth door in frustration, Teal'c lurched deeper into the complex. He had no sense of where he was in relation to the outside world. Behind him he heard a klaxon sound. They had obviously found the bodies.

Two more right turns and he found himself standing in front of another rusted iron door. Behind it he heard the hiss and clatter of machines. Behind him he heard the guard running. There was no going back. Hoping it would open, Teal'c pushed at the door. It groaned inward. Teal'c stepped through quickly, closing it behind him.

The room was twenty degrees hotter than the corridor and filled with a madness of noise. Steam vented and hissed, clouding the room in white. Through the steam he could see machines, and around them, women. It took him a moment to realize that he had stumbled into the laundry room, great vats of water hissed and bubbled while the women stirred them with long wooden sticks. The constant motion agitated the detergent and kept the clothes both wet and soapy. One of the women looked up. Her face was sheened with a film of sweat. She wiped her forehead with the back of her hand and stepped away from the vat. She held the stick in front of her like a makeshift weapon. She lowered it as she recognized him.

Teal'c had seen her before, one of the wretches from the food line.

"What are you doing here?" Her voice was as broken as her spirit; too many years down here breathing in the chemicals, the steam and the dyes.

"I mean you no harm."

"I didn't say you did," she said, setting aside her stirrer. None of the other women broke from their routine. The sound of the wooden sticks clanging against the sides of the metal vats was like some peculiar music of slavery.

"I need to find a way out."

"There isn't one, not for the likes of you."

Teal'c raised an eyebrow curiously.

"A prisoner," she said, filling in the silence.

"There is a way out of everywhere there is a way into," Teal'c assured her. "It is the nature of doors: the way out is the way in."

"But you don't want to try and walk out of the front door, believe me. They'd cut you down before you took a second step."

"I will take the risk."

"No you won't."

Again Teal'c arched his eyebrow.

And again she filled in the silence, "If you haven't looked in the mirror recently, let's just say you don't exactly look like one of us."

"That is true."

"Meaning you do not really blend in. You can't exactly

sneak out the front door disguised as a guard." Before she could finish her train of thought there was a bang at the door. "Give me one good reason why I shouldn't hand you over to them. Quickly. One reason?"

Teal'c shook his head — trying to clear it, to think — she took it to mean he had no reasons to tell her.

"Quickly," she urged, this time reaching out to drag him deeper into the steam. Still shaking his head, Teal'c followed her. Behind them the door opened.

"Where is he?" one of the guards bellowed, his voice venting with the same angry hiss as the steam. Not one of the women answered. Teal'c followed the guiding hand of the woman as she drew him down behind her huge laundry vat. She pressed a finger to her lips. "We'll find him," the guard said, "and when we do, we'll kill him, and we'll kill anyone we find helping him."

"That means you," another voice said, making it clear he meant each and every woman in the room. Teal'c felt them stiffen. He waited for the betrayal, expecting it at any moment. It didn't come. He knew it wasn't him they were protecting; it was the woman helping him. That made him all the more determined to deliver a reckoning on their behalf.

"We know he's in here," the guard repeated. Teal'c could hear him moving about in the steam.

Still the women said nothing.

The footsteps came closer, slowing ominously as they neared the unmanned vat. "Where's the woman meant to be working this load?"

"I'm here," his helper said, moving around to stand between the man and Teal'c's hiding place.

"Why weren't you at your station?"

"Call of nature," she said. "That, or maybe I was helping the poor wretch you're chasing get away. That'd be just like me, wouldn't it?"

Teal'c stiffened.

"Yes, Namaah. Just like you. What did you do?"

"I washed him up with the boil wash and shrunk him real small like a pair of your skivvies, dried him out and popped him in one of the fresh laundry baskets. I'll roll him out later and none of you will be any the wiser."

"You've got a smart mouth, woman," the guard said. Teal'c didn't like the way he sounded when he said it. He heard the slap of hand and flesh and, shifting his position slightly, saw the guard grabbing at the woman. "Maybe I should tell Keen that I'm claiming you. What do you think?"

"I'd rather boil my ovaries in vinegar," she said, sweet as could be.

"It can always be arranged," the guard promised, matching the woman's tone. "Now, just this once, how about you tell me the truth?"

"No one came in here 'cept you," one of the other woman said, putting an end to their little dance of lie and flirt.

"That so ladies?" the man grunted. When none of them said anything different he moved on, walking down the line. Still they talked, their voices like ghosts. Teal'c couldn't make out half of what was being said, but what he heard was enough to know they'd found the guard's bodies. Finally the door closed and they were gone. Teal'c heard one of the women come up and berate his helper, voice low, tongue sharp. He didn't move from his hiding place until she came to get him.

"You need to get out of here," she said, stating the obvious.

He followed her as she led him further into the huge laundry room. There was a second door, and through it a set of servant's stairs that led back up to the ground level. He followed her up.

"Why did you help me?"

She didn't answer him. She moved with a curious limp he noticed, and between steps the fabric of her simple dress slipped back enough for him to see the withered flesh beneath.

She pulled it back across quickly, but not quickly enough to hide the hard white lattice of scars that had been cut into her calf and ran all the way up to her thigh.

"Who did this to you?" Teal'c asked.

"They said they were trying to help me," she said. It was enough.

"Come with me," he said, meaning it. He could not imagine what so-called help could cause such scarring. It was barbaric.

She shook her head. "No."

"This is no life."

"This is my life. Go. There is a door halfway down that passage. It opens into a service room. There is a small window at the back of the room. You will need to break it. None of the windows in this place open. This one looks down upon the garden maze. It will be unguarded now; Keen has had his fun for the day. It's probably the safest place in the city for you. Skirt the maze and make for the buildings on the far side. You'll be in what used to be Eltis, the old temple district. Aim for the largest of the buildings, you'll see one with a brass weathercock, behind it the ground dips away. Follow the slope down. There are barbed fences, you'll need to go over or under, and then you have to cross the railway tracks. As you come up the slope on the other side you should see the first of Keen's ravens. They're painted all along the walls. Head for the birds. They mark the streets as unclean. In the ghetto you'll find others, they'll help you."

"Come with me," he repeated.

"I can't," she said, shaking her head. This time he realized how much she wanted to go through that window with him, and guessed what was holding her back. "My son is here. If I'm not back at my station in a few minutes they'll know I helped you and he'll be made to suffer."

Teal'c understood. She turned to walk away before he could stop her, but at the corner she turned to look back.

"You want to know why I helped you? Find Kiah, she will help you understand it all."

"Why would she risk herself?"

"Because my mother is a better woman than I am. Now go. Please. Or this will all be for nothing." And then she was gone.

Teal'c did not wait to see who came around the corner next.

CHAPTER TWENTY-SIX

Fall At Your Feet

THE MUJINA sat alone amid the bones of the temple.

It had chosen to make its nest among the dead — it gave the creature a unique connection to the place. The memories of the fallen clung to the marrow of their bones. If it closed its eyes, the creature could lose itself in all of it, in all of the sadness and joy of the dead, from the first touches of skin against skin, the first kisses, the first nights as lovers — firsts that affirmed and reaffirmed life — to the lasts: the last kisses, the last sighs, the last breaths and last goodbyes. The bones remembered. All of those intense moments were written forever on the bones of the dead, along with so many more triumphs and tragedies in between. All it needed was someone with the gift to read them and set them free so that they might never be forgotten.

The Mujina did not forget. Not once. Not one memory. It remembered.

And in remembering, it consumed, taking on the loves and hatreds and petty jealousies of the dead as though they were its own. All of those emotions lived once more, this time inside his skin. They vented with their own voices, clamoring inside his skull. The chorus of the damned was as maddening as it was compelling. It needed to be heard and the Mujina needed to hear it. That was new. It had lived such a long time, so much of it alone, but this was the first time it had nested among the dead, the first time the bones had shared their secrets.

Of course the dead were no sort of company. They did not need it, not the way it needed the others. The way it needed the woman. Its loneliness never faded. It had thought that in her it had found someone who cared. It had sung to her. It had wept at her touch and her promise. It had waited. But she had not returned. Was she out there now, looking for it, trying to make good on her promise to come back? Was she as lost as it was? Or had she forgotten it?

The Mujina did not forget. Not once. Not one memory. It remembered.

And in remembering, it hurt.

All of these others crowding around its nest, they meant nothing compared with her. It was all for her. When it remembered the woman it hurt, but the hurt was beautiful as much as it was cruel.

The creature looked up from the fibula it cradled in its lap to the high walls. It truly was an amazing construction, a temple raised from human bones. Skulls set one atop another and another formed the pillars with which the walls were supported. The bones had yellowed, some more than others, giving each curve and angle a subtle hue. The shades came together to merge into the color of decay. Some of the bones were childishly small, barely formed, while others showed the effects of bone-eating sickness and age. The Mujina sat with its back against the altar, the pelvic bone of a dead mother pressing into the base of its spine. It shared the moments of birth with her, the echo of her screams coming down through the centuries to swell inside its head. So much hope and so much pain. And for what? Her son was interred in the pillar beside the nave. He didn't live into his second year. This necrotic temple didn't discriminate against age or disease; every corpse was welcome to add to its twisted majesty. The only aspect shared by the dead was their heritage; they were all Kelani. The temple was a mocking monument raised by Corvus Keen to show the world that even in death the Corvani were masters.

The Mujina drank it all in, bloated on it.

But it was not enough.

It was never enough.

Because she was not there.

The others were outside, the superstitious and the sacrilegious, waiting to fall at its feet in their devotions. They came because it was a gift from the gods themselves, a thing worthy of worship. They brought it gifts, things they thought it might like or deem worthy, chipped and battered relics, sacred stones, parchments of lost wisdom, lucky charms, coins, but all it craved was their love. No, that wasn't true. It had craved their love, but now it had come to savor something darker, something it had not tasted for so long: fear.

It was such a potent thing. They adored it, but even that was not enough to mask their terror; they feared it every bit as much as they adored it. The Mujina contented itself with that duality. But it knew it wasn't enough, not when there were worlds out there, thousands upon thousands of them, that could both love and fear it. The thought was potent. Toxic.

In its mind the Mujina imagined worshippers spread all across the galaxies, infinite in their devotion, thousands upon thousands of their bone churches erected to glorify it, their icons fashioned in its own shifting image. There was glory in that, but more, it would be able to help them all; every story of suffering and pain it heard could be soothed. All it wanted to do was use its gifts to help.

And one day it would find her. It could go to her if she could not find her way back; they could still be together.

Then it would not be alone.

It had carved the faces of its saviors into the bones of the altar, to honor them; to the Mujina the faces of O'Neill, Carter, Teal'c and Daniel Jackson were nothing short of icons. And then, it had rendered *her* beauty in bone — an exquisite recreation of its Madonna. Its love and its weakness. A terrible, fatal beauty etched into the dead of this place. All of the carvings were loving representations, they could be nothing less, after all these were its most cherished disciples: the ones who had set it free.

The Mujina rose slowly and walked across to the door, content to let the devotions begin for another day.

CHAPTER TWENTY-SEVEN

Ghetto King

THE CITY beyond the railway tracks was a desperate place.

It wasn't merely the architecture of despondency, the weeping brickwork with its bullet striations and the crumbling façades with no building left behind them, it was so much more. The spray painted ravens marked the beginning of the ghetto, the spread-winged birds looking down upon the Kelani like so much carrion. The desperation was ingrained in every face Teal'c saw. Every line was weathered in hard, none of them down to laughter. Sallow-faced women hunched over cracked and broken stoops scrubbing at the bald stone with wire brushes as though they could scour the despair out of their lives.

He walked the streets for hours, not sure what he was looking for. He had no idea how he was supposed to find the old woman, Kiah.

With the night drawing in, a young girl in a tight red dress half-skipped half-walked down the center of the road, following the remains of the white line. No one else looked at her. That in itself interested Teal'c. He watched the people not watching the girl. A boy, all skin and bones and broken promises sat hunched over the curb playing with a tin soldier, his rat-at-tat death knells gunning out to punctuate the rhythm plated by the wire brushes. Across the street a hag beat away at a hanging rug with a stick, great clouds of dust billowing out with each whack. She coughed up a lungful of phlegm as Teal'c walked past her. She watched him with an ugly sneer on her lipless face. Teal'c nodded to her. The hag ignored him, taking her aggression out on the threadbare carpet. An off-white pigeon settled on the rope beside it. Two more settled on the broken glass that topped her wall. Teal'c studied the birds with a detached curiosity. They showed an almost domesticated disregard for humanity. More birds settled along the guttering of some of the nearest tenements as he walked down the center of the street.

He felt rather than saw the curtains twitch and the curious stares behind them.

Teal'c followed the girl in the red dress.

It felt like the only thing he could do — and part of him was sure she was leading him to wherever these people wanted him to be, so it made sense, too. She looked over her shoulder as she neared the corner, to be sure he was following as she skipped across the street and disappeared between two tumbledown houses. Their windows were boarded up. The doors hung drunkenly on broken hinges. Behind the houses, the girl in the red dress squeezed between slats in one of the broken fences. Teal'c was more than twice the size of the opening. He didn't need to worry, before he could stoop to peer into the gap three men emerged from the building opposite. They were roughly dressed in layers of dirty rags and coats. Each wore at least five coats, one on top of another, like armor. Not that any amount of wool could have saved them from a bullet or shrapnel form a bomb blast. The coats bulked them up, but even so, none of them were a match for the Jaffa's powerful physique.

"You're not welcome here, stranger," one of the men growled. He stepped forward, crossing his arms over his chest defensively. Teal'c studied the man.

"I was told to seek out Kiah," he said, watching all three faces for any flicker of recognition the name might bring.

"Were you now? And who would have told you to do that, eh?"

"Her daughter."

That earned a sharp exchange of looks from the men. The

second sniffed, hawked and spat as he stepped forward. He brushed his coat aside to reveal the stock of an old shotgun. It wasn't much of a weapon, but it was a weapon just the same. "You were in the compound? How'd you escape?"

Teal'c looked down at the wad of phlegm on the cobbled stone at his feet. "She helped me."

"Did she now? And tell me, why would she want to do a thing like that?"

Teal'c said nothing. Instead he maintained steady eye contact with all of them, weighing up the threat they posed. None of them looked particularly well nourished with their stark cheekbones and hollow-eyed stares. If it came down to a fight the first blows might hurt, but the second, third and forth would be lacking strength — meaning they would attack with an explosive burst of fury or not at all. Teal'c looked down at their thighs; the muscles appeared relaxed, not tensed. "I was told to seek out Kiah in this place because she might help me. You are not Kiah so I am not looking for you. Take me to her and I shall not harm you."

The leader laughed. It was an open and surprisingly honest sound. He looked at his partners in crime. The second man shrugged. The third had what looked like an old pair of night-vision goggles dangling around his throat and a pistol tucked into the rope belt keeping his trousers up. They were dressed for war. "Well would you listen to the big fella? Maybe we should teach him a lesson in manners, hey boys?"

Still Teal'c said nothing.

"Nah," the third man finally spoke up. "If Namaah's willing to stick her neck out to get this joker out of the compound, I reckon he's worth taking to Kiah."

"You always did have a soft spot for that girl," the leader said, but Teal'c noticed his casual stance and knew the risk of fighting was past. Violence was easy to read if you knew the signs to look for. He turned back to Teal'c, "So what do we call you, big fella?"

"I am Teal'c, son of Ro'nak."

"That's a right mouthful. What say we call you Bob?"

"I am Teal'c."

"Okay, big man, it was just an idea. Keep your hair on."

"Jubal Kane what brings you to old Kiah?" The woman inclined her head oddly, following the sounds on the old wooden boards of the stairs with her ears. It took Teal'c a moment to realize she was blind.

"Namaah sent us a little helper," the leader said. His voice was different now, softer. Deferential. This old blind woman was obviously important to them. That in itself made Teal'c curious. What could an old woman with no eyes offer to their war effort? She did not look like a warrior, neither did she carry herself like one. He knew enough to understand that looks could intentionally be deceptive and that warriors could not rely on strength alone. Because of that, he did not dismiss her.

"Did she now? Well come up here and let me get a look at you. Don't be shy."

The others stood to the side, pushing Teal'c up the middle of the staircase toward the waiting woman. She held out her hands. She had surprisingly strong hands, thick with calluses. They were worker's hands, shaped by honest graft. Teal'c took them and raised them to his face, allowing the old woman to feel out his features. Her rough fingers lingered over the gold of his tattoo. "Strong bones," she said, appreciatively. "But, tell me, what is this?" Again her fingers returned to the gold of his tattoo.

"It marked me as First Prime of Apophis." His lip curled. "Though that was another life."

"Ah, we each of us have those," Kiah said, with surprising compassion. "But I did not ask what the markings meant, I asked what they were."

"My apologies, ancient one," Teal'c said, earning a splutter of laughter from Jubal Kane. "It is a tribal marking of my people; as we approach manhood we are thus tattooed to mark our service to the false gods. It is the 'honor' of First Prime to have his inlaid with gold."

"Barbaric," Kiah said, but she didn't take back her touch. "A slave brand, that is what you are saying, yes?"

Teal'c followed the train of her thoughts; she was drawing a parallel between his tribal tattoo and the raven brand used by Corvus Keen to subjugate the Kelani and mark them as outsiders. She was, in other words, letting Jubal Kane and his cronies know that they were not so different. They both had their supposed masters who profited at the expense of their people. He nodded. "Yes."

"There is no honor in these brandings. These are not badges of war, no matter what they tell us. They are marks of hate meant to show the world we are less than we are."

"Your people carry their own brand," Teal'c said.

"Not ours." She spat on the floor. "The raven was a plague carrier in the not-so glorious past of our people. The bite of the fleas they bore carried the blood plague. It decimated our people. To use the raven now is to bring back memories of that black time. It tells the world we are unclean."

Jubal grunted. "And that Corvus Keen is a bloated parasite feeding on the corpses of decent people."

"They hide us away here and turn our homes into a ghetto, thinking they will break us. They do not understand that all of this only makes us stronger."

Teal'c bowed his head in agreement. "As it is with the Jaffa."

"This city is our home. Our parents and our grandparents gave everything they had to carve this place out of the dust. He knows that. He knows all of it. And yet he spurns everything they were — everything he is — his heritage and his inheritance, in his quest to expunge us from history. It isn't as though he is anything more than I am, or Jubal or Jachin here. He was always one of us. That is my greatest shame."

Teal'c realized she was talking about Corvus Keen himself.

"You have no reason to be ashamed, mother," Jubal Kane said. "You did not make him the way he is."

"Didn't I?" the old woman said, bitterly.

"Of course not."

"But he is my flesh and blood, sweet Jubal. How can I not blame myself or wonder how it might have been different? Everything he uses now, all of the history he throws in our faces, he learned at my knee. He is my son every bit as much as he is your brother."

"Which means he isn't your son at all, because he is no brother of mine," Jubal said. "The day he put your eyes out is the day he lost the right to call himself that. You didn't put the sickness into him, mother. You didn't make the monster. He was born wrong."

The old woman had no answer for that.

And Teal'c understood now exactly why this blind woman was so important to the resistance fighters hiding out in the ghetto, and why Namaah hadn't been willing or able to flee with him.

Kiah was the mother of the tyrant.

She was a symbol, every bit as much as the raven or the gold tattoo.

Teal'c hid in the darkness. Every nerve and fiber bristled. He wanted to fight, not hide, but the old woman had insisted he trust her. He did not feel like he had a choice. She led him into the bedroom and lifted a trap in the floor, ushering him down. He had to crouch, curling his legs in to his chest as she lowered the floor over his head. Less than a minute later he heard the floorboards groaning as heavy feet walked slowly across them. They seemed to linger for a perilously long time directly over his head. He did not dare breathe. His tell tale heart beat against his chest, so loud he thought they must surely hear it. The voices raised. He couldn't tell what they were saying, but the tone spoke volumes. They knew the old woman was sheltering the fugitive and they would find him. She could play her games and hide behind her kinship with Keen, but there would be no mercy for her treachery. If they could prove she had sheltered the man everyone and everything she held dear would be taken away from her.

Teal'c flinched at the sound of the slap and her old body slumping to the floor. It took every ounce of restraint he had not to erupt out of his hiding place and tear the man limb from limb. Instead, he let his rage smolder. There would be a time for reckoning. The man would be held to account for his cowardice.

And then, even as he expected the light to invade his hiding place as the trap door came up, they moved away.

He risked opening the trap a crack and saw the woman lying on her side sobbing. He slipped out of his hiding place and moved across to the window. He crouched low, careful not to be seen, and watched as the two Raven Guard walked out into the street. He let his silent fury burn both of their faces into the back of his mind so that when the time came he would know them and they would pay.

Like the man who now called himself Corvus Keen, Teal'c learned some of the history of the Kelani at Kiah's knee. She told of how they were the older race of this world, and how they were slowly being exterminated for their peaceful ways by the man she couldn't bear to call son.

"Son," she said the word like a curse, which Teal'c supposed it was, in a way. "I fell in love with the wrong man. It was as simple as that," she explained, shuffling about her candlelit hovel, keeping herself busy as she talked. She was stubbornly independent, refusing his help to fill the water pot as she set the stove to boil. "Much to the chagrin of my father, I gave my heart and body willingly to Zellah, a Corvani soldier. Even then plenty thought it was a crime to mix the blood, even if they didn't say it out loud. That was my crime. I fell in love with the wrong man," she repeated, as though saying it over and over often enough could somehow lead to absolution. "Zellah loved me well enough, but he was no real husband. It was too much for him, I suppose, the constant sniping and snide comments, the whispers and the looks. They never stopped. We thought they would. We thought people would accept us for what we were, but they never did.

"That was the world my son was born into. Is it any wonder he hates the people who drove his father to suicide? Zellah was weak. He left me alone with a half-breed boy and no home to call my own. I will never forgive him that. It's easier to forgive Zarif than it is to forgive his father — yes that was my boy's birth name, Zarif. Not this stupid affectation he's given himself. Corvus, the crow, and yet he daubs the world with ravens as though he doesn't know the difference between one bird and another! As if I didn't teach him better than that! Zarif's a product of his environment, twisted by the world around him, filled with so much hate, but it was the hate the world kept feeding him. There's always a reason, isn't there?"

She was right. He had visited many worlds and there were always reasons, no matter how shallow, for the greatest good and the basest wrongs.

"Zellah was just a coward who couldn't stand the way people looked at him all the time. We were taken in by a good man, Jamal. He was Jubal and Namaah's father. He took us off the streets out of pity, but he came to love us eventually. At first it was only pity, though. I have never flattered myself into believing he could not resist my looks." She laughed at that, and so it went on.

Kiah needed to talk and, for a while at least, he could listen. If she sensed his urgency she did not let on.

"Perhaps it is a mother's blind love refusing to die, but I can't believe this is all his doing. Yes, he had his faults growing up but this thing he has become… it is monstrous, Teal'c. That is the only word for it."

Teal'c nodded.

"Your silence condemns an old woman," Kiah said, not cruelly.

"My apologies. I did not think. But you are correct," he said, offering her the lifeline she needed. "There is a creature in his company capable of great evil. It is possible that this creature has twisted the darkness already inside your son. That is how this particular enemy works."

"Do you speak the truth, Teal'c? Do not lie to an old woman… Do you mean that my boy might not be—? That this might not all be down to him?"

"There is evil there, I will not lie to you, but I believe the Goa'uld are capable of corrupting a good man."

"This thing you called Goa'uld, tell me, what is it?"

Teal'c took her hand and raised it until her fingers brushed up against the gold of his tattoo. She flinched as though the branding had burned her.

"The monster that did this to you is here?"

"One of his kin," Teal'c said.

"And so the evils of your life and mine collide."

"Evil is drawn to evil."

"It was ever so," Kiah lamented.

It wasn't until she began into the litany of her son's crimes against his own people that she mentioned the death trains and the facilities he had set up in the outlying districts, and the evils perpetrated there in the name of racial purity. "It's ironic, isn't it, that a half-blood be so obsessed with purity?"

"I believe so, yes. But is it not also the case that we crave that which we cannot have, and by doing so torture ourselves into self-loathing?"

"Are you a warrior or a sage, Teal'c?" Kiah said, with something approaching a smile.

"I merely speak the truth."

"There is nothing mere about the truth, believe me. Only the truth can set us free."

"You have great wisdom, old woman," Teal'c said.

She chuckled at that. "Am I so old to you? Perhaps I am. It has been years since I last saw my face. In my head I am forever a thirty-three year old woman, not beautiful but by no means ugly. Tell me, Teal'c, when you look at me what do you see? I would know myself through a stranger's eyes."

He thought about it for a moment. "I see hope and stone," he said. "I see the foundation of this place. It is solid and unflinching. Stone is the cornerstone of these people. In the lines carved deep into the stone I see the remembered beauty of youth and the hope that the world might one day be that way again."

"Flatterer." She touched her face, her fingers lingering on the deepest wrinkles. "These lines are nothing more than where grief has chipped away at me year after year, but thank you. For a while at least I shall pretend to be what you see in me."

"I merely speak the truth," Teal'c said again, inclining his head slightly.

"And I will happily pretend that is so."

They sat a while in silence. Outside the broken window the sounds of her son's war raged. The gunfire was sporadic, the screams horrific. Together they made an ugly symphony. In the distance Teal'c heard the melancholy sigh of a train's whistle.

"Tell me about the death trains," he said.

"What is there to tell? We are being exterminated one by one," she explained. "They make us wear silver ravens on our arms when we walk the streets. Anyone caught without their armband forfeits their freedom — such as it is. We can only walk where they let us walk, when they let us walk."

"A prison without walls, your daughter called it," Teal'c said.

"Namaah always did have a way with words. The trains run day and night. There are too many of us for it to be any other way. My son wants us gone — out of sight out of mind, I suppose. As if it could ever be that easy to wipe out all of those years of hurt. He has set up facilities in the provinces. They used to be factories, now they're 'facilities'. I shudder to think what's happening there. The fact that no one who's dragged off to one of those god forsaken places has ever come back tells me all I need to know."

Teal'c took the old woman's hands in his, moving forward to kneel at her feet. "I would like to see these trains."

"It's too dangerous." She shook her head. "We can't afford unnecessary risks, I am sorry."

"You need not fear for me, old woman."

"I don't," she said. "I fear for myself, for my children. If you're caught you'll bring the wrath of the guards down on all of us. There'll be no petty vengeance from my son. He'll cleanse each and every last one of his family. I cannot allow you to take such a needless risk. I am sorry."

"I fear my friends have been taken on one of these death trains."

"Then they are dead and nothing you could do now can bring them back. I am sorry."

There was nothing he could say to that.

Still, as night's dark masters stole in, Teal'c broke the promise he had never made. He crept down the stairs, past the curls of flaking whitewash and the splintered boards, out through the door and into the cold. The street was dark on one side where the silver of the gibbous moon failed to shine. Teal'c clung to the shadows. Window after window was blind. He trailed his fingers across the old stone, won-

dering what stories it might tell if it could speak. He felt out
the pits of bullet holes and the chalky dust inside them, and
followed them to the corner.

He listened before he stepped out, expecting to be challenged. It was only common sense to think that Jubal Kane
must have set up some sort of night watch to patrol the streets.
The man was too cautious to leave his family's safety up to
chance. After a few minutes of quiet listening, Teal'c heard
the soft shuffle of worn-down soles nearing. There was no
discipline to the step. He waited in the shadows.

It was Jachin. The small man smoked a thin roll-up and
exhaled a raft of smoke that corkscrewed up across his face.
Two more drags and he scuffed the cigarette out underfoot. He
looked up, straight at Teal'c's hiding place, and for one heart-
stopping moment seemed about to challenge him, but then
Jachin turned away and moved on. Teal'c crossed the street,
crouched low, moving fast. On the other side, he sought out
more shadow. And so it went from street to street, alley to
alley, stopping at every corner, listening, following the shifting shadow cast by the moon to the very edge of the ghetto.

Logic dictated that any death train needed tracks or it
wasn't going to get anywhere — and he knew where at least
one set of tracks were because he had crossed them coming
into the ghetto. He scrambled down the bank, scuffing up
dust and dirt, then scaled the chain link fence.

The iron rails carved through the dark of the city, a straight
line all the way to where he wanted to be.

Teal'c kept low, running point to point, breathing hard. In
the distance he heard the deep-throated growls and barks of
mastiffs or some other breed of watchdog. There was nothing he could do if they got his scent, so it was pointless worrying about them. He looked back twice; once to see if he
was being followed by Jachin, once because his shadow suddenly stretched out before him, elongated and exaggerated

by lights in the sky. He saw flames but had no way of knowing whether they were common in the ghetto or if the violence had escalated to some new flashpoint high. He turned his back on the fire in the sky and ran on.

On either side of the railway banks the shadows changed. Behind them the buildings became gradually more decrepit, covered with invective and daubed with rebellious slogans and angry fists. The walls crumbled but the graffiti remained.

The barking of the dogs intensified as he neared the station house. He didn't need to get any closer to appreciate just what kind of hell Corvus Keen had fashioned. Thousands upon thousands of broken people huddled up against the darkness, coughing and whimpering and crying or simply sitting in silence, enduring. None of the faces had features — they were wiped clean by the distance and the moonlight shadow. He didn't need to see the infinite sadness or the grim despair, it was enough to see the sheer mass of Kelani trapped in this filth-ridden squalor waiting for the next train to ship them out to their deaths. It was barbaric. That was the only word Teal'c could find that came close to encapsulating the horror of it all.

Careful to be sure the moon wasn't at his back to play traitor, Teal'c crouched down, digging in for the long haul. He watched the life signs of the camp, the routines of the guards and the movement of the water carriers. There were pockets of prisoners that were completely ignored by the water carriers, he realized quickly, and assumed they represented the old and infirm. The guards up in their watchtowers took sadistic pleasure in their task. When a woman ran toward the gates of the station a single staccato rattle of gunfire cut her down. She twisted and spun and fell like a discarded rag doll and lay in a puddle of her own making. Worse, by far, no one down there dared go to her side so she died alone.

Teal'c rose slightly, his face twisting into a snarl.

There was no way he could make it unseen to the watchtower and he couldn't see the murderer's face, so he added an unseen enemy to his mental list. It weighed heavily now.

O'Neill and the others were down there somewhere; they had to be. Down there or already shipped off on one of the death trains. He needed to give them a sign. Something to let them know he was out there, but what? What would O'Neill be looking for?

He resisted the urge to string up a dozen of Keen's Raven Guard, despite the fact that it would have delivered his message loud and clear. Not every man in the black and silver deserved to die. That was a lesson he had taken with him from Chulak.

In the end he decided to try one of O'Neill's animal calls. He crouched, cupping his hands over his mouth and pursed his lips. He gave three short bleats that were meant to sound like the hoots of an owl but sounded more like the death throes of a tomcat in heat.

A moment later a howling wolf answered him. Only there were no wolves in any city he had ever encountered; they preferred the solitude of the forests or the wide open tundra. O'Neill had heard him. Teal'c was torn. Part of him wanted to break from cover and run to O'Neill's side, to stand together, but another part of him was so horrified at the sheer volume of suffering all around him that the only stand it wanted to make was against Corvus Keen and the monster that lurked in the man's shadow: Iblis.

They were alive — and gathering that intelligence had been the entire purpose of his mission. He hadn't come to rescue them barehanded. He was no fool. Any rescue attempt would need numbers and careful planning. It was enough to know that O'Neill and the others were alive, and the railway tracks told him exactly where they were going.

He ran back toward the rising flames.

They had been betrayed.

He knew that the moment he saw the thick black smoke.

He crawled back up the railway embankment and stared at the painted raven. Behind it angry red tongues of flame licked at the black sky. He knew with dread certainty it was Kiah's home that burned. She had foretold it… and even as he walked down the center of that lonely road, Teal'c knew he had brought it down on her. Not by creeping out, but by seeking her out in the first place. Her hand of friendship had cost her dearly.

There was no sign of Jachin. Teal'c crossed the street, no longer worrying about the shadows. There was no safety there anyway.

They were throwing buckets of water at the rising flames when he reached them, his worst fears made horribly real. Red ghosts burned gauntly across their beaten faces. These people had suffered too much already, and this one fire burning right at the heart of their home threatened to consume their final talisman — the thing they believed held the wrath of the tyrant Keen at bay. They had invested so much — too much — in the blind woman, and now with the flames devouring stone, flesh and bone, it was no wonder they were broken.

"Is the old woman inside?" Teal'c shouted. One of the Kelani turned, saw him, and turned away, throwing his bucket at the trailing flames. The water hissed and steamed to nothing before it could reach the stone wall.

Jubal Kane was trying to force his way into the burning building only to be battered back by the ferocious heat, and then Teal'c looked up at the window and saw Kiah's frightened face pressed up against the glass as she struggled with the frame. She couldn't force it open. All around Teal'c people were urging Kiah to break the window and jump for her life, but she wouldn't — couldn't — do that. The only mercy would be that the smoke would take her long before the flames reached her — and that was no mercy at all. Her hand beat weakly against the glass. Eventually the heat would shatter it but by then it would be too late for the old woman.

Jubal Kane lurched away from the doorway, tears of frustration and grief stung from his eyes by the smoke. Choking black clouds of the stuff engulfed the doorway. Inside the house a series of small detonations rocked the foundations one after another. A deep crack resonated through the very core of the building as one of the main braces buckled and finally snapped beneath the anger of the heat. Jubal Kane saw Teal'c and for a moment didn't seem to know whether to curse him or beg for his help. His lips moved. Teal'c read them: *you brought this down on her...* But he might just as easily have been transferring his own guilt onto the soundless screams of Jubal Kane's frustration.

Teal'c looked away — anywhere but at the grieving son.

The young girl with the red dress was there with them, running at the flames with her small bucket of water. Again and again she ran back to the water pump on the street corner and back to the flames, spilling more than half of the slopping water as she did. Teal'c turned his back on the burning house. He followed the girl to the water pump and knelt at her feet. "Pour water on me, child," he said, with his head bowed. She didn't ask why, she just did it, pumping the handle hard, water splashing everywhere. She soaked him to the bone. Teal'c rose, nodding his thanks to the child, and walked toward the burning house. The heat of the conflagration was fierce even twenty feet away. Before he was halfway up the tenement stoop it had scorched most of the water out of his clothes and he felt it burning his skin and the roof of his mouth as he tried to breathe. That didn't stop him. Teal'c walked forward, into the fire.

The heat of the blaze fused the clothes to his skin even as they shriveled away to a blackened nothing.

He took the stairs carefully, walking at the outside of the risers, not the inside where the fire would have weakened them. He didn't touch the walls, didn't look back down even as the flames bullied his back, he just walked deeper and deeper into the heart of the burning house. He knew which room she was in. It was the same one she had hidden him in earlier that day. The smoke was thick, cloying. It rippled in black eddies across the ceiling. The door on the landing was closed. Teal'c pressed his hand flat against it and felt the heat built up behind it. He knew that opening it was the last thing he wanted to do, the backdraft from the oxygen sucked into the fire, gorging it, would vent out in a huge explosion: but he had no choice. He had to go through the door if he wanted to reach Kiah.

He aimed the blow level with the lock and drove the flat of his foot hard into the wood. It splintered inward, the latch torn from its mounting. Even as it crashed open Teal'c heard a series of short high-pitched pops and hurled himself out of the line of the blast. He hit the floor hard, hands covering his head. Still, the explosive force of the backdraft tore out through the door and swelled to fill the corridor for a full five seconds before it shrank back inside the doorway. Teal'c rolled over. His back burned, agony searing deep beneath his skin. Biting down on the pain, he pushed himself to his feet and plunged through the open door.

He could not see Kiah for the smoke.

Teal'c crouched low, looking beneath the blanket of roiling smoke for any sign of the woman. He found her lying unconscious beside the bed. She had obviously been trying to climb into it when she finally succumbed to the relentless choking of the smoke burning through her lungs. He knelt beside her, leaning in close to try and feel her breath on his face. Her eyes were closed. She looked almost peaceful — as though she had come to terms with the fear, faced it and prevailed, and finally accepted what the blaze meant. He felt the softest feather of fitful breath against his cheek. That was enough. Teal'c gathered her into his arms. Kiah was painfully frail, light. He felt every bone as he lifted her.

Behind him, the glass in the window shattered outward, raining searing shards onto the street below.

The flames roared through the small room, consuming everything in their way. They ate through the soft fabrics, chasing up the curtains to frame the broken window. They consumed the bedding, climbing the heavy flock paper on the walls to rage across the ceiling and across the doorway, forcing Teal'c to plunge through the flames. They burned at him, into him, so hot he felt his grip on consciousness scorched away as he staggered down the stairs, flames raging all around him. He hit the wall. Hit the banister. It splintered beneath his weight, breaking away treacherously. Teal'c barely stopped himself from going with it, lurching away from the ragged edge of the wooden rail even as it blackened and burned.

And then the air hit him. With it came the strength to manage another step and another. He clutched Kiah to him. His eyes stung with smoke-tears. He stumbled toward the door. Every inch of his flesh shriveled tighter around his bones. Ablaze, Teal'c emerged from the burning house.

He managed three lurching steps before he fell to his knees.

The young girl in the red dress was the first to rush toward him with her bucket slopping water.

The fire burned out, but not before taking the house and much of the street with it. There was no doubt it had been deliberate. Jubal Kane had suspected the black-skinned newcomer until the stranger had plunged into the flames and carried his mother out. Now the man lay in the other room being tended by his daughter, Nat. She pressed cold compresses to his skin, trying to take the heat out of him but the man was on fire inside. Jubal had looked in on him an hour ago. His skin suppurated, yellow blisters swelling even as hard skin cracked and wept. Jubal had seen burns like this once before — and then the victim had died before sunrise.

His wife, Elli, sat with his mother. She was awake. The smoke had taken its toll but she would live, thanks to the heroism of the stranger, Teal'c. That he would risk his life for his mother absolved him of all suspicion as far as Jubal was concerned.

No, there was only one man responsible for the fire: Corvus Keen.

What this meant for his sister, Namaah, there was no way of knowing. Keen kept her close. He had an unnatural obsession with her even though he treated her like some worthless piece of crap. The way he had always looked at her, even when they were young, made Jubal's skin crawl. He could only hope that for once this fixation of Keen's would keep her safe.

He called Jachin through. They were joined by Basry, Sallah and Nadal. "It's obvious who is responsible for this," Jubal Kane said. "The question is what do we do about it?"

"We cannot fight a war against them single handed," Nadal said, voicing the simple and most obvious truth. They were not equipped to go toe to toe with the Raven Guard. They did not have the men or the firepower. They had survived this long on token resistance — being too small an irritant to be worth Corvus Keen's time to crush. That, and in no small part, the last lingering traces of love for his mother had stayed his hand. The fire burned that last illusion of safety away. Keen didn't care about any of them, and to fight him now would almost certainly mean their own damnation.

But Jubal Kane was prepared for that.

Hungry for it, even.

He wanted an end to this.

"We've lived under this false shadow of protection for too long, but one fire has burned it all way. And stripped of it, we're as vulnerable as all those others who've been dragged away to his bloody 'facilities'. And if we aren't careful, we'll end up just as dead."

The damning words hung in the air unanswered for the longest time.

"What do you suggest we do?" Sallah asked, finally. Sallah was a lanky figure with an almost epileptic fidgetiness. He squirmed in his seat, looking from face to face for answers. "We can't fight a war, Nadal is right."

"Not toe to toe," Jubal agreed, "but there are other ways to fight."

"What do you mean?"

"Cunning over brawn, courage over numbers. Look at that man next door if you want to know what I expect from you now, brothers. That a stranger would do this for us, without a thought for his own safety, that shows us the way."

"You want us to burn with him?" Jachin said, aghast.

"You always were too literal. No, I mean we spread the word to Kray and those others like him who still stand against my brother. It's time for our passive resistance to become active. Together we can hurt Corvus Keen. He rules by fear. We don't need a war, we need simply to make him fear us instead."

"But why should he fear us? What can we possibly do to him? He has an empire, for God's sake. All those guns. It's too much, Jubal."

"All it takes is one spark, one fire, one little victory."

"You have a plan, don't you?" Nadal said, leaning in.

"What fate are you most afraid of for your family?"

"The train," Nadal said, without hesitation.

Jubal Kane nodded. "We hit the death trains. We stop thousands from reaching his facility and in saving them add their numbers to our cause."

"Thousands of starving, desperate wretches," Sallah said. "They're as good as ghosts already. They aren't going to stand up to Keen."

Jubal shook his head. "You underestimate the power of redemption, my friend. They might be ghosts today, but tomorrow they will be avenging spirits. Instead of entering the facility as prisoners, they will march side by side with us as liberators. Can you imagine the effect it will have on Keen's men watching thousands march across the fields toward them?"

"You're mad," Sallah said, shaking his head. "He'll crush us before we get within one hundred miles of his precious facility... You plan on facing automatic rifles with pitchforks and broken pipes? We aren't playing soldiers here, Jubal."

"You're right Sallah. We're not playing at all. We're fighting for our lives."

By rights Teal'c should have died.

His symbiote worked aggressively to counter the debilitating effect of the burns, nourishing his skin even as the girl soothed it with water and soft words. It salvaged his system from inside out, supporting organs that would otherwise have failed as his skin failed to absorb the oxygen they needed to survive. He lay in a pool of his own sweat as the heat still burned inside him. The sweat-yellowed sheets clung to his naked body.

He tossed and turned all night and into dawn, slipping in and out of consciousness. Every time he closed his eyes he saw the flames burning again.

The girl soaked her towel and pressed it to the gold embedded in his forehead. She touched it almost reverentially.

He opened his eyes.

She pulled her hand back as though slapped.

"I will not hurt you, child," Teal'c said "There is no shame in curiosity."

"What is it?" she asked, hesitating before reaching out again.

"It is a slave marking. It says I was once owned by a Goa'uld called Apophis."

"But you are free now?"

"I am free now," he agreed, struggling to sit up.

"No, you need to rest. The girl tried to stop him but he had no intention of lying there meekly and waiting for the healing to happen. His symbiote would treat the worst of his injuries, time would heal the rest.

"I am well enough, child."

"I have a name, you know," the girl said, shaking her head in disgust at his stubbornness.

"I am sure you do."

"It is Nat. Thanks for asking."

"I did not ask."

"I know. It's called sarcasm." She peered at him. "Are you simple or something? I mean, did the fire melt your brain and leave you stupid?"

"That's quite enough of that, young lady." Jubal Kane leaned against the doorframe, an intense smile on his handsome face. The Kelani possessed an almost magnetic charisma, Teal'c realized, feeling the brunt of that seemingly easy smile for the first time. He had misjudged the man. He was a born leader, like O'Neill. He had that same affability that masked a fierce intelligence and ruthless cunning. Jubal Kane was a man you wanted on your side in a fight. Looking at him, whip-lean and hard, Teal'c could not help but wonder how much like his brother he actually was? To look at, one was in effect a shadow of the other: the black and the white, the bloated and the athletic, the compassionate and the cruel. But for a childhood of love instead of festering hate he could have been looking at Corvus Keen. "How are you feeling?"

"I have been better."

"Truly. I don't understand how you've recovered so quickly, third degree burns across more than eighty percent of your body should be a death sentence."

"In another, perhaps. But I am Jaffa."

"I'm not going to complain. I would much rather you didn't die."

"As would I." Teal'c pushed himself up to his feet. He was

decidedly unsteady. After a moment he accepted the girl's hand and allowed her to support him.

"I can't begin to thank you for what you did back there, for my mother."

"Then do not," Teal'c said. His bluntness surprised the man. "I merely repaid my debt to her. We are even."

"Not yet. You may have repaid her, but there is a debt still between you and I. Kiah told me about your friends. I know where they have been taken. I can help you find them. Let me do that, then we can call it even."

"That is not necessary," Teal'c said, raising a hand to forestall Jubal Kane's objection, "but it is most welcome. I believe they have been taken to the encampment to await the death train."

Jubal Kane nodded. "Six wagons and three trains shipped out this morning heading to the Rabelais Facility. The camp is empty now. I believe that is where we will find your friends, if they are still alive."

"Then that is where we will go," Teal'c said. The little girl squeezed his hand. He squeezed it back.

It was an effort to walk. Breathing was hard; every inhalation felt like death by a thousand cuts as the air itself stung his smoke-damaged lungs.

"You don't look so good," Nat said.

"I will be fine," Teal'c assured her. He could feel the symbiote compensating for the weakness in him. What his body needed was Kelnorim, but he did not have the luxury of time so any real healing would have to wait until O'Neill and the others were safe.

They joined the rest of Jubal Kane's crew in the main room. "Nadal, move your hefty buttocks and let Teal'c sit," Jubal said. Nadal made to move but the Jaffa shook his head. "Thank you, I will stand."

"Another stubborn fool," the Kelani muttered. The man was fat and he did not carry it well, but there was a hardness to his eyes that the warrior in Teal'c appreciated. For all the extra weight, Nadal was a fighter. There were too few of them in the Kelani ghetto. "Well I for one am not too proud to park my backside down in a soft chair and enjoy it."

Teal'c looked at the others, recognizing Jachin, but not the fidgety stick insect of a man who sat across from the corpulent Nadal.

"We have business to discuss, gentlemen," Jubal Kane said. "Nat, go play in the street." He ruffled her hair as she screwed up her nose. When she was gone, he continued: "All right, we've got one question to answer, so that shouldn't be too difficult. My friends, tell me, how do we stop a train?"

"Is that supposed to be a riddle?" Sallah asked, scratching at the scrag of beard that had grown through his sallow cheek.

"I can think of a few ways," Jachin offered. "Short of hijacking the train or parking a truck across the tracks, we're looking at damaging the rails themselves. Given the momentum of a packed train at full speed we're talking about very little damage. A simple explosive charge would do it. Hell, a sledge hammer and a little time would."

"Okay, let's put it this way—can you do it?" Jubal Kane asked.

Jachin grinned. "I might not be much of a fighter, but I know my way around a detonator. Trust me, I can do it."

"That's all I wanted to hear."

They listened to him as he outlined his plan for derailing the Rabelais Death Express.

CHAPTER TWENTY-EIGHT

Downbound Train

DANIEL JACKSON lost himself listening to the music of the train, the driving pistons and the belching steam and all of the other rattles and creaks in the dark. It wasn't exactly an orchestra of hope but that was because he knew what it meant — they were hurtling down the rails toward their final destination. With that in mind, the driving clatter of the iron wheels hitting the cracks in the tracks was more akin to the melancholy of a funeral dirge.

All around him the stink of desperation sweltered. Strangers pressed up against him. Their misery was palpable. The selection process had stripped them of their dignity and any illusions they might have had. They might just have been riding down into Hell.

Why don't they fight back? It was an obvious question and it rang in Daniel's mind. They allowed themselves to be ushered onto the death train and herded like lambs to the slaughter. There was a fatalistic resignation to it all. And now, in the filth and the dark, all he could smell was defeat. This was their lot; this was what Fate intended for them. That hurt Daniel more than any of the slings and arrows of supposed outrageous fortune Shakespeare had railed about. How could this kind of treatment ever simply become 'acceptable'? And of course, how many other trains like this one were there out there in the night? Ten? One hundred?

He wanted to rally them into rebellion. *Maybe Jack could say something to whip them up? What though? If knowing that their loved ones were being sorted out for death wasn't enough to make this worm turn, what on earth could be?*

On earth? Daniel grunted. It was a bitter sound in the blackness. And in the echo another thought resurfaced:

What if we don't make it home?

Daniel had thought it — or variations on it — a hundreds times or more. How could he not? Each time they stepped into the gate there was a very real chance none of them would return, they all knew that, but this was the first time it genuinely felt as though it might be true.

And curiously, he wasn't scared.

He pushed his back up against the hardness of the wood side.

Outside, beyond the carriage, Daniel heard a bang — a short, sharp detonation. It took a moment for his brain to register that it was an explosion, and a moment longer to understand the implications of it. He felt the shift in the train's momentum shiver up through the timber all the way from the wheels to the roof, and then the screech as the wheels locked and the roll became a slide. His balance was pulled away from him by the unexpected slide, he clawed at the straw and hard wood lining the bottom of the carriage but couldn't stop himself from pitching back.

And then the world around him descended into chaos.

"*Jack?*" he called out. It was buried beneath the sudden rage of impact as something wrenched one of the carriages further up the train off the rails. The violence of the derailment tore through the prisoners. They were so tightly packed into the death trap that they couldn't protect themselves, they couldn't so much as raise their hands as they twisted and fell, slammed into the wooden sides even as the walls ruptured lethally. Then the world lurched away beneath him, hurling Daniel upward as the wagon jack-knifed. His face slammed into the splintering roof and he reached out, trying to find something to hold on to. Metal and wood contorted violently, twisting into a web of jagged pains. Around him the screams were contagious. Daniel could hear so many more sounds, the gut-wrenching sobs of the injured; the angry barks of the guards trying to make sense of the accident and instill some sort of order; the grating of the train's wheels still spinning on uselessly and the melancholy wind that blew through the wreckage.

Daniel fell into a sharp hardness of bodies.

Hands pushed at his face and chest. He smelt the heat of blood. Felt the hot dribble of it into his face. He pushed back against the bodies, trying to find his feet.

The carriage lurched again, and for a moment it seemed to hang there, suspended by the thinnest of threads, then the weight shifted and the entire carriage yawed. It was a graceless topple, the slide into oblivion only arrested by the sudden and shocking implosion of jagged wooden spars and metal braces that bled moonlight and agony as the forces pulling at the wreckage finally tore it apart.

Daniel fell.

A long tooth of ragged wood tore through his upper arm as he came down on it and the press of bodies crushing down on him meant he couldn't drag himself free. Another twist in the darkness drove him further onto the wooden stake. He screamed but it was only one more frightened sound in the all-consuming dark. He tried to think rationally: a few more inches and it would be all the way through his arm and piercing deep into his side! He screamed again, trying to yell for Jack or Sam or anyone who might hear and help, but like the first one it was lost amid the others. Voices cried out. Bodies kicked and thrashed. He felt himself being hit and kicked by people desperate to crawl over him and out through the ruined siding into the fresh air. Those less fortunate lay still, bleeding or already dead. Daniel struggled to push down against the floor — or was it the ceiling? The derailment had him utterly disorientated. It didn't matter. He stared out through one of the broken panels. A full moon hung in the black sky. He fixated on it. Agony blazed through his arm as he tried again to move it.

And then he felt the first tear of wood entering his side and the pain put out the moon.

CHAPTER TWENTY-NINE

How to be Dead

THE GOA'ULD, Iblis, raged silently.

He could not abide incompetence in those around him. Kelkus was dead. His disciple had paid the price for his own stupidity but that did not appease Iblis' fury. The Shol'vah had escaped him, not once, but twice. It would not happen a third time.

No.

The time had come to step out of the shadows.

Iblis stood at the threshold of the vile bone mausoleum the Mujina had chosen for its nest. The place was rank with decay and old death. Ugly. Some few pilgrims still waited on the steps and among the graves clutching their offerings like the treasures they were not. It amused the Goa'uld that even in the face of such bleakness the humans managed to cling to their death rituals. Behind the corrugated iron roofs of the old factory buildings smoke belched into the black sky. Kelani bodies fueled the fire. Everyone in the Rabelais facility knew that, and yet still they found some cold comfort in building their graveyards and observing their rituals.

It was a suitable place to hide the ring transporter that allowed him to move freely between the capital and the various facilities he had instituted. It gave him a power the others could not grasp — the ability to seemingly be in two places at once. It was a simple deception, but the rumors it spawned were frequently amusing.

He heard the mewling of the Mujina, a desperate melancholy loneliness in its cry. It was like some wolf howling at the moon to attract a mate. Pitiful. Iblis had no interest in the creature tonight.

No, tonight he intended to visit Corvus Keen and put an end to this charade once and for all. Keen had made his own nest on the third floor of a derelict building in the heart of the old production buildings, close enough to the incinerators to smell the fires all day and all night. Even outside the air was putrid. There was so much death here, even just scratching at the surface. What went on behind closed doors thrilled the Goa'uld.

The bulbous body of a black rat fled into the shadows as he swept by.

He left the bone garden and came out onto what they laughingly called Main Street. The pouring rain drummed a maddening percussion on the corrugated roofs. Behind him the watchtowers loomed like specters. Despite its obvious decay the Rabelais Facility was perhaps the last truly majestic building in Corvus Keen's Empire. It was a relic of better days. Five stories tall, row upon row of windows, some blacked out, some bricked in, others gazing blankly across the filth-strewn streets like the blind eyes in the face of a once noble patrician. The thick walls hid the screams. But lights still burned in the first floor laboratories, meaning the master of Rabelais was still at work. The man's thirst for knowledge was impressive. The man's thirst for pain, more so. He seemed to devise a new torture with every coming dawn. There were so many Corvani here who excelled, that it made Kelkus' failure all the more galling.

Iblis wearied of this body. It was neither ugly nor beautiful, indeed it was utterly unremarkable.

He took the rusty old freight elevator to the fifth floor, the car rattling and wheezing as it struggled with his weight, and then walked down the deserted passageway toward Corvus Keen's chamber. Bare bulbs flickered in and out of light, casting shadows across the floor. By the time he reached the forth bulb they were all dead. He wasn't surprised that no one challenged him or blocked his way. It was a mark of his supreme arrogance — after all who would dare try to kill him? That was the way Corvus Keen's mind worked. Where some might have fallen into paranoia and surrounded themselves by soldiers, Keen simply refused to believe anyone would have the temerity to try and kill him.

How wrong could he be?

Iblis didn't wait for permission to enter.

He swept into the dank smelly room. It was a sty, every bit as slovenly as its occupant. "How can you live in this filth?" he demanded of the tyrant. There was no 'sire' now, no unctuous bowing and scraping.

Keen was marooned in his chair, struggling to stand. His face relaxed visibly when he saw Iblis come through the door. The wolfhound at his feet stirred, opening an eye to see who disturbed its slumber. Its jowls curled back on yellowed teeth at the sight of the Goa'uld but its snarl settled quickly into a sigh and the dog closed its eye once more, content to sleep the rest of the day away.

Iblis smiled and closed the door behind him.

"Your mutt is neither faithful nor watchful, it seems." The words sounded like one long sigh as he ghosted up behind the tyrant's chair.

"He's tired," Corvus Keen answered gruffly.

"Indeed, yes, yes… Tired. Aren't we all? Tired of incompetence. Tired of other people failing."

"What do you want, Iblis? I am in no mood for games tonight."

"Want? Like you, I want the world. Actually I want more. I want worlds. I want the stars. Even the way you talk reeks of indolence, do you know that? Be more specific with your questions, Keen. You never know which one might be your last. It would be a pity to die uttering a foolish question. What do you want *with me*? So much more pertinent don't you think?"

"Can't you go and play with one of your corpses? There must be fires to light and bodies to burn. I am in no mood for this." The ridges along the top of the fat man's skull had begun to ripple, his skin mottling with a turgid blue tinge as his face flushed.

"No, or rather yes, if we are being precise. I can and I will play with a corpse — but I won't be going anywhere to do it."

"Why is it your kind delight in riddles, Iblis?"

"Ah, you are quite right. I should speak as plainly as I would have you speak. Yes, yes, yes. I should speak plainly for the stupid fat man on his pretend throne."

"How dare you!" Corvus Keen struggled to rise, his arms shaking from the exertion of trying to lift his colossal frame out of the chair. He was livid. Flecks of spittle sprayed from his mouth and his eyes blazed with anger.

"Kneel before your god and beg for your wretched hide. Do it. Now!" Iblis stared at Keen and saw the fear in his eyes.

"You're mad…"

"No, merely weary. It is time to end this game."

"You mean to kill me? You can't hope to get away with it…"

"I can't? Why ever not?"

"Because… because…" Corvus Keen spluttered, craning his neck to look.

Iblis reached out slowly and pressed his fingers into the flabby flesh of the half-breed tyrant's throat, twisting them so that the nails dug in painfully. "Go on, I'm waiting to know why I can't do this. Yes, yes, yes. I am waiting. So tell me before I wring your stupid fat neck for you."

"I am… THE RAVEN KING!" Corvus Keen gasped, struggling for every breath he took. Keen's eyes bulged comically in their sockets and the skin around them began to turn purple. Still Iblis' fingers tightened their relentless grip.

"Why?" It was less than a croak. Keen's hands were up at

his throat trying desperately to wrench away Iblis' fingers but the Goa'uld's grip was like iron.

Iblis threw back his head and laughed. "Why?" he mimicked. "Why? Because I am your God."

Iblis smiled. His smile widened, and widened, and did not stop stretching until it had transformed into a deathly rictus. From between its lips a gray scaly worm wriggled. The ridge of its spine was slick with blood.

Iblis' eyes rolled up inside his head, the host body dead before the Goa'uld had fully extricated itself. All Corvus Keen could do was scream as the thing squirmed and slithered toward him, and then, lightning fast, whipped around his neck and in, through the skin as it wrapped around his spine and pierced his brain stem, taking control. The fat man convulsed in his chair, then sat up straight, sneering down at his own flesh where food crusted against flaccid skin.

For a long moment Iblis simply absorbed all that had been Corvus Keen and Zarif before him. So much hatred. So much anger. No wonder the human had allowed his body to crumble beneath him; it was nothing short of mercy that he was liberated from the mass of fat and blood. Iblis absorbed it all, all of the knowledge — his father, his blood, the step-sister he coveted, the daughter that might have been his, the brother he loathed, the mother he had burned and blinded — all the hopes and fears that had driven Corvus Keen. And he turned them into something more potent: power.

"Better," he said, steel in his voice as he pushed himself to his feet. This form was at least interesting if not attractive, and for now it suited Iblis' schemes.

He walked across to the window and surveyed what had become his new domain. It was not beautiful, but that did not matter, it was deathly.

And dreaming of death, soon it would be time to open the Stargate.

Now, at last, he could emerge from the shadows. The

irony of this new body amused him. Instead of some beautiful butterfly emerging from its cocoon he was a swollen, bloated moth. But moths always had been the true kings of the night, Iblis thought, dragging the corpse of his last host toward the door.

Wheezing in his new skin, the Goa'uld cursed the arrogance of the man it had become and vowed to keep guards close to hand in future.

"You!" Iblis shouted, trying out his new voice. At the far end of the passageway a black and silver clad guard turned, about to spit a curse his way before he saw Corvus Keen dragging a dead man toward him. "Dispose of this thing before it stinks up the place."

The guard looked down, recognizing the corpse despite the damage to its stretched face.

"He out-lived his usefulness. Be sure you do not."

CHAPTER THIRTY

Runaway Train

TEAL'C WALKED toward the wreckage.

Jachin had been right, it had been disturbingly easy to derail the train. A single charge had blown out one of the tracks, buckling the iron rail so that when the engine hit it at full steam it was lifted and twisted and slipped the tracks. Within fifty feet the lead carriages had snaked out uncontrollably and gone over onto their sides, skidding and sliding through the grass and dirt of the embankment. That in itself would have been enough, but not for Jachin. The impact that turned the derailment into a wreckage was even simpler: the Kelani rolled an old flatbed truck down the slope of the embankment into the path of the sliding train. The gas tanks on the truck were full, promising an explosive impact.

Teal'c had stood side by side with Jubal Kane and watched the engine slide into the wall of flame only for the carriages behind it to jack-knife as the full horror of the crash unfolded. Now they walked toward the little man who had caused so much devastation. Jachin looked inordinately pleased with himself as he dusted his hands off. "Told you," he said.

"Excessive, don't you think?" Jubal frowned down at the ruined train as the shocked and wounded tried to claw their way out of the wreckage.

"Is it stopped or is it stopped?"

"It's stopped."

"Which is exactly what you asked for. The rest, as they say, is just a bonus."

Jubal stared at the man. "The rest is not a bonus, the rest is a lot of wasted humanity. Sometimes you frighten me.

Sometimes you just make me seethe."

Jubal had sixty-eight guns with him. It was all the ghetto could muster — all that were willing to throw their lot in with him and make a stand against Keen. It was hardly enough to take on an army, but sixty-eight guns were enough to sound out one hell of a battle cry. They would shake Corvus Keen's world to its rotten foundations before they were through.

"Who wants to stay forever young?" Jubal Kane said.

Teal'c believed he was talking to himself so did not answer. He stared at the wreckage, horrified by the senseless destruction and the unnecessary loss of life. He clenched his fist, needing the sting of pain as his nails dug into his palm to stop himself from lashing out at the idiocy of Jachin. Surely this was every bit as evil as anything perpetrated by the so-called enemy. How could it be anything less as far as the dead on the train were concerned?

"Come on, my friend, tonight we fight, tomorrow we break fast with hell's demons."

"I believe I have lost my appetite," Teal'c said.

Jubal Kane laughed. "You know, the more I get to know you, big man, the more I like you."

And the rain came down. Teal'c savored the cold on his upturned face. He could not dwell upon the tragedy of the prisoners. He had to set about the business of saving his friends.

The train had at least twenty Raven Guard on it that needed to be neutralized. Jubal gave the signal and his men streamed down from their hiding places along the embankment and fell upon the dazed guards as they stumbled along the side of the train, trying to work out what had happened and to stop the Kelani prisoners from escaping. Gunshots rang out brutally in the night. That was the signal chaos had been waiting for.

Teal'c ran from carriage to twisted carriage looking for any sign of his friends. Bodies lay broken and every bit as ruined as the wooden timber frames of the wagons. People crawled about on their hands and knees, moaning and groaning as they tried to drag themselves away from the wreckage toward the safety of the grass verge. The rain turned the dirt into sucking mud, making everything much more of a trial as people slipped and slithered and slid and fell, barely able to pick themselves up again. In the confusion it was impossible to tell friend from foe. The Raven Guard had lost their guns in the hysteria after the crash and panicked under the onslaught. Now, blinded in the rain and the red glare of the burning truck, they were crawling about, every bit as dazed and confused as their prisoners.

Teal'c stood over a wounded man who had fallen face first and was sucking up mud and rain with every breath he took. He would have helped him, only he recognized the man as one of the two who had come looking for him at Kiah's house just before it had been set aflame.

"Were you the one who hit the blind woman?" he asked, kneeling down close enough that the struggling man might hear. He need not have worried. The man heard all right.

The fool tried to nod again, lying through his teeth to save his own skin. "It was Gant. He made me do it. I tried to stop him. You have to believe me."

"I do not have to believe you at all," Teal'c said. "But it is not my place to believe or disbelieve, neither is it up to me to dispense punishment. Jubal Kane," he called, his voice rising above the agony of the wounded and the anger of the wreckage.

Kane turned to see who called his name.

With his free hand, Teal'c gestured for the ghetto warrior to come. "This is one of the men who burned your mother's house."

"No, no, please, no…" The guard struggled to rise.

"Shut up!" Jubal Kane snapped. And to Teal'c, "How can you be sure?"

"He is one of the two I saw leaving after she sheltered me from their search earlier in the day."

"One of the ones that beat her?"

Teal'c nodded.

Without a second thought Jubal Kane stepped in and snapped the man's neck in single savage motion. The brutality of it shocked the Jaffa. "That is the justice of the ghetto," Jubal Kane said, as though intoning judgment on the damned. He turned his back and walked away in search of another Raven Guard to put down. Teal'c did not need to be able to read his mind to know what he was thinking: the second man who had tried to murder his mother could be among them. There was no mercy in the man's face.

Teal'c found Carter first. She was sitting with her back against the underside of the train carriage. The wheels had long since stopped spinning but they were still hot enough for the rain to steam as it hit the metal. She had her arms up around the long axel and appeared to be using it to brace her back. Her face was covered with blood that streaked in tears of rain, like a fury torn from the stuff of nightmare and given flesh. She smiled up at him through the bloody tears as he hunkered down beside her. "It's good to see you, Teal'c."

"It is good to see you, too, Major Carter. Are you well?"

She saw his concern and touched her cheek. Her fingers came away wet with blood. "This? It's not mine. I'm fine," she assured him. "Starving but fine. Honestly."

"That is good."

She shook her head. "It's horrible, Teal'c. This whole world is horrible. I never thought I could think that. But…" she grunted. "I don't understand it. How can people do this to each other?"

Teal'c said nothing. He had no answer for the cruelty of humans. Instead, he asked, "What of Daniel Jackson and Colonel O'Neill?"

Carter shook her head again, as though trying to shake

off some mental malaise and clear her mind. "The Colonel is fine, a few cuts and bruises, no broken bones. He's looking for Daniel."

"I should join his search, if you do not mind?"

"Help me up, we'll go together."

Teal'c continued his search moving from carriage to carriage, Carter at his side. The rain and mud made it difficult to tell one face from another, and mixed with the pain, it became impossible. Up and down the line Jubal Kane's men moved with brutal efficiency. They dragged the unconscious black and silver clad guards out of the twisted wreckage and dumped them on the embankment, and marched the conscious few at gunpoint. A fight broke out, dying before it could become more than a flurry of fists, as fat Nadal pistol-whipped the Corvani guard, laying him out cold. With grim satisfaction Jubal Kane's man finished him. It turned Teal'c's stomach. War was one thing, but this, this was slaughter. It had no place in honorable war. It was the kind of monstrosity the Goa'uld had forced him to perpetrate as First Prime. The psychology of it was simple: they had been beaten, their families tortured and killed, treated like scum, made to eat scraps from the dirt at the feet of these men, and now the worm had turned. The punishments they inflicted on the guards were less cruel, less unusual, but no less final once meted out. More gunfire ran out, this time single shot execution style.

When the anger had burned out, the righteous fury that demanded blood justice, then mercy would have its chance to win out, but for now there was a reckoning to be had. That, at least, was the kind of thinking the Jaffa could understand.

Teal'c walked away.

"You look like hell, buddy."

He turned at the sound of O'Neill's familiar voice behind him. The colonel had found a compact automatic pistol — that made sixty-nine guns — and was crouched down beside

Daniel Jackson. He leaned in and had his hands — one over the other — pressed down hard over a deep wound. On the floor beside him lay a bloody wooden stake. More gunfire rattled the night.

Even through the rain and the dark, Teal'c could tell that his friend was in a bad way.

"Gonna need to brush up on my field medicine," O'Neill said.

"I'd really rather you didn't," Daniel managed through clenched teeth.

"Quit being a girl, Daniel, and let me save your life. I can give you a bullet to bite on if you like?"

"Not necessary," Daniel winced.

"Let's get you patched up. We'll let Fraiser handle the tough stuff."

"I'm glad to hear it," Daniel Jackson said. He didn't make another sound as O'Neill ripped strips from his shirt to pad the wound, and then bound it up with what was left. Without their kit there wasn't much more he could do.

While O'Neill finished patching up Daniel Jackson, Teal'c debriefed them on what he had learned of the Goa'uld, Iblis, of Kiah, and of the tyrant Corvus Keen and the nature of the Rabelais Facility.

"Oh this day just keeps getting better and better," O'Neill muttered, tying off the makeshift field dressing. "I don't suppose you happened to overhear where this Goa'uld has hidden the Stargate, did you?"

"I did not."

"Pity. Could have done with some good news right about now."

"I found you alive, is that not good news?"

"Yeah, I guess it is, bud. I guess it is."

The sixty-nine guns at Jubal Kane's disposal became ninety-three. Five of the Corvani carried a second piece.

They had saved over nine hundred Kelani from the train. The numbers staggered Jack. Nine hundred. Jubal Kane's men ushered them toward some unseen point in the distance. Jack knew the plan, what there was of one. He couldn't argue with it because there wasn't much to argue with. There had been fatalities, of course. Aside from the twenty Corvani Raven Guard, thirty-seven of the prisoners had proven too old and too weak to survive the crash. Another hundred or so were carrying injuries, broken bones, cuts, bruises. Some would die, most would make it.

The walking wounded helped with the worst of the victims, fashioning makeshift stretchers and the like to help bear them. Daniel had insisted on walking until the blood loss had made him all but pass out and O'Neill had insisted that, actually, no, Daniel couldn't 'walk just fine', and made him take a ride on one of the stretchers.

Jubal Kane pointed at a dark smudge on the horizon. To Jack it looked no different than all of the other dark smudges he had seen as they walked. "The Rabelais Facility. It used to be a chemical processing plant until six months ago. Now it processes people. My people. That smoke, that's some of them after they've been processed, if you catch my drift."

O'Neill did. It wasn't a particularly difficult drift to catch.

"The way I see it," Jubal Kane continued, "we have a choice. Not much of a choice, I'll grant you, but it's still a choice. We can take these nine hundred hungry, sick and frankly beaten people back to the ghetto and await Keen's retribution, or we can go about causing him some real pain. Those are our people in there, O'Neill. I think that makes it our call, don't you?"

"And, let me guess, you've already made up your mind?" Jack squinted toward the smudge as though he might be able to make something else out of it. It stayed a black smudge no matter how much he screwed his eyes up.

"I have. We wouldn't be walking this way otherwise."

"Yeah? Well, good luck with that. All I want to do is get my people home. This isn't our war."

"Yet here you are in the middle of it, with no way to get your people home." Kane stopped, a hand on O'Neill's arm. "Help me win, and I will do everything I can to help you return home."

"Those are long odds."

"The Kelani are a strong people, O'Neill. Do not underestimate us." He held out his hand. "Do we have a bargain?"

Jack looked at the offered hand, but did not take it. He didn't trust this joker, not for a minute. There was stuff going on here he wasn't party to, but just because he didn't know what it was didn't mean he couldn't tell it stank. "Let's talk to this explosives guy of yours and hear what he has to say for himself, shall we?"

The rain hadn't let up in the last hour. Indeed, if anything it was worse now than it was when they had crawled out of the wreckage.

"Jachin, come here and explain to the colonel what we have in mind."

Jack turned and gestured for Carter to join him. "Sir," she nodded, wiping at the blood still smearing her face.

Jachin's grin as he explained what he had in mind was wholly inappropriate. "Right, so, this place used to be a chemical processing plant. Most of the stuff has been cleaned out, the vats turned into holding cells, or worse. Anyway, we have intel that leads us to believe several of the chemicals they used to work with here were highly volatile in nature — and more interestingly for us, according to our man they aren't exactly easy to clean away. We're talking fumes eating into the metal of the vats themselves, and believe me, plenty of those pits are still lined with exactly the kind of explosive stuff we need for the fireworks."

"Fireworks?" O'Neill said.

"Hasn't Jubal explained?" Jachin shrugged, and then grinned. It was an infectious smile. Jack didn't share it.

"Why don't *you* tell me?"

"Well, we need a distraction, right?"

"Right."

"We're just talking about a lot of flash and bang, these are our people in there, after all."

O'Neill nodded along with the reasoning but he still didn't like where this was going. It wasn't the plan so much as the people behind it; the lack of discipline of the Kelani's, the gung-ho attitude of some of them, and, no bones about it, Jubal Kane. The man just rubbed him the wrong way. He trusted him about as far as Daniel could throw him.

"Basically, big tank go boom," Jachin said, matching the 'boom' with an expressive gesture. "And while the guards flap around trying to put the fires out, we go in. Simple as that."

"Providing nothing goes wrong," Carter said.

"Nothing can go wrong. I know my explosives."

Jack grunted. "Something *always* goes wrong."

CHAPTER THIRTY-ONE

Somewhere a Clock is Ticking

IN THIS CASE it didn't so much go 'wrong' as it did 'too well'.

Jachin did indeed know his explosives. He wired up a small device with a big enough charge to do more than singe a few eyebrows, and gave explicit instructions as to exactly where Carter should place it. Carter had drawn the metaphorical short straw. With O'Neill needed on the sharp end, ready to go in guns blazing, it was down to her as the smallest and fastest. She had argued O'Neill blue in the face. There wasn't a viable alternative. He couldn't be in both places at once. It was as simple as that. Still he had fought her on it every step of the way. It was his job to put his life on the line, not hers, was how he had so succinctly put it. That had ended the argument, but not in his favor. He didn't trust Jubal. That distrust outweighed his protectiveness. That same distrust had steered him toward intervention in the first place. In a perfect world it would have been the insurgents attacking the encampment, the team not interfering with the history of this world. But there were times when it was impossible to merely observe, and this was one of them. There were too many lives and risk, and too many echoes of Earth's own history to be ignored. So they had not only taken sides, they had become involved. And once involved, they were never going to sit back. They were committed to seeing this through to the bitter end.

She scurried forward, keeping as low as she could, head down looking at her feet as she moved, then back down to a tight crouch. Only then did she look up to scout out her next resting place. The rain had eased off, but hadn't stopped.

It made it easier for her to move unseen, but harder for her to hear anyone who might have gotten a little too close for comfort. All she could hope, as she offered a silent prayer to whatever god, demon, devil, imp or sprite, watched over bombers, was that it meant they couldn't hear her either. Fair was fair, after all.

She dropped down flat onto her stomach and crawled on elbows and knees through the short grass. Searchlights from the watchtowers strobed across the facility erratically, lacking any kind of identifiable pattern. Either the soldiers manning the lights were exceptionally disciplined, or they were chasing moths with the bright beams. Either way, it made her job of slipping in under the fence unnoticed that much more difficult.

Sam counted out three minutes. In that entire time the searchlights didn't cross the same patch of ground once. Sometimes they played out toward the dark corners, other times they ran along the edge of the perimeter fence or right through the center of the yard. Once, midway through the count, one of the lights worked its way up the wall of the five story building and illuminated the entire roof.

It was an elaborate dance. She half expected hippos in tutus to pirouette their way from super trooper to super trooper.

There were seven chemical vats. They were huge cylindrical containers lined up like bowling pins that towered over the complex more than ten times her height. Full, one of those going up was going to provide more than fireworks. God only knew what the residual fumes would do — God only knew what the residual fumes *were*.

Her instinct was to hit the first one at the front of the diamond — in terms of line-of-least-resistance it was the easiest both to reach and to escape, but it was also the easiest one for the searchlight to pick out, so she discounted it.

She moved forward to a grassy knoll, ten feet closer to the fence, where she could better see the comings and goings of the guards. Right then she would have killed for a pair of binoculars never mind night vision goggles. She had nothing but the moon.

Sam lay there for another ten minutes watching the men to see if they were any less erratic than the lights. They weren't. Two of them, she saw, walked a short distance away from the compound's fence into the shadows of nearby trees — she couldn't be sure but they appeared to be necking back a bottle of something, meaning they wouldn't be too interested in what happened to their little strip of fence for the next few minutes. It was moving faster than she was ready for. Sam pushed herself to her feet. The wet grass soaked through her BDUs, making them cling uncomfortably. She checked off to the right once, and then ghosted down the hill toward the length of fence she'd decided to cut through.

Every step of the way she expected to hear the blare of a klaxon going off and for the searchlights to all swivel around to focus on her. It didn't happen.

She hit the fence and fell to her knees, digging quickly with her hands to scuff up enough of the bottom wires for her to start cutting through them. Each individual link took her seven seconds to sheer through using the wire cutters the Kelani had given her. They were blunt almost to the point of uselessness. She needed to cut through six to be able to squirm underneath the fence, seven or eight to be on the safe side. In less than one minute she was through and on the other side.

As Sam dragged herself through the dirt — kicking out with her feet almost as though she were swimming — the first dogs barked. It was the other sound she hadn't wanted to hear. She tried to judge how far away the animals were; there was no way to know if they were running free or if they had handlers reining them in. Either way, she had to run — difficult in her weakened state — sending all of her time calculations out the window. "Just great."

She looked over her shoulder. The drinkers were still drinking, but it looked like they were about to put the cap back on their bottle. She didn't wait to see if they decided to light up a smoke: she didn't need to, they were already reacting to the barking dogs. She ran. Straight across the dirt yard toward the chemical vats, arms and legs pumping hard. Three hundred yards at a full sprint — it should have been comfortable, even running hell for leather, but she couldn't remember the last time she had eaten. Halfway and her head was spinning. Fifty yards from the drums and she was running blind, her eyes refusing to focus. The last ten had her stumbling tangle-footed and falling, picking herself up only to fall again. How no one saw her was a miracle.

She unwrapped the explosive with shaking hands, willing her head to stop spinning. It was a primitive device, little more than two sticks of dynamite and a timer really, and she primed it quickly, giving herself two minutes to get clear. It would have to be enough.

Sam pressed it onto the metal casing of the drum, wedging it up against the welding on the lower stanchion exactly where Jachin had told her to. The force of the explosion would tear the weld apart and leave a gaping hole in the outer casing of the drum. The fumes would leak out, come into contact with the smoldering fragments of the bomb and everything would go up in a second lethal explosion.

Or at least that was the theory.

Sam made it all the way back to the opening in the fence and hunkered down, waiting for it to blow. The effort of running made her nauseous and she squeezed her eyes shut against the world's queasy spin, taking deep breaths. After a moment she peeled open one eye. The searchlights roved across the roof of the building and up and down the yard as she counted the seconds off in her head. After one hundred and fifty seconds it still hadn't blown. Cursing, she checked her watch, hoping she'd miscounted with the adrenalin pumping. She hadn't. The timer hadn't triggered the detonation. Which meant she had to go back and either fix the timer or set it off manually. Neither particularly appealed. She didn't even have a radio to call in to O'Neill and let the others know what the hold up was. She stuck to the shadows this time, not running so much as ghosting. She kept low and ran in short staggered intervals.

The searchlights swept across the yard. She almost ran headfirst into one of the beams and barely managed to check herself before she did.

One of the wires had come lose from the timer. Unfortunately the countdown device has almost run its course, and was stuck one second from true, so reattaching it was out of the question. She'd have had an entire second to contemplate the life flashing before her eyes, before 'boom'. Not ideal. But she had nothing with which to jerry-rig a new timer either, or work out a way to circumvent the old one.

Or did she? Her feet squelched in the run-off from the downpour that had collected in a muddy puddle around the bottom of the chemical vat and she realized that she'd already seen the solution — the thirsty guards had been kind enough to demonstrate. All she needed was their bottle. She didn't even need that: she had her water flask. Working quickly, she filled it from the rain puddle, and pried the explosives away from the metal drum. She wedged them in against the side of the drum as best as she could, then stripped away the wires from the timer, leaving them exposed and bare. Next she balanced the water flask as precariously as she could, the mouth of the bottle less than an inch away from the wires. She held on to it while she steadied her nerves. The idea was pretty simple. It was like the old game Mousetrap, really. One thing connects to another. Cause and effect reduced to water, wire and hopefully an explosion. She would let go of the flask and eventually gravity would take its toll, the weight of the water would tilt it as the rain continued to fill the flask until it reached the brim — it would either fall, or spill its contents, meaning it could play out one of two ways: the steady flow of water would complete the circuit and count down that last second, or the bottle itself would force the wires together, and making contact complete the circuit. There wasn't really a great deal of margin for error, the bottle couldn't fall the wrong way, she'd compensated for that, but it could fall short or wide of the mark and miss the wires all together, but by rights either way ought to work and she really wasn't fussy. As long as the thing blew, mission accomplished. She could sort out that idiot Jachin later.

But — and there was always going to be a but — there was no way she would make it all the way back to the fence. Not a prayer. She'd be lucky to make it behind the next vat, which meant there was no running away this time. She hoped the explosion bought the others the time they needed to get inside the compound. And even more fervently she hoped she would be there to greet them when they did.

With another silent prayer to the patron saint of bombers, Sam took her hand off the water flask and started to run.

The explosions tore through the night.

O'Neill had expected a single double-shock detonation and a few fireworks; the charge had been a small one, barely more than a flash-bang, according to Jachin. But what they got was no simple double-shock. That first concussion ruptured the silence and was followed by a second much larger detonation as the vat itself went up — only it didn't simply ignite. The trapped fumes turned the entire structure into a huge grenade, the force of the detonation tearing the metal drum to razor sharp shrapnel that it spewed across the compound. It sliced into the surrounding drums, scoring through the metal casing, and seconds later causing a third and forth explosion.

Flame ripped out blanketing the sky above them from

horizon to horizon, turning night into day. He could feel the battering heat on his face even this far away from the blaze and all O'Neill could think was that Carter was down there in the middle of it. She didn't have a radio or any other way of letting them know she was okay, she didn't even have a weapon to protect herself now that she'd drawn all attention her way… If she was even alive after the Fourth of July light show down there. "Goddamn sonofabitch!" O'Neill turned on the grinning firebug, grabbing him by his ragged shirt. "You said a small controlled explosion!"

"But isn't this so much better?" The flames reflected in Jachin's eyes, making him look crazed.

"Better?" Jack shook him. "Carter is in the middle of that goddamn mess!"

Searchlights roved wildly through the darkness, looking for the saboteur, and klaxons blared into discordant life. Doors opened and guards and prisoners alike streamed out into the yard. It was chaos, which was exactly what the pyrotechnics had been meant to achieve.

Down the line, Jubal Kane gave the signal and his ninety-three guns rushed the gate. The rest of the refugees and prisoners followed barehanded, screaming and whooping as they charged the Facility's chained gates.

In disgust, O'Neill let go of Jachin and watched as Jubal fired the first shot. The bullet took one of the watchtower guards in the side of the head, sending him sprawling backwards over the low wall of his ensconcement. He was dead before he fell. There were no pin-wheeling arms or terrified screams. It was all very surreal. He simply fell. And as though that were some prearranged signal, ninety-two other guns roared.

Suddenly the compound was filled with screaming, flames, and the angry bark of gunfire — all notes in the music of war.

"Is that a hand cart I see on its way to hell?" O'Neill said to no one in particular.

"I do not believe so, O'Neill," Teal'c said. "There are no wheels."

CHAPTER THIRTY-TWO

Under Your Skin

THE MUJINA emerged from its nest into a world of fire. All of the memories of its imprisonment swarmed up to overwhelm it; they had found it, but rather than transport it back to hell the Ancients had chosen to turn this new world into one of flames and death. Could they hate it so much, so blindly, that they would damn an entire world to make sure it was alone? Yes, it thought, yes they could.

It stared at the seven metal towers, at the angry flames consuming them, and at the shadows they threw across the compound and its friends, those who came to worship it and offer devotion. They crawled on their hands and knees in the dirt, unable to flee because the gates were chained and there was no way out, nowhere to run. The rain could not touch the fire. It burned and burned, eating into the metal. Spreading. It would not take long for one spark to catch the wind and be carried to the main building. That was the way of fire: it ate and ate and ate, never sated. They would all die, it knew, everyone in this place, everyone that it had allowed to become close to it, and all that would remain would be their bones.

"No!" it screamed, consumed by the fear of being alone once more. Its voice was lost amid the pandemonium.

It reached into their minds, wanting to help, wanting to calm them. But all it found there was fear and anger and hate, and all it could do was recoil, reaching out from mind to mind to find something. It didn't know what. Just something, someone it could help, someone it could save so that it didn't have to walk into the fire alone.

It staggered out through makeshift graves, head turned to the sky. The black smoke still burned from the incinerator fires, but it was swallowed up in the conflagration. Everything burned. Everything.

It was a horror the creature had never thought to see again.

It saw a slack-skinned woman trying to batter the flames away from an old man. It saw the two of them fall to the floor, burning.

The Raven Guard struggled to establish some kind of order. They dragged the Kelani out of their barracks into the yard area, as far away from the burning drums as possible. They marched down the line, barking bigoted epithets as they pistol-whipped any fool too slow falling into line. Others fanned out like ants marching to fight the rising flames — a hopeless, pitiful task.

"I didn't do it," the Mujina said, grabbing the closest person. She was a shell person, hollow cheeks, dark eyes and breasts shriveled away to nothing, like the rest of the meat on her bones. She shuffled, trying to pull away from the Mujina, but there was no fight in her. So instead the woman stared imploringly at the creature, begging it to let her go. But then her eyes flared wide open with hope as she thought she understood, thought that the Mujina was here to save her, when all it wanted was forgiveness. "I didn't do it," it repeated. "This isn't my fault. It isn't. I didn't do it."

"Save me," she said, and it wished it could help her. It really did. It wished that it could help all of the Kelani that had been gathered here to die.

But it knew that it could not.

That knowledge undid something within the Mujina's mind. Some fundamental piece of its identity, its sense of self, sheared off. All it had ever wanted to do was help. It lived to help. And now, when it was most needed, it could not.

And then, through the mass of suffering that threatened to

overwhelm it, the Mujina touched another mind, something strong, glorious, and like a moth it was drawn toward it.

O'Neill was side by side with Jubal Kane when the Kelani fighter breached the gate. The chains couldn't hope to withstand the sheer mass of bodies hurling themselves at the gate; Kane pulled his pistol and fired a single shot into the hasp, blowing the lock wide. Howling triumphantly, they poured into the death camp. They didn't care if the searchlights found them. Guns spat, bullets streaking through the burning sky.

O'Neill took out two of the gate guards, and made an eyes right gesture to Kane. Jubal didn't miss a beat. He hit the wall, counted off three, one, two, three, on his left hand, and spun around the corner, firing once. His single shot took the defender between the cheek and jaw, burying itself in the man's head. Kane nodded back to Jack, giving him the thumbs up.

He only had one spare clip and O'Neill felt no great rush to waste human life, be it Corvani or Kelani. They were still human. If he could get through the next few minutes without firing another shot he'd be a happy man.

Nadal and Teal'c came up behind them. The Kelani moved with surprising athleticism for a man of his size. The others came in behind them, spreading out to form a wedge that drove deep into the ranks of the defenders. The place reeked of blood and sweat and all of the other stenches of confinement and torture.

The yard was in chaos, the Raven Guard struggling to impose any kind of order. The Kelani prisoners weren't fighting. Days without food, days filled with systematic mental and physical torture, had beaten the fight out of them. But Jubal Kane's raucous war cry galvanized them — the knowledge that after all this time someone had come to save them. There were no gods in places like this, O'Neill knew that all too well, but it didn't matter. Their prayers had been answered by the dark and hungry avenger that was Jubal Kane. That was answer enough.

"I'm going to look for Carter," O'Neill said. "You go do whatever it is you have to do, hero."

Jubal Kane nodded. "I will find my brother and end his atrocities once and for all. Wish me luck."

"Just a hunch, but I've got a feeling you aren't going to be the one needing it."

Kane grinned at that — and his grin was every bit as mad as Jachin's had been as he stared into the fire. These people scared him.

"Teal'c, come with me."

Something had come over the prisoners.

It felt the shift in their minds.

The fear was there still, but it was no longer the driving emotion.

It took the Mujina a moment to realize what this long forgotten emotion was: hope. It felt it coming up in waves from the thousands of stoop-shouldered and beaten-down Kelani. Nothing changed in their faces. They did not punch the air and cheer. They did not fight back. But deep down inside, in the secret place they had nurtured and clung to during the dark days of their confinement, they had dared to hope. That hope had been crushed, battered, tortured and experimented on, but somehow it had not burned out. It was a curious thing, hope, it took almost nothing to revive it. And now, striding into the compound was the very first gift the liberators brought with them.

The Mujina wanted to weep. The emotion was so intense. It couldn't keep them all out of its head. It lurched forward under the weight of hope, trying to see, to find the bright and brilliant mind it had touched. "Neryn Var," it called out to her but she wasn't there. It called out again and again but it was so loud. There were so many cries. Shouts. It couldn't concentrate. Couldn't find that glorious mind again. "Don't leave me," it whispered. "Not now…"

It scanned the faces of everyone near it, pushing deeper and deeper into the press of bodies, and ignoring the imploring looks and grasping hands that clawed at it.

"Don't leave me," it said again.

"I won't leave you," a voice said out of the noise. It turned, filled with its own bright and burning hope, and saw Iblis's slug-like smile on Corvus Keen's borrowed face. "Not now, not ever."

·The Mujina reached out. Something was wrong with the Raven King's mind. It… it did not belong under this skin. The Mujina tried to focus, reach down, reach in. No, that wasn't right. Some of it did. That made no sense unless…. Two minds in the same shell, one dominant the other almost gone, superseded by the new bright, glorious mind. It had sensed this once before in the woman, Nyren Var. She had been the same, two somehow fused into one, but her second mind was every bit as alive and bright as the first, not like this.

And then, the most curious of thoughts crept into its own mind: could it also share this gift? Could it become like them? Could it open itself to another and never again be alone inside its own skin? Could it turn into something beautiful inside of its plain emptiness? Would she come back to it, would she share its life, if it did?

"Will you help me find her?" it said.

"Who?"

"The woman, Nyren Var. The Tok'ra. Will you help me find her? She promised to come back to me. I miss her."

"Tok'ra?"

"She is like you, two inside one, the shell and the real mind. She has such a beautiful mind."

"I will help you find her," the Raven King promised. "But first we need to leave this place."

"Together?"

"Together."

The word was like nectar to the creature.

It reached deeper into the Raven King's mind, brushing aside the shallow memories of the fat man, rooting all the way down to the memories of stone that Iblis had locked away in the darkest part of his psyche — tortured memories of his centuries long imprisonment within the Kelani artifacts. "You understand." The Mujina gloried in the fact that, amid all of this suffering, it had found a kindred soul: a true prisoner. And like it, Iblis had only recently tasted freedom for the first time in millennia. It tasted so many of the same hungers in the Goa'uld's mind. "We are the same," it said, truly believing it. "We are the same, you and I."

"Come with me." Iblis held out his hand and led the Mujina back into the shadows.

Samantha Carter lay on her back looking up at the stars. They seemed to be on fire.

She couldn't hear anything.

She hadn't been able to since the explosion. Her head rang with a percussion of tinnitus in her own blood. Every inch of her body hurt. The shockwave from the explosion had punched her violently from her feet, throwing her more than ten feet through the air, and she had come down hard, face first into the wet earth. She'd barely managed to crawl into the shadows and roll over onto her back. All she could think was that at least she was alive. The drums burned out of control.

She heard gunshots. Retaliatory fire. Sporadic bursts, single shots. The searchlights stopped beaming down the fire and turned on the yard. She could see people, though from the ground with the light streaming down into her face they were all featureless shadows.

The colonel and the others must have hit the gates. It was only a matter of time before one of them found her. "This sure isn't Kansas," she said, closing her eyes.

"Damn right it isn't, Major. Now up you get before a tornado comes and dumps us on our asses in Oz and we're both left feeling rather stupid."

"Good to see you too, sir." She reached out a hand for O'Neill to help her up, wincing as she moved.

He hauled her up to her feet. "How bad are you hurt?"

"I'll live."

"That's what I like to hear. Now let's make like a pair of shepherds and get the flock out of here."

Teal'c came around on her other side and she walked between them. "How's Daniel?"

"Whining like a baby," O'Neill said. "Which I take to mean he's doing just fine. It's only when he shuts up that I worry."

"O'Neill," Teal'c said suddenly, pointing at something in the shadows. It took Sam a moment to realize that it was actually a pile of bodies slumped up against the side of the main building.

"What is it, Teal'c?"

"The Goa'uld I spoke of: Iblis," Teal'c said. He walked across to the pile of bodies and dragged Iblis' corpse aside. The body was a mess, its face twisted.

"He doesn't look so good," O'Neill said.

"He is dead, O'Neill." Teal'c made sure by wrenching the head until the vertebrae cracked. He held on to the corpse a moment longer than he needed to.

"You sure about that?"

"I am." He stepped away from the body, letting it slump to the ground.

"Well, that's one less thing we need to worry about then."

"I do not think so, O'Neill. I believe we have one *more* thing to worry about: the Goa'uld has abandoned this host body."

"Well that's just peachy."

Jubal Kane saw his brother through the people. No, he

amended silently, they weren't people, not anymore. They were living dead, shamble-footed corpses stripped of dignity, stripped of life, stripped of everything that made them human. It made Kane sick with rage.

The rain had soaked into his layers of coats, more than doubling their weight on his shoulders. He didn't care, he only had eyes for his brother, Zarif, or Corvus Keen, or whatever he was calling himself today. The so-called Raven King stood with his swollen knuckles planted on his ample hips, deep in conversation with one of his minions. Jubal licked his lips and started walking toward him. He kept his pace measured, almost leisurely, as he moved between the living dead. He had no eyes for them, no kind words. The rest of his men could play rescuer, Jubal Kane had a purpose — and that purpose was execution.

He stripped the first coat as he walked, leaving it in the dirt behind him, and the second and third as he sidestepped the body of a woman. Dropping the coats was like shedding skin, being reborn with each layer less, leaner, harder, more powerful. More dangerous. He shucked off the forth coat, a gray military greatcoat, and as he emerged from the ring of Kelani prisoners being held back by the Raven Guard, he threw the fifth coat into the face of a thin-faced Corvani.

Everything seemed to slow down then, each second drawing it out and out until it finally snapped into the next. The black sleeves of his fifth coat fluttered like raven's wings as it flew into the face of the guard. The man cried out, his words unintelligible as they stretched into meaninglessness.

"Brother mine," Jubal Kane called, twenty-five feet from the corpulent tyrant. Keen's head came up slowly, looking over the shoulder of his lackey. Kane was surprised his brother had waddled out alone. On any other day he wouldn't have been able to get near the bastard. There was no recognition in his too-blue eyes. That was galling. Jubal Kane took another step toward him. He held his arms down loosely at his sides, fingers wide, stretching the tension out of them. He had imagined this moment countless times, in every scenario imaginable, brother against brother, the final showdown.

But there wasn't a single one of them in which Corvus Keen didn't know exactly who it was striding toward him.

"We never were good enough for you, were we Zaf?" He hadn't called him that in years. The nickname burned in his mouth. Jubal took another step, raising the revolver in his right hand. It had six shots in the cylinder. He had reloaded it when he had first caught sight of the man he had come here to kill. "But this? This is too much. These are your people, your blood, Zaf. Your blood! What happened to you? What could make you do this?" He swept his left arm out to encompass everything around them, the broken souls, the burning buildings, the guards and the liberators: all of it. "And don't you dare blame it on mother, you worthless whoreson. She loved you every bit as much as you deserved, so I don't want to hear any of your pitiful moans about being cast out."

"Quite the monologue," Corvus Keen said, his slug-like lip curling into a sneer. "Are you finished?"

Jubal Kane squeezed the trigger once, the bullet slamming into his brother's right shoulder. The impact of the shell bullied him back a step and a blood red rose flowered where the bullet had torn through. He fired a second shot, this one into Keen's left shoulder, matching the first. The fat man jerked back like a marionette having its strings cut one after the other. The lackey his brother had been talking to howled, trying to put himself between Jubal Kane and his target. Kane squeezed off a third shot, taking Keen through the stomach. The blood leaked down over his gut.

"Stop him!" Keen roared but his voice was lost beneath the report of Jubal's fourth shot that blew out his left knee-cap. The fat man went down, pole-axed. He walked closer. Everyone around him moved so slowly, unable to save the tyrant from his own flesh and blood. The bullets robbed

Keen of the control over his own limbs. His arms spasmed as he tried to raise them, though whether to ward off a blow or strike out at the air between them Jubal Kane neither knew nor cared. This was his time. Here. Now.

Jubal raised the revolver for his fifth shot, and as he did the air between them seemed to thicken and shimmer. He took his time, drawing a bead on his brother, thumbing back the trigger for the final shot. It was all about this bullet. He weighed the gun in his hand, realizing that now, when it came right down to it, this was all his brother's life and his people's suffering was worth, a few pounds of metal and a trace of gunpowder.

"This last one, this one is for me."

Something strange was happening to his brother — an unearthly radiance seemed to burn up his eyes. Was this death? The soul arching out of the body looking for heaven?

Jubal Kane realized something profound then: he really didn't care.

He put the sixth shot right through his brother's heart, ending it once and for all.

He walked away, and the Raven Guard let him.

The Mujina screamed as the final bullet tore into Iblis.

It scrambled forward on its hands and knees, trying to press down on the wounds that had opened so many holes in the man's flesh. It didn't care about anyone or anything else. It didn't want to be alone. Not now. Not when this one had promised to stay with it forever.

"Don't leave me," it begged. That was all it could think. Hands slick with blood it tried to push the life back into Iblis' bloated gut. It reached out with its mind, and touched the twin minds of the dead man. It felt the last flicker of intelligence from the suppressed host mind fail, the motor functions of the body shutting down. The other still burned gloriously, but it could not burn forever, not now that its host was gone.

"Please," it whispered to the second mind, the one it thought of as its friend, and suddenly it knew what to do.

Leaning in close it kissed those bloody lips and welcomed the Goa'uld into its flesh, giving the greatest gift it could: life. In return Iblis fulfilled that bittersweet promise — the Mujina would never be alone again.

It shuddered as the Goa'uld wrapped itself around its cerebral cortex and sank into his mind.

Opening their lips, they — Mujina and Goa'uld — tasted the air and felt *whole*.

A black-feathered bird settled on the ruined gates of the Facility. It was not a raven. It was a crow, a proper crow.

Jubal Kane saw it and took it for an omen: there would be no more ravens.

The liberators counted the cost of their victory. Of the ninety-three guns Jubal Kane had commanded, twenty-seven had fallen. These would be remembered, Kane swore at their graveside. They were buried amid the bones of the other Kelani.

The Corvani fared worse. Despite O'Neill's protestations, Nadal and Kane gathered up the men who had tortured and tormented their people and told them to beg for mercy. They begged. They got down on their hands and knees in the dirt and begged. It didn't save a single one of them. None of the Kelani prisoners shed a tear for the Corvani dead. Some shuffled over simply to spit on their bones. It was some small psychological payback for the hell they had put them through. O'Neill understood it but he didn't like it — but, as he kept telling the others, they weren't here to rebuild a society, they weren't the galaxy's police. These people had to be allowed their own justice. It was important.

They tore down the Mujina's nest, interring those other bones along with the new dead. "It is time for this to end, all of it," Jubal Kane said, "the dead deserve to rest."

All of them except for Corvus Keen. The tyrant's corpse was dragged outside the compound, into the center of the field, and left to feed the crows.

The fires took days to burn out.

In that time Jubal Kane tried to get word back to the ghetto. The Rabelais Facility had fallen and Corvus Keen was dead, but that didn't mean their fight was over. Far from it, there were a dozen other facilities, thousands of black and silver soldiers every bit as twisted by the bigotry of the doctrine, willing to continue the tyrant's work in his name. But this one victory was not so small. In time thousands of survivors would march with Kane's guns to the second facility and the third, and the Corvani would be the ones running in fear.

While Kane fought the good fight, Sam, Jack, Daniel and Teal'c searched the ruined facility. They were looking for one of three things: the point of origin glyph, the Stargate or the Goa'uld. They found none of them. Instead, what they did find were logs of the experiments the Corvani scientists had been working on. Sam poured over them with grim fascination and revulsion. So many of them seemed to be obsessed with testing the stresses that the human body was capable of withstanding — tests conducted in similar situations — tortures that offered vital clues as to the effects of G-Forces and such on the test subjects. The columns were all neatly filled out, the data recorded, including the final stresses at which the test case expired. It made gruesome reading. Sam explained what she had found.

Jack reached out and closed the log book. "Move on."

In another part of the facility they found the treasure room — it was more like a graveyard of lost things. Wallets, purses, shoes, belts, anything that might be of value, was piled in the center of the room by the new arrivals to be sorted later. O'Neill closed the door, wanting nothing to do with this macabre horde.

And then they found the rooms where Kelkus carried out his experiments on those brought in to the facility. This was the worst of it by far and only Teal'c had the stomach to enter.

They all knew what he was looking for: the Goa'uld.

Teal'c refused to believe the creature was dead, and until he'd seen the body neither did O'Neill.

They didn't find the Goa'uld. Somehow it had found a way out of there before the noose could close around its neck — which meant it had a way out. If they couldn't find the creature at the very least they could find that and the hunt could continue.

What they did find, stashed away in the loot was the GDO.

Iblis had left the facility soon after taking his new host.

It was all part of his plan, allowing himself to seemingly be taken by surprise by the man with the low velocity weapon. Of course he could have raised his personal defense shield. He could have crushed the human like some insignificant ant, but Iblis was playing a long game — a shell game. It didn't matter which shell the Goa'uld inhabited at any given time. That last one had served its very brief purpose, getting him closer to the Mujina. The creature had some very peculiar mental barriers that protected it from direct invasion: he had needed it to welcome him in, to surrender itself. In essence, to love and trust him. It had welcomed him in, and now it was his and all because it was lonely. How simple the creature was to manipulate. By the time his shield shimmered into effect the fifth bullet had undone his old host body. Nothing could have stopped the last one. Had the man shot him in the head, well then there would have been no rebirth, but he did not. He wasted his bullet stopping the pump rather than shutting down the brain. It was typical of the sentimental way the humans thought of their flesh, distilling both love and hate and placing them within the heart despite the fact that they had no place being there. Those were cerebral emotions, born in the brain. It was inevitable that the betrayed brother would aim his last shot for the heart.

This new form was more appealing, and had some rather unusual benefits that would be well worth exploring further, but for now Iblis concerned himself with the secrets locked within the creature's head. The Mujina shared all of its memories willingly, allowing Iblis access to the thousands upon thousands of souls it had tasted, all of those dreams and fears and memories. And in those stolen pasts he found the Shol'vah. He took the traitor's life and devoured it. Know your enemy. Know his weaknesses. Know his strengths. That was the art of war at its simplest. And through the Mujina, Iblis knew Teal'c. It knew them all: Colonel Jack O'Neill, the man who had failed his own son, Daniel Jackson, the man who could not save his wife, and Samantha Carter, the woman forever a disappointment to her own father, Jacob... the Tok'ra! Her flesh and blood had been taken as a host by the wretched queen's spawn — that was worth knowing. It would have to stay away from this one lest she sense its presence within this false flesh. These were its enemy. These Tau'ri who failed everyone around them when they needed them most. It did not fear them. Indeed, through the Mujina, it felt another emotion all together: pity. It pitied them. Iblis closed off that part of his new host. In normal circumstances it would not have allowed any trace of its host to survive, but the Mujina was different. It was more than human. Its gift was useful to the Goa'uld.

Iblis used the rings to transport himself back to the city.

They were looking for the Stargate. Of course, it wasn't there, and without the correct glyph they would not be able to return home. Iblis wrestled with the desire to simply snuff them out as opposed to simply expediting their return home.

Keep your enemies close, keep your treasures closer still. It seemed that it had much to thank them for as they waged their war on the System Lords. They could be an unwitting tool. This was a new way of thinking for Iblis. It was almost, dare he admit it, human. It was devious and cunning and lacked the god-given rightness of Goa'uld beliefs. He smiled as he delved deeper into the Mujina's memories and understood, recalling its traumatic escape from its prison. The gate had not merely lost contact and slipped, the wormhole had failed catastrophically. This intrigued the Goa'uld. It was rare for a gate to fail, rarer still that the travelers should survive. Of course, as a result, they were stranded. This changed things. No one would be looking for the Tau'ri. They would assume they were already lost. They were already dead to their world so no one would miss them if he finished the job. Already wheels spun within mental wheels. Kill or be killed. That was the way of life. Death was not such a bad place for them to be.

But there was an alternative. The Mujina's voice was strong inside him. It wanted to help them. He felt its loyalty to its liberators. It was quaint. The creature was so used to showing everyone their heart's desires now it had a chance to not only show, but to give the Tau'ri everything they wanted. It could open the door that would take them home. By absorbing the Mujina and opening up his mind to it Iblis had given the creature the one thing it knew its companions wanted: the glyph that represented this world on the Stargate. It was ironic, if nothing else. The Mujina knew it was inside him, it fought Iblis for what it wanted. The creature was no simple host. It was strong in ways that Iblis was not used to. It resisted in ways Iblis was not used to countering. But the gifts it granted far outweighed the difficulty the Goa'uld had in subjugating its personality. It gave the Mujina what it wanted. It would not kill the humans unless it absolutely had to.

In the two days before Iblis revealed himself, careful to

never be close to the woman, Carter, the Goa'uld made calculations and complex predictions based upon the star charts and other data constructed by Corvus Keen's astronomers. The fool had been so sure it was his destiny to rule the stars themselves, as though his impure blood could ever be a match for the might of the System Lords. Still, the obsession had proved its worth. With the charts, Iblis was in a position to replicate the conditions that dragged the wormhole off course.

Even with the Mujina to soften his psychology, Iblis did nothing that did not serve his own purposes. That was the nature of the beast.

So for two days Iblis worked to save them, and then finally, when he was ready, he emerged from the shadows.

"I know where the Goa'uld hid his laboratory," the Mujina said, seeing the distrust on the Daniel's face. It was sat cross-legged on the floor when they found it, drawing glyphs in the dirt. It knew he would recognize them for what they were. "Let me help you."

Over and over he marked out the glyph for Kushmara. It was almost laughable how blind these humans were.

"I don't think so," O'Neill said. "You'll stay very still and speak when you're spoken to unless you want to end up with your head in a sack again. Understood?"

"I only want to help you," the Mujina said. This time he scraped out the sign of the Earth. He couldn't have been more obvious if he tried. "That is all I ever wanted. I swear to you. I did not ask for you to see your dead son's face in mine. That was your need, not mine. I only wanted to help you."

O'Neill refused to look at the creature and his anger was sharp. "No more helping."

Daniel Jackson sat down beside it. It could smell the blood on him still. And inside, the grief that losing his wife caused. "Jack, you should see this."

The Mujina masked its smile. Daniel traced the outline of the earth glyph. He knew what it meant.

"What is it now, Daniel? Has your pet monkey written a line of Shakespeare in the dirt?"

"As good as," Daniel said. "I think he's telling us how to get home."

That caught O'Neill's attention.

"Do you know what this is?" the earnest young human asked the creature. It shook its head. "Where did you see it?"

"It was inside the fat king's mind when I touched it."

"Is it possible?" Jack said, looking at the lines traced in the dust. "Could Corvus Keen have known the glyph for this planet?"

"It's possible he knew it without even knowing what it meant," Daniel said, then he traced a couple of sharp lines around the symbol and suddenly it looked uncannily like the symbol of the Raven Guard.

"Well, I'll be damned," O'Neill said.

Daniel leaned in close. "Tell me, have you seen this?" He asked the Mujina as he drew a circle in the dirt. It was a crude rendition of the Chappa'ai. The creature smiled. It knew what he wanted more than anything in the world. He wanted to go home. It nodded, "Yes, yes, the big eye that looks from place to place, that is where Iblis took it. It is there now. I can take you to it. I can show you."

But it wasn't the Mujina that met them, it was Jubal Kane.

The man held out his hand to O'Neill, shaking it. "You have done a great thing for my people, but the fight is not yet won."

"But you're the right man for the fight," O'Neill said.

"Perhaps, but I would be a fool not to ask you to stay and help."

"We've got our own war going on, Jubal. Speaking of wars,

where's the damned Mujina got to?"

They had no way of knowing what the creature had offered him to lie for it. "It is dead."

"How the hell did that happen?" O'Neill asked.

"I don't know. I found it in the old chapel where it had made its nest. It had cut its own throat and bled out. I will see to it that the poor animal is laid to rest." He looked at Sam. "Perhaps you would stay?" He asked, with a smile that said he knew she wasn't going to say yes.

She ducked her head slightly, returning his smile. "Where they go, I go," she said.

Jubal Kane turned to Teal'c. "What about you big guy? You know Kiah's not stopped talking about you since you carried her out of her house like that. You're the kind of hero I could use as a Number Two."

O'Neill and the others looked at Teal'c. He hadn't mentioned anything that had happened while they had been parted. "I am honored, Jubal of the Kelani, but I must return with O'Neill."

"Well, you guys know where to find us," Jubal Kane said.

Together they walked through to the chamber where Iblis had had the Stargate stored.

"You're going to want to keep this covered," Daniel said. "You don't want any more Goa'uld coming through."

"I was thinking of burying it," Jubal said.

"That would work."

The DHD had been broken open and had a number of Goa'uld crystals wired into it. Sam had no idea what they did, but assumed it was something Iblis had done to power up the gate so that it was able to dial out.

"Is it going to work?" O'Neill sounded dubious.

"There's only one way to find out," Sam said, punching in the first co-ordinate the Mujina had scratched out in the dirt. The chevron locked into place. She smiled back at the others. "Looks like we're going home." She punched in the rest of the co-ordinates for the SGC, each chevron in turn locking into place. The ambient glow behind the chevrons themselves flared red as the final one encoded. And then the familiar quicksilver film stretched across the eye of the Stargate, the crystal blue surface agitated as the event horizon of the wormhole established itself at the destination. The ripples surged, exploding outwards in an unstable vortex, before being sucked back in to the churning surface. The difference in the dialing sequence puzzled her, but with the gateway home established she wasn't going to question it.

Sam stared at the rippling blue portal, knowing she was only five steps away from home it was hard not to just run through it.

"Send the signal, Major Carter. We're going home."

Sam activated the GDO, sending SG-1's call-sign out through the ether.

The Stargate wavered, the wormhole flickering as though about to lose contact. It held but there was no way of knowing how long it would continue to do so.

"What the hell just happened?" O'Neill demanded.

"I don't know," Sam said.

"What I mean is: 'is it going to hold or is it going to collapse when we're halfway home?'"

"I don't *know*!"

"Fine," O'Neill narrowed his eyes. "Daniel, Carter, Teal'c. Go go go!"

"What about you sir?"

"Last one through turns out the lights. Now go!"

Sam watched Daniel go through, took a deep breath and followed him into the blue.

The Mujina-Iblis waited outside, listening to the conversation of the Tau'ri before it entered the old laboratory. He saw the Shol'vah follow Carter through the Chappa'ai and black anger surged up inside him. He set his mouth in a grim rictus-smile and walked toward the Stargate. It was all he could do to restrain himself when every muscle and nerve ending cried out to strike down the infidel and be damned with subtlety and plans. Vengeance there and then promised its own pleasures. No. Now was not the time.

"What the hell?" the colonel's gaze darted between Jubal and the Mujina.

"Sorry, O'Neill," Jubal said. He couldn't hold the Tau'ri's eye. They were simple creatures, the Mujina-Iblis thought, savoring O'Neill's shock at Jubal's betrayal. It was almost as fulfilling as the Sol'vah's blood would have been.

O'Neill reacted instinctively, throwing himself toward the wormhole. It was a pathetic attempt at escape and only served to deepen the Mujina-Iblis' anger. The temerity of the Tau'ri, to think that it could simply run. The Mujina-Iblis stepped forward, its grin cruel now as a faint snick met his footstep. His weight depressed a hidden pressure plate set into the floor. The air crackled with life as the stasis field activated.

He had used his two days well.

He had prepared.

He had taken apart the components of those vile tablets that had held him captive for so long and rebuilt them in this room, turning the area in front of the Chappa'ai into a trap. The aspect of the twin that was all Iblis savored the irony that the technology that had imprisoned him for so long would save him now.

The force field rose up around O'Neill even as he screamed, as his face froze in that moment of outrage and fear, trapped in that backwards glance at the open Stargate. So close to escape, the rippling blue of the Stargate's eye taunted him.

O'Neill couldn't move no matter how desperately he fought against his invisible bonds.

Mujina-Iblis allowed the silver in his eyes to blaze, making certain that O'Neill could see just how thoroughly he had been deceived.

He turned to Jubal. "You served your God well, human."

O'Neill's expression darkened as realization crawled across his features. "You can't manipulate it," he warned Jubal, struggling against the hold of the force field. Each word cost him. Iblis could have silenced the Tau'ri had he wished, it would have been easy enough, but he liked to hear his victims beg. It added to the enjoyment of the kill. "You can't control it."

He was right, of course, but that didn't matter because Jubal didn't care. He wasn't interested in control. He had no desire to harness the Mujina like some beast of burden. All he wanted was vengeance — and right now, he believed the Mujina could deliver his heart's desire.

"Do you know what it is to see your people exterminated, O'Neill? To be helpless while a monster murders your family before your eyes?" Jubal jerked his head toward Iblis. "With him on our side, we will never be helpless. We will never be slaves again."

O'Neill ground his teeth, trying to force the denial out: "You're wrong," he rasped. "You're already a slave."

Mujina-Iblis walked up to O'Neill and placed his hands against his chest. "Enough. I should kill you now for your crimes against my brethren," he said, noticing the way the man's eyes narrowed. "Yes, yes, I know your mind, Jack O'Neill. I know what you have done — to Ra, to Apophis, to Seth, to Cronus..."

"You promised he'd be allowed to leave unharmed," Jubal objected, stepping forward. He reached out, not quite daring to touch his new god. As it should be. Mujina-Iblis smiled coldly, baring his teeth.

"So I did. Death is too simple a fate for a slayer of gods, after all, and I am a patient creature."

He stepped away, permitting Jubal Kane to approach O'Neill. Any guilt the Kelani man might have felt was masked by his blazing conviction — the Mujina's talents were, indeed, fascinating.

"You understand," Jubal said to O'Neill. It was a statement, not a question. "I know you do. With him at our side, we can destroy the Corvani evil forever. He can save us."

O'Neill shook his head. "Don't you get it? All you're doing is trading one monster for another. This isn't living. Freedom? Don't make me laugh."

Jubal didn't answer. Jaw set tight, he shoved the colonel backwards into the wormhole.

Iblis nodded approvingly.

He had a world to enslave and time enough to devise a million ways for O'Neill pay for his crimes against the Go'auld. The God Slayer would beg the next time they met. For now, the anticipation of his suffering would have to suffice.

He turned his back on Jubal.

There was an entire world waiting to hurt.

What God could ask for more?

ABOUT THE AUTHOR

STEVEN SAVILE is the author of the *Von Carstein Vampire* trilogy *(Inheritance, Dominion, Retribution)* set in Games Workshop's popular *Warhammer* world, and re-released collectively as *Vampire Wars*, as well as *Curse of the Necrach*. He has written the best-selling original audio novel *Torchwood: Hidden* for BBC Audiobooks, read by Naoko Mori who plays Toshiko Sato in the BBC series. He has also written the first novel based in the *Primeval* universe, extending the adventures of Professor Nick Cutter and his crew out beyond the limits of the British Isles. He has re-imagined the bloodthirsty Celtic barbarian *Slaine* from *2000 AD* in a new duology of novels for Black Flame *(The Exile, The Defiler)*. He has also written for *Star Wars, Jurassic Park*, and four incarnations of *The Doctor*.

Most recently he has written *The Black Chalice*, Book One of the *Knights of Albion*, soon to be released by Abaddon, whilst *Silver*, his religious thriller, debuted in hardcover in the US in January of 2010.

Steven's other original novels and short story collections include: *The Hollow Earth, Temple: Incarnations, Laughing Boy's Shadow, Houdini's Last Illusion, Angel Road*, and the forthcoming *The Odalisque and Other Strange Stories*, published by Dark Regions Press in the US.

Steven has edited a number of critically acclaimed anthologies, including *Elemental*, Redbrick Eden, and *Doctor Who Short Trips: Destination Prague*. He also compiled *Smoke Ghost & Other Apparitions* and *Black Gondolier and Other Stories*, the collected horror stories of Fritz Leiber.

He was a runner up in the 2000 British Fantasy Awards, a winner of a 2002 Writers of the Future Award, and won the 2009 Scribe Award for best young adult original novel for his book *Shadow of the Jaguar*.

Fantastic TV, a study of genre TV shows from the last 50 years was recently released by Plexus.

He is currently working on *Gold*, the follow-up to *Silver*, and writing the script for one of the world's most popular computer games with DICE/Electronic Arts.

SNEAK PREVIEW

STARGATE SG-1: SUNRISE

by J.F. Crane

THE NIGHT had grown dark and when Teal'c looked up he could see no stars through the dome that shielded this city from what lay beyond.

He did not speculate as to what that might be, but his instinct—what O'Neill would call his 'gut'—told him that it was dangerous. Too much was hidden in this place, too many lies told in the guise of truth, for him to believe that all was well on the world of Ierna. And so he kept his guard raised, his attention ranging out beyond the whispered discussions between his team and into the city at large. Even from this distance he could see the white flicker of the screens that projected the Message onto the vast sides of towering buildings, he could hear the distant hubbub of a city, and beneath it all he could detect the tramp of booted feet. Teal'c did not doubt that they were being hunted by the men who served the Elect.

But they did not come close to the place Rhionna Channon had selected as a meeting point, which made him at once thankful and suspicious. Daughter of the Pastor, her loyalties remained unclear despite her protestations. The Jaffa on Chulak had a favorite expression for such situations—bait your trap with Satta-cakes, not gruel. He would be vigilant.

They awaited her in a deserted plaza beneath a vast, empty tower. At the center of the space a flat rectangular structure, about as high as his waist, sloped down toward a circular area surrounded by a low wall. Once, perhaps, it had been a fountain trickling into a pool but now both were dry and dusty. O'Neill sat on the edge of the slope, swinging his legs to mark his boredom, however the tight grip he maintained on his weapon belied his feigned nonchalance. Major Carter had her back to them all, covering the other entrance to the square. And Doctor Jackson was studying the footage he had taken on his camera, his face ghostly in the light shining up from the screen.

"…really, it's quite remarkable," he was saying, gaze intent and brow creased. "We're looking at a culture that apparently dates its existence from a hundred and fifty years ago."

"Yes, apparently," O'Neill said. His eyes were hidden beneath this cap, shadowed in the dark night. Teal'c did not need to see his face to hear the cynicism in his voice. Neither did Daniel Jackson.

"I'm not saying they sprang into being a century and a half ago," he said, his tone skirting irritation. "But there's clearly been a significant loss of knowledge about their own history. And a retrograde step of that magnitude is almost always the result of some kind of societal cataclysm — war, plague, disaster. Huge population loss."

"Collective amnesia?" O'Neill had stopped swinging his legs and sat very still. "Wouldn't be the first time."

After a silence Daniel said, "There are plenty of reasons why people forget their own past, Jack. Almost none of them involve memory stamps."

"Yeah, and almost all of them involve some smart-ass in a suit rewriting history to make himself the good guy."

Daniel Jackson switched off his camera, the small light disappeared and left him in the shadows. "That's a fair point — history, as they say, is written by the victors."

"Question is, who's the enemy here?"

"That's what we're here to find out, isn't it?" Daniel Jackson stood up and stretched. "That's why we're meeting Rhionna."

"Is it?" O'Neill didn't move. "Is that why we're here, Daniel? Because I thought it was to get hold of the shield."

"They're not mutually exclusive aims."

"Daniel's right, sir," said Major Carter. "Rhionna may be able to help us find out more about the shield."

"Sure," O'Neill said. "At a price."

"You don't know that, sir."

"Oh, I think it's a good bet." He jumped down from the fountain, his boots echoing dully as they hit the bottom of the empty pool. "There's always a price."

"Now you just sound cynical," Daniel Jackson said.

"Yes," O'Neill agreed. "That's because I *am* cynical!"

"It may be a price worth paying, sir." Major Carter had half turned from her post. Teal'c could see the gleam of her eyes in the dark. "If that shield really could help defend Earth from attack by the Goa'uld…"

"A price worth paying." It was a muted echo. "And what if the shield turns out to be a crock, then what? What if all that happens is we end up saving some other screwed-up world from itself while we get— Then what? You still think that's a price worth paying, Major?"

She was silent a moment. "Yes, sir," she said. "I think it is."

O'Neill didn't answer, just muttered something indecipherable under his breath.

"Come on Jack," Daniel Jackson said, "you've never made this just about the standing orders before."

"Yeah, well P3R-118 changed my mind!"

In the silence that followed Major Carter turned back to her watch, but Daniel Jackson was not so wise. "That's just one place…"

"They were in our heads, Daniel! They were screwing around with our minds. And what did we get out of it? Nadda. Zilch." He slammed his fist against his chest. "Nothing but a pain in the goddamn ass!"

"We saved those people from slavery," Major Carter said, her back still turned. "That counts for something."

"Not enough," O'Neill growled. "And, just so we're clear, this time we're here for the shield. And that's all. Got it?"

"Well, you can't just…"

The rest of Daniel Jackson's protest faded from Teal'c's ears as he saw a shape detach itself from one of the buildings in the darkness beyond the plaza. "O'Neill." He raised his weapon and dropped into a defensive crouch. "Someone approaches."

"Carter?" Teal'c heard the snap as O'Neill unsaftied his weapon.

"Nothing this side, sir." Her voice was tense, but calm.

Then, from the shadows, stepped the slender figure of Rhionna Channon, her hands raised. "It's me."

"Are you alone?" Teal'c peered into the darkness, but could see no other movement.

"Entirely," she said, stopping some distance away. "I'm sorry to have kept you waiting for so long, I was obliged to dine with my father tonight. He would have been suspicious had I not attended."

Keeping her covered, Teal'c rose. Behind him, he sensed O'Neill moving forward. His boots made a dull noise against the ground. "I imagine they're already wondering where we are."

"Yes," she said. "The Elect Guard have been deployed to search. We must leave this place before sunup."

"Must we?" O'Neill stepped forward, his weapon leveled. "And where *must* we go?"

At his side, Daniel Jackson let out a long breath. "Jack…"

"*Daniel.*" He shifted his weapon, using it to indicate Rhionna Channon. "I've got a better idea. We stay right here and you tell us what you know about the shield."

The woman lowered her hands. No longer dressed in the gown in which she had attended the service, she was once more attired as if for hard work. "I cannot tell you all you wish to know," she said, her gaze holding O'Neill's. "However, I will take you to a woman who can."

"Bring her here."

"Impossible."

"Why?"

She hesitated. "You must trust me, Colonel O'Neill. The Elect will tell you nothing of *Sciath De* — it terrifies them. But I can. I can help you, but you must come with me — you must trust me."

"And why should I do that?"

Folding her arms across her chest, Rhionna Channon appeared as intransient as O'Neill. "Because, if you want to find God's Shield, you have no choice."

The city after dark was just plain weird, and Jack couldn't help thinking back to Daniel's talk of war, plague, and disaster. There was definitely something post-apocalyptic about the dark, silent skyscrapers that loomed along the fringes of the city while its tiny heart flickered with the cathode-glare of vast screens hanging from the sides of buildings.

Rhionna kept them far away from the light as she led them through the city, and Jack was grateful — if only to avoid having to watch more of the God-awful soap being pumped out into the streets.

"You'd think they'd get bored," Sam murmured as she walked by his side.

"Beggers can't be choosers," Daniel said. He was a couple of steps in front, head turning every which way as he tried to take it all in at once. "If this is the only entertainment they can get, the only culture permitted…"

"It's the only culture they want," Rhionna said, turning her head to look back at them as she walked. There was anger in her dark eyes, a flare of frustration. "They are like pigs at the trough, eating only what they are given without question."

"But you question," Daniel said. "What makes you different?"

Her expression sharpened and she looked away. "What I have seen," she said with a frown. "What I will show you."

It was the truth, Jack thought, but not the whole truth. There was something she wasn't telling them...

Ahead of them, a knot of people suddenly came into view from around a corner. Rhionna stopped dead, breathing something under her breath. In the dark it was difficult to make out details, but Jack knew a soldier when he saw one and instantly raised his weapon. Teal'c and Carter did the same, only Daniel lifted empty hands. "Daniel," he hissed, jerking his head in a 'get-behind me' motion.

Daniel ignored him, of course. "Who are they?" he said to Rhionna.

"The Elect Guard. Stay here." Over her shoulder she glanced at Jack. "Lower your weapon."

"I don't think so."

The soldiers had also stopped, taking up a defensive posture as one man detached himself from the group.

"Captain Tanner," Rhionna said, walking toward him.

"Goodman Tynan thought you would have some hand in this business," the captain said. He spoke quietly, more anxious than angry. "Would that I had not discovered you."

"Then look with blind eyes, Captain," she said. "I am taking them to the Badlands."

Badlands? Jack exchanged a glance with Daniel who just shrugged.

The soldier spared them a glance. "To what end?"

"To..." She hesitated, and Jack had the distinct feeling she was holding something back. "They need information. Does not the Message teach that we should help those in need?"

With a snort, Tanner said, "I had not thought you paid so much attention to the Message, Rhionna."

"Only when it is in my interest to do so." Reaching out, she touched the man's arm. "They seek *Sciath De*. If they can find it..."

The captain looked from her face back toward SG-1. "You have no reason to trust them; did they not come from the Other Place?"

"Tanner, you know we must question all we are told. Everything we know of the Other Place is told to us through the Message, how can we trust it?"

He let out a breath and looked down at his boots, thinking. At Jack's side, Carter mouthed 'Other Place?' When Tanner spoke again, it was in a voice so low Jack could barely hear him. "Very well, this night my eyes are blind to you and my men will keep their silence. But go quick, Rhionna Channon, the Elect fear these strangers."

"I know," she said. "And that is why we should trust them." She squeezed his arm. "My thanks, Captain Tanner, to you and your men. I know what you risk."

Then she turned back to Jack, the vibrant red of her shirt standing out against the gray as she beckoned them forward. "We must hurry. This way."

With that she disappeared around a corner.

Carter broke into a jog to follow, Daniel and Teal'c on her heels. Jack brought up the rear, sparing a glance for the soldier watching them with serious eyes. Neither spoke but in the gloom Jack saw an honest face and gave the man a nod. Tanner did the same, then turned on his heel and returned to his men.

Clearly there was much more going on in the Ark than met the eye.

And Jack hated that.

READ MORE IN...

STARGATE SG-1: SUNRISE PUBLISHED OCTOBER 2010

STARGATE UNIVERSE: AIR

by James Swallow
Price: £6.99 UK | $7.95 US
ISBN-13: 978-1-905586-46-2
Publication date: November 2009

Without food, supplies, or a way home, Colonel Everett Young finds himself in charge of a mission that has gone wrong before it has even begun. Stranded and alone on the far side of the universe, the mismatched team of scientists, technicians, and military personnel have only one objective: staying alive.

As personalities clash and desperation takes hold, salvation lies in the hands of Dr. Nicholas Rush, the man responsible for their plight, a man with an agenda of his own…

Stargate Universe is the gritty new spin-off of the hit TV shows Stargate SG-1 and Stargate Atlantis. Working from the original screenplay, award-winning author James Swallow has combined the three pilot episodes into this thrilling full-length novel which includes deleted scenes and dialog, making it a must-read for all Stargate fans.

Order your copy directly from the publisher today by going to www.stargatenovels.com or send a check or money order made payable to "Fandemonium" to:

<u>USA orders:</u> $10.95 ($7.95 + $3.00 P&P).

<u>Rest of world:</u> $13.95 ($7.95 + $6.00 P&P)

Send payment to: Fandemonium Books, PO Box 2178, Decatur, GA 30031-2178 USA.

Or check your local bookshop – available on special order if they are out of stock (quote the ISBN number listed above).

A new danger lurks in the Pegasus Galaxy

STARGATE ATLANTIS

HOMECOMING
Book one of the Legacy series

Jo Graham & Melissa Scott

Based on the hit television series created by
Brad Wright & Robert C. Cooper

Series number: SGA-16

STARGATE ATLANTIS: HOMECOMING

Book one in the new LEGACY SERIES

by Jo Graham & Melissa Scott
Price: £6.99 UK | $7.95 US
ISBN-10: 1-905586-50-7
ISBN-13: 978-1-905586-50-9
Publication date: October 2010

Atlantis has returned to Earth, its team has disbursed and are beginning new lives far from the dangers of the Pegasus galaxy. They think the adventure is over.

They're wrong.

With the help of General Jack O'Neill, Atlantis rises once more – and the former members of the expedition must decide whether to return with her to Pegasus, or to remain safely on Earth in the new lives they enjoy...

Picking up where the show's final season ended, Stargate Atlantis Homecoming is the first in the exciting new Stargate Atlantis Legacy series. These all new adventures take the Atlantis team back to the Pegasus galaxy where a terrible new enemy has emerged, an enemy that threatens their lives, their friendships – and the future of Earth itself.

Order your copy directly from the publisher today by going to www.stargatenovels.com or send a check or money order made payable to "Fandemonium" to:

<u>USA orders:</u> **$10.95 ($7.95 + $3.00 P&P).**

<u>Rest of world:</u> **$13.95 ($7.95 + $6.00 P&P)**

Send payment to: Fandemonium Books, PO Box 2178, Decatur, GA 30031-2178 USA.

Or check your local bookshop – available on special order if they are out of stock (quote the ISBN number listed above).

STARGATE ATLANTIS: BRIMSTONE

**by David Niall Wilson &
Patricia Macomber**

Price: £6.99 UK | $7.95 US
ISBN-10: 1-905586-20-5
ISBN-13: 978-1-905586-20-2
Publication date: September 2010

Doctor Rodney McKay can't believe his eyes when he discovers a moon leaving planetary orbit for a collision course with its own sun. Keen to investigate, he finds something astonishing on the moon's surface – an Ancient city, the mirror of Atlantis…

But the city is not as abandoned as he thinks and Colonel Sheppard's team soon encounter a strange sect of Ancients living beneath the surface, a sect devoted to decadence and debauchery, for whom novelty is the only entertainment. And in the team from Atlantis they find the ultimate novelty to enliven their bloody gladiatorial games…

Trapped on a world heading for destruction, the team must fight their way back to the Stargate or share the fate of the doomed city of Admah…

Order your copy directly from the publisher today by going to www.stargatenovels.com or send a check or money order made payable to "Fandemonium" to:

<u>USA orders:</u> $10.95 ($7.95 + $3.00 P&P).

<u>Rest of world:</u> $13.95 ($7.95 + $6.00 P&P)

Send payment to: Fandemonium Books, PO Box 2178, Decatur, GA 30031-2178 USA.

Or check your local bookshop – available on special order if they are out of stock (quote the ISBN number listed above).

STARGATE ATLANTIS: DEATH GAME

by Jo Graham
Price: £6.99 UK | $7.95 US
ISBN-10: 1-905586-47-7
ISBN-13: 978-1-905586-47-9
Publication date: September 2010

Colonel John Sheppard knows it's going to be a bad day when he wakes up in a downed Jumper with a head wound and no memory of how he got there.

Things don't get any better.

Concussed, far from the Stargate, and with his only remaining team mate, Teyla, injured, Sheppard soon finds himself a prisoner of the local population. And as he gradually pieces the situation together he realises that his team is scattered across a tropical archipelago, unable to communicate with each other or return to the Stargate. And to make matters worse, there's a Wraith cruiser in the skies above...

Meanwhile, Ronon and Doctor Zelenka find themselves in an unlikely partnership as they seek a way off their island and back to the Stargate. And Doctor McKay? He just wants to get the Stargate working...

Order your copy directly from the publisher today by going to www.stargatenovels.com or send a check or money order made payable to "Fandemonium" to:

<u>USA orders:</u> $10.95 ($7.95 + $3.00 P&P).

<u>Rest of world:</u> $13.95 ($7.95 + $6.00 P&P)

Send payment to: Fandemonium Books, PO Box 2178, Decatur, GA 30031-2178 USA.

Or check your local bookshop – available on special order if they are out of stock (quote the ISBN number listed above).

STARGATE SG-1: OCEANS OF DUST

by Peter J. Evans
Price: $7.95 US | £6.99 UK
ISBN-10: 1-905586-53-1
ISBN-13: 978-1-905586-53-0
Publication date: March 2011

Something lurks beneath the ancient sands of Egypt. It is the stuff of Jaffa nightmares, its name a whisper in the dark. And it is stirring…

When disaster strikes an Egyptian dig, SG1 are brought in to investigate. But nothing can prepare them for what they find among the ruins. Walking in the dust of a thousand deaths, they discover a creature of unimaginable evil – a creature the insane Goa'uld Neheb-Kau wants to use as a terrible weapon.

With Teal'c and Major Carter in the hands of the enemy, Colonel O'Neill and Daniel Jackson recruit Master Bra'tac to help track the creature across the galaxy in a desperate bid to destroy it before it turns their friends – and the whole galaxy – to dust…

Things get hot as SG-1 search for a mythical shield

STARGATE
SG·1

SUNRISE

J.F. Crane

Based on the hit television series developed by
Brad Wright and Jonathan Glassner

Series number: SG1-17

STARGATE SG-1: SUNRISE

by J.F. Crane
Price: $7.95 US | £6.99 UK
ISBN-10: 1-905586-51-5
ISBN-13: 978-1-905586-51-6
Publication date: October 2010

On the abandoned outpost of *Acarsaid Dorch* Doctor Daniel Jackson makes a startling discovery — a discovery that leads SG1 to a world on the brink of destruction.

The Elect rule Ierna, ensuring that their people live in peace and plenty, protected from their planet's merciless sun by a biosphere that surrounds their city. But all is not as it seems and when Daniel is taken captive by the renegade Seachráni, Colonel Jack O'Neill and his team discover another side to Ierna - a people driven to desperation by rising seas, burning beneath a blistering sun.

Inhabiting the building tops of a long-drowned cityscape, the Seachráni and their reluctant leader, Faelan Garrett, reveal the truth about the planet's catastrophic past — and about how Daniel's discovery on *Acarsaid Dorch* could save them all...

STARGATE SG-1: FOUR DRAGONS

by Diana Botsford

Price: $7.95 US | £6.99 UK
ISBN-10: 1-905586-48-5
ISBN-13: 978-1-905586-48-6
Publication date: August 2010

It was meant to be a soft mission, something to ease Doctor Daniel Jackson back into things after his time among the Ancients — after all, what could possibly go wrong on a simple survey of ancient Chinese ruins? As it turns out, a whole lot.

After accidentally activating a Goa'uld transport ring, Daniel finds himself the prisoner of Lord Yu, the capricious Goa'uld System Lord. Meanwhile, SG1's efforts to rescue their friend are hampered by a representative of the Chinese government with an agenda of his own to follow - and a deep secret to hide.

But Colonel Jack O'Neill is in no mood for delay. He'll go to any lengths to get Daniel back — even if it means ignoring protocol and taking matters into his own hands.

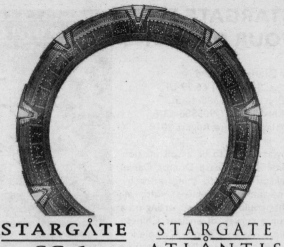

STARGÅTE
SG·1.

STARGATE
ATLÅNTIS.

STARGATE UNIVERSE.

Original novels based on the hit TV shows **STARGATE SG-1, STARGATE ATLANTIS** and **STARGATE UNIVERSE**

AVAILABLE NOW
For more information, visit
www.stargatenovels.com